# BOYFRIEND IN A BODY CAST

Nicole Schubert

Earnest Parc Press

Boyfriend in a Body Cast
Published by Earnest Parc Press
Copyright © 2024 by Nicole Schubert.



Earnest Parc Press
Earnestparcpress@gmail.com

Publisher's Note: This is a work of fiction. Names, characters, places, and incidents are a product of the author's imagination. Locales and public names are sometimes used for atmospheric purposes. Any resemblance to actual people, living or dead, or to businesses, companies, events, institutions, or locales is completely coincidental.

Cover Design by Carolyn Nicole

Boyfriend in a Body Cast/Nicole Schubert.--1st ed.

ISBN: 979-8-9873441-6-3

For Kathy, best buddies forever

# 1 FALL TALENT JAM

Excitement swept through the high school gym as Beatrix Plumb—barely-sixteen, budding idealist, full-fledged romantic, chronic self-doubter—manned a spotlight pointed at her annoyingly outgoing fourteen-year-old sister, Paige, belting out a song on the stage directly below the "FALL TALENT JAM" banner, eclipsed by the "FLEET 2 BEAT THUNDERBIRDS 4 CHAMPIONSHIP! GO LIONS!" banner. Fleet was Owen Fleet, the team quarterback, and Beatrix, aka Bee, had been seriously crushing on him forever. It gave her a thrill just thinking about him, in spite of the fact that her sister's confidence on the talent show stage at that very moment was eclipsing Bee's thrill big time.

And so, to compensate for her annoyance at her sister, Bee did what she always did: She began to narrate her life with optimism to get herself back on track. It was a fabulous life hack. She did it all the time. Well, she'd done it for as long as she could remember. And it worked! She narrated in her head as if someone special were actually listening, someone who would get her. Immediately. Hear her. Love her. See her. Just as she was.

You see, Beatrix "Bee" Plumb had a famously weird—as in totally brilliant—and bright outlook on life, full of popping colors and sounds and useful ideas.

"Life wasn't perfect...," Bee began inside her optimistic and romanticized imagination, lifting her brunette-bobbed head a little higher as she kept the spotlight on Paige. "...not with a little sister everyone loves more than you. Or gushy parents who give said sister all the attention she needs, while leaving you in the dust."

Bee glanced over at her parents, Judy and Hank Plumb, standing in the aisle at the side of a row of students with their blue, green and gold spirit wear and eyes on Paige. Her parents both had their phones up filming Paige, beaming with pride at their younger daughter as she rocked the high school talent show. And Paige was only a freshman!

"And life wasn't perfect thanks to an embarrassingly high I.Q.," Bee continued describing herself and her situation, "that makes you appear overly capable and able to fend for yourself—to everyone, especially said parents. Even when you have no idea what you're doing and just wish someone would tell you what to do and guide you through the ups and downs of your days and the many awkward moments, like at school and now and all the time...instead of looking at you like the rock-solid goddess of wisdom in the family, and also carpooling sherpa, making you drive your stupid sister everywhere and insisting you help other people with their homework when you were long done with yours—when you just really need to space out or scroll or hang with your BFF."

Bee deftly adjusted the sound and lights as Paige finished her talent-show performance and her parents jumped up and applauded for Paige like crazy.

"Life also wasn't perfect thanks to an excruciatingly huge crush on Owen Fleet...," Bee narrated in her head as Owen Fleet—her sixteen-year-old, charismatic, lovable, attention-junkie crush—bumped Bee on his way to the stage, his gorgeous green eyes flashing flirtatiously at her as he mouthed "sorry" and deftly passed with a grin, "...hot quarterback and my true love and boyfriend since kindergarten...," Bee continued then mouthed "I love you" to Owen's back. "...I mean, *boyfriend* in my dreams."

"Give it up for the Owen Fleet Quartet," boomed the master of ceremonies—two-time State Humorous Interp Speech Champion Mason—from the stage, breaking Bee's blissful fantasy narration for a moment. "Smokin' rappers and mangy Thunderbird tail kickers!" Mason continued.

The crowd and Lions' cheer squad went nuts as Owen ran up on stage with his best friend, Nick Wells—also sixteen, recently returned to town and a regular nice guy, confident, funny—and two more football guys.

Owen riled up the crowd, "Three games to State Championship! Who's gonna win?"

"Lions!!!" the crowd cheered, then roared like big cats.

Owen ran over to his buds on the stage in the spotlight, and they started their talent show rap number with awesome and goofy lyrics.

Bee was desperately smitten as she watched Owen ham it up with hip hop mastery. "No, life wasn't perfect," she continued in her head to her imaginary listeners. "But it was okay, thanks to Kate, my best friend since fifth grade. We do everything together."

Across the auditorium, Bee admired her wise, pragmatic, loyal best friend—sixteen-year-old Kate Towers—as Kate manned another spotlight. Bee and Kate were totally in sync, and they moved their respective spotlights in tandem, smoothly, like a symphony, following Owen on the stage, sharing a BFF bliss moment.

"...until now," Bee's happy voice cracked with now-fake optimism about Kate —

—as Kate stopped moving her spotlight because her new boyfriend, Torian, appeared next to her and moved in for a kiss.

*Gross*, thought Bee.

Kate was over-the-top happy to see Torian.

Bee deflated. "Yes, everything was always okay because of Kate until now...now that Torian joined Entertainment Club, the club Kate and I founded, and he found Kate." Bee watched

Kate and Torian start to make out. "And I was left alone. With no one finding me. Not even close."

Bee turned away from Kate and Torian's blissful annoying love to watch Owen work it onstage with his rap number and football team crew. She took a deep breath in to recover and exhaled slowly and steadily then continued. "Luckily, I have hope. And dreams." Bee lifted the mic on her headset to talk to Kate, "Okay, I'm going for it."

Kate pulled away from Torian—not an easy task—barely getting her mic up. "Okay. Go! Do it! You're awesome!" Kate encouraged Bee.

Bee felt a surge of hope again from Kate's enthusiastic support. "And I'm going for it with my best friend Kate at my side—in spite of Bore-ian," Bee added then took another breath, grabbed a hand-written poem from her bag and headed down the side aisle, past the crowd of students and families, to the side of the stage, ready to go up next in her talent show debut—

—just as Owen finished his rap number, and the audience went nuts.

Master of Ceremonies Mason stepped forward to the mic. "Next, give it up for a last minute add," he encouraged, then got confused when he read the name, "Flatfoot...Poet?"

Everyone—the whole school and guest audience filling the auditorium—laughed.

And Bee, the Flatfoot Poet, froze. She looked to Kate for assurance, but Kate was making out—*again!*—and her spotlight was pointed at the ceiling not at Bee, who was nervously standing on the side of the stage now and ready to go on for her talent number. Bee's heart sank.

"Flatfoot Poet?!" Master of Ceremonies Mason repeated. "Anyone?"

Bee's heart started to pound—*panic, panic, panic!* She couldn't move. Frozen. But she needed to move. She needed to step forward out onto the stage to perform her number, the one she'd prepared for night after night, the hip hop song she'd written and the flatfoot dance steps she'd choreographed to tap out the beats of the song. It was the song she'd worked so hard to perfect, even though it wasn't perfect, but it was really, really great.

But Bee just couldn't step forward. She was paralyzed by fear. Fear that Owen would see her and not like her performance and fear that everyone would see her and laugh, because she was so used to being invisible. And what if her song, her performance was just too weird for all of them? Too different? Too odd? She couldn't think clearly all of a sudden—especially not without Kate. Normally, Kate would back her up and love her no matter what and make her feel proud and right-sized, but Kate was making out and Bee was all on her own and the audience was laughing at her Flatfoot Poet introduction.

Bee quickly hid behind one of the stage curtains instead of stepping out onto the stage.

"Flatfoot Poet?!" Master of Ceremonies Mason called out one more time, now using a funny, deep baritone voice, which got a huge laugh, which just made it worse for Bee—

—which is when Owen ran back out from behind the curtains on the side of the stage to the center of the stage and hammed up a tap dance to fill the void of Bee, the Flatfoot Poet, not appearing. Nick joined him. "Romeo, oh, Romeo," Owen recited as he fake tap danced.

"Wherefore are thou...Romeo?!" Nick and Owen continued together, both attempting to tap dance, which was hilarious on its own.

The crowd ate it up, cracking up at the two clowns.

"Alright," Master of Ceremonies Mason stepped in. "No Flatfoot Poet? Then Fab Five Dancers it is!" And he humorously shooed Owen and Nick away from the mic.

Owen and Nick barreled offstage, which is when Nick slammed into Bee hiding in the curtains.

"Oops, sorry," Nick apologized.

"Sorry," Bee apologized back, flustered by the whole ordeal and not recognizing Nick because he'd just moved back to town and hadn't been there since third grade. "I was just..."

"Hiding in the curtains?" Nick teased with a friendly smile and steadied her.

Bee blushed and wondered, *Who is this guy?*

Then, Owen appeared and playfully grabbed Nick in a headlock and knuckle rubbed his head. "Nick's working on manners," Owen told Bee, teasing his best friend, Nick. "But how 'bout that verse?!" Owen shot her that charming grin and shamelessly winked.

Bee was more flustered by Owen's sparkly smile and charm than anything that had just happened and hurried back to her spotlight station and crumpled her poem. Out of her headset sitting on the light stand, Bee heard Kate's voice demanding, "What happened?!"

Bee grabbed her headset and replied, "You bailed on me!"

"You chickened out!" Kate defended.

"You were making out!" Bee defended right back.

"I was waiting for you to go on!" Kate insisted.

"You hate poetry!" Bee reminded her.

"Doesn't mean I can't support you!" Kate cried.

Bee heard Torian do a growl-esque purr through the headset. And then she heard Kate giggle.

Which was just too much to deal with. So, Bee reached over, attempting to slam the "HEADSET OFF" button. Instead, she accidentally hit "MAIN OFF."

The room went dark—as in the *entire* auditorium. Gasps and cries of confusion rang out from the crowd. No one could see the stage. No one could see anything.

"Doesn't mean I can't hate your boyfriend for ruining our friendship!" Bee shouted to Kate into the headset in the dark and slammed it down.

And Bee felt her heart squeeze and her stomach clench, like she was about to lose the most important person in her life. And she was going to make it worse by walking out. Like what if there was no return? But she was just so angry and hurt so she stormed out of the auditorium leaving everyone in the dark, literally, and not feeling any better for it.

# 2 BEE PLUMB'S PERSONAL & PRIVATE JUNIOR YEAR MANIFESTO

Bee continued to feel awful after the debacle with Kate at the talent show and like she never wanted to talk to anyone ever again. She gloomed around in her room that night and dreaded coming out the next day. What was everyone going to say? But then, it was like nothing ever happened. Her family said nothing about the auditorium going dark and didn't even notice that Bee had been upset.

And when they got to the car for carpool, Kate just said, "Dude, you didn't have to get so agro. Mr. Bradshaw fixed the lights and it was all good." And then, Kate got in back with Torian, and Paige got in front, and they drove to school like nothing ever happened.

It was as if Bee were invisible. Or didn't count. Or her feelings, her insides were invisible. And her outsides seemed normal to everyone.

And it made Bee feel even more alone than before. Like maybe she was going to be alone forever. Which is when her eternal optimism kicked in and she knew she had to find a solution so she could get through this. She leaned hard into this positive thinking for several days and came up with a plan.

And now, several days after the talent show fiasco, Kate was in back with Torian reading Bee's fabulously optimistic plan on her phone as Bee drove out of the school parking lot after Entertainment Club in her beloved old red Chevy—a 1967 Impala sedan 327—and was leaning into how much she loved driving this car.

Bee got the Chevy to drive "for now" from her Nana Jana when Nana Jana bought herself a brand-new Jaguar with all the bells and whistles. So, technically, the car was on loan to Bee indefinitely from her grandma.

Bee's parents always complained that Nana Jana drove too fast and worried that the Jag wasn't going to help that situation. But Bee knew where her grandma was coming from. *Having a car that you love gives you instant freedom*, she thought now and every time she drove. Yes, Bee loved that car from Nana Jana, aptly named the Strawberry Firecracker Bomb Mobile by Nana Jana—or SFB Mobile for short. The SFB Mobile made Bee feel like she finally had something that was all hers—something that she could control—at least until Nana Jana took it back, which hopefully would never happen.

Originally, the SFB Mobile was a present to Nana Jana from Papa Robbie, Bee's grandfather. Papa Robbie was super into cars and had suped it up and made it fancy for Nana Jana already back when they lived in Granada Hills, California. Papa Robbie was a film editor and always drove the coolest old cars. Nana Jana used to do makeup for the movies and loved having a stylish, fast ride. She also liked new things, so she'd go back and forth between driving the SFB Mobile and some other brand-new fast vehicle that she would buy willy nilly on a spree.

After Nana Jana and Papa Robbie moved up to Whitefish, Montana, Nana Jana got new cars more often. She said she needed more excitement now that they were in "the Flathead," aka the Flathead Valley, up in the Northwest. She did love that the Flathead was secretly famous for its fab ski resort—Whitefish's Big Mountain—which she skied in the winter, and Glacier National Park, which she loved to drive through in the spring, summer and fall but never hiked because she wasn't an outdoors person unless it involved speed. Hence, no hiking, camping or cross-country skiing.

Papa Robbie still worked on movies as an editor, and sometimes after the movie was filmed, the director would come up to Whitefish and work with him on his editing machine at their home. Other times, Papa Robbie would go down to Hollywood to work or go "on location" wherever they were filming the movie. Nana Jana usually went along when Papa Robbie was on location for the excitement. While he was at work, she'd play, and if they were in Los Angeles, that often involved speeding up the PCH in her newest roadster.

So, yeah, Bee got lucky with the cool grandparents and cool car, which she'd gotten as soon as she could drive. And right after she got her license, she started driving carpool. Bee loved driving carpool when it was just to school and back and matched her schedule. It usually was Paige and Kate in the mornings, and then, Paige would get some other ride home because Bee and Kate stayed late for Entertainment Club or went and did other stuff after school.

Now, unfortunately, Torian drove with them in carpool too even though he didn't need to. He'd park his own stupid car on their street in the mornings then go and get Kate from her house, and then, he and Kate would walk across the street to Bee's house so Bee could drive them. Kate said it was because Torian knew how much Kate loved to ride with Bee and he didn't want to disturb their time together or make Kate unhappy.

*Yeah, right*—Bee didn't believe it for a second. She figured he just wanted more time with Kate and didn't care about infringing on their friend time together. *So annoying!* she thought.

This whole situation really did make Bee unhappy. So, even if Torian were being altruistic regarding Kate and Bee's friendship, him driving in carpool wasn't exactly a win-win. Though possibly, it was better than Bee never seeing Kate again except when she sat on her lawn across the street making out with Torian Bore-ian. But at this moment, with Kate and Torian in the back seat on the way home from school, it was a tossup.

Bee drove past workers cleaning TP and purple and orange graffiti off their high school. The graffiti read: "THUNDERBIRDS RULE! LIONS DROOL!" Obviously, the crosstown rival team, the Thunderbirds, had done this naughty deed. It was a big rivalry, especially in football and basketball.

Bee glanced in the rearview mirror to the back seat to see if Kate and Torian had noticed the TP and graffiti, but they hadn't. *Why?* Because stupid Torian was kissing Kate's neck as she read Bee's write-up of her plan on Bee's phone, which Bee had just handed her right before they'd started driving.

Bee was getting more and more annoyed with Torian and his stupid PDA. "Yes, for sure, I hated Kate's boyfriend for ruining our friendship," Bee started up with her inner narration to her imaginary audience to assuage her distress. "Especially after the talent show! And now, there's Kate back there in the back seat reading my supposed private writing, and somehow, everything is becoming super clear. Yes, now I know! Things have to change. If I want a life, I have to take destiny into my own hands, without Kate." This was painful, but Bee continued, forcing herself to sound persuasive to herself, trying desperately to convince herself, "Kate doesn't care anyway. And I'm never going to tell her anything personal ever again!"

"I like it," Kate said cheerfully, looking up from Bee's phone, meeting eyes with Bee in the rearview mirror. "Junior Year Manifesto. Nice ring to it: JYM."

"Really?" Bee chirped, totally surprised by this unexpected positive reaction to her plan from Kate, which made her very, very happy.

But then, it got bad. Because Kate started to read what Bee had written in her Junior Year Manifesto aloud. Her very private, inner hopes. *Out loud!* From Bee's phone! While Torian was right there! *"Bee Plumb's PERSONAL & PRIVATE Junior Year Manifesto. Number One,"* Kate read.

"No!" Bee shouted at Kate. "What are you doing?! Stop!"

Kate didn't stop. She just kept going, right from Bee's

manifesto, *"Go after what I want in an esteemed and respectful way."*

"I don't want him to hear!" Bee cried desperately, meaning she didn't want Torian to hear her personal thoughts and personal goals, and she reached back unsuccessfully to grab her phone from Kate.

Kate continued reading Bee's manifesto, "And *Two, be awesome enough to like myself and my life so I can get Owen to notice me.* Nice!" Kate beamed, pleased with her friend's sudden bravery.

"You have no respect for my personal space," Bee scolded. "Either of you!" Then, she screeched up to her cookie-cutter tract house in North Kalispell and tried to grab her phone from Kate again, reaching into the back seat.

Kate held Bee's phone out of reach as she got out of the car. "He's not even listening," Kate defended her actions regarding Torian. "Torian doesn't care about your manifesto or if Owen notices you." Then, she looked over at Bee's sister, Paige, and Paige's boyfriend, Tommy, sitting on the stoop.

On the lawn, the Plumb family's Spanish exchange student, Diego—a hot, passionate, fifteen-year-old artist, obsessed with Bee—sculpted a life-size statue/installation of his love: Beatrix "Bee" Plumb.

"Mom! Bee's here!" Paige shouted back into the house.

Bee and Torian got out of the Strawberry Firecracker Bomb Mobile, and exchange-student Diego snapped a Polaroid of Bee's annoyed face.

Bee's mom, Judy, appeared at the door.

"Hi, Honey!" Judy exclaimed to Bee. "I need you to take Paige to get new toe shoes after you help Diego with math. Unless you have something."

Bee shook her head *no,* as if she didn't have any other things that she'd rather do and some that she needed to do. She was a sucker, and every time her mom asked her to drive Paige to her stupid classes, she was too chicken to stand up for herself, and she always agreed. Same thing with tutoring Diego.

"Great! Super helpful! Thank you!" Judy chimed and disappeared inside.

Bee, Kate and Torian watched Diego rip off Statue Bee's

clay nose, slam a new clay blob on Statue Bee's face and go at the nose. *Totally weird.*

Kate whispered to Torian, "So glad my parents aren't into the whole exchange student thing."

"I can hear you," Bee snipped at Kate, annoyed.

Kate held up Bee's phone with a grin, deflecting, "And I am so psyched about your manifesto!"

Bee tried to grab her phone back from Kate.

Kate held it away, playing keep away. "You just have to come up with a great way for Owen to notice you," Kate cried as she whipped around, holding the phone out of Bee's reach.

Bee persisted, jumping around Kate, almost getting it.

But Kate was fast.

Bee and Kate wrestled for the phone.

"Put yourself out there!" Kate continued as they jostled about. "Like we did with Entertainment Club! And look what happened!"

Finally, Bee stopped trying to get the phone, totally out of breath. She glared at Torian. He grinned. Bee turned back to Kate. "*We*, emphasis on *we*," Bee reminded her friend. "*We* started Entertainment Club. Then, he joined, and now, everything's different." Bee quickly grabbed the phone and shot Kate a "there!" look before reluctantly turning to Diego. "C'mon, Diego, let's do your math," she barked then started into the house.

Diego dutifully followed.

Kate yelled after Bee from the sidewalk, "We'll help you! Tomorrow at school! We'll come up with a plan. To execute your plan. I mean, manifesto. We'll get you noticed."

Bee stopped; she so wanted to believe that Kate would help her, while in her ear from behind, Diego sang like a nouveau love-obsessed Sting, "Don't stand so, don't stand so..."

And Kate cheered, "You'll see! JYM!" And she smiled at Bee, pleased, as Torian pulled her across the street to the Towers' house with the beautifully manicured lawn and railroad ties along one side, marking the edge of the small hill covered in that tiny kind of cute ice plant.

# 3 BEE SCHEMES TO GET OWEN IN HER CARPOOL

The early morning sun peeked through Bee's east-facing bedroom window as Bee smoothed her favorite flirty dress in front of her stand-up mirror. She liked dresses, especially ones with flowers on them. This one was green with little yellow buttercups. And she liked that she was carrying out her plan, embracing her manifesto, going for it.

She stood tall and smiled at herself in the mirror as she clutched a clipping of a newspaper photo of Owen as the Lions' quarterback from the previous year and continued narrating her life to her invisible listeners, "So, that was it, just me and my manifesto. No Kate, no more. But that was okay. Because I was going to rock my destiny, by myself. In fact, I already had! Right, Owen?"

Bee looked at Owen in the newspaper clipping as if he could hear then held up the news-photo Owen so "he" looked in the mirror with her and at her and could hear her even better. "I mean, just yesterday I got you to see me," she told news-photo Owen. "Right?"

Which is when Bee flashed back in her mind to "yesterday" after school when she was standing outside on the front high school walkway by the parking lot waiting for Kate and Torian so she could drive Kate home. Torian had to stay late for some stupid music thing, and Bee felt totally left out because Kate and Torian were making out right then because they stupidly couldn't stand to be apart ever—*For what, like five seconds?!* Bee complained in her head.

Suddenly, out of the corner of her eye, Bee spotted Owen approaching her with his football friends.

Bee froze as Owen passed and headed towards a suped-up truck waiting for him curbside. She heard the words, "C'mon, Bee. JYM! JYM!"—in her head and felt an electrifying surge of confidence and fear course through every cell in her body, and she ran after Owen, yelling, loud, determined to get his attention, "Hey! Owen! I heard your car's in the shop!"

Owen stopped.

Bee gasped. Then, awkwardly, nervously, forced herself to speak, "So, um, if you need a ride to school....! Since we're neighbors...! Practically!" She laughed nervously. "Lemme know. You know, like if I just happen to be driving by. Carpool. In the red Chevy. SFB Mobile. And I just happen to see you. It'd be easy. Just shout out, whatever." Bee smiled, trying as hard as possible to be cute and nonchalant.

Owen shrugged, "Sure, why not?" Then, he shot her his gorgeous grin and hopped in his friend's truck, and they peeled out.

"Ohmigosh!" Bee exclaimed to herself. "He said 'why not?' He SAID WHY NOT?!!!!"

Bee came back to the present from remembering this flashback of this fabulous moment from the previous day. It was still super early morning, but Bee had left her house and gotten in her car while thinking about this awesomeness, and she was now driving, pulling away from her house as she continued narrating her story to her imaginary listeners, "And here we are. Bright and early to give Owen a ride to school." Yes, her manifesto was being put into action, and she was about to get Owen to notice her, like *really notice her.*

Bee glanced at the time on her phone on the seat next to her in the SFB Mobile: 7:03 a.m. And she justified to herself,

"Giving him a ride to school so he doesn't have to walk." Her plan was to catch him as he exited his house to walk to school.

Bee put on one of her favorite disco-y R&B songs, "September," by one of her favorite funky R&B bands that she was super into at the moment—Earth, Wind & Fire—and sang as she turned the corner in this quiet, older residential neighborhood in North Kalispell, just east of Whitefish Stage Road, where Owen lived, while Bee and her family lived just west of it in the newer tract-home neighborhood.

She waved to a morning jogger. "Hi, Mr. Jones!...Hi, Owen's house!" Bee added as she waved to Owen's ranch-style house that looked similar to the others except that it had old strands of TP in the big tree in front.

Bee continued round the block then stopped just round the corner from Owen's again. "Super perfect," she told herself. "And super...Owen?" Bee gasped, totally confused by what she was seeing: There, right down the street on the other side, was Owen, sitting shotgun in a sporty purple Cabrio, talking to the driver, sixteen-year-old Jade Brand, the hot-headed cheerleader of the Lions' crosstown rival team, the Thunderbirds. "Huh?!" Bee wondered to herself in shock from this sight. She knew the driver was a girl but didn't recognize Jade at first.

Meanwhile, inside Jade's Cabrio, Owen, oblivious to Bee, was watching Jade, who was also oblivious to Bee. Jade was focused on a just-opened gift box she was holding, revealing gorgeous blue Italian glass earrings that Owen had just given her. Owen's look said that he was totally smitten with Jade and gushy in love.

Jade's eyes said that she was superbly happy with the gift. She shut the box. "May the best team win," she asserted with a mischievous smirk.

Owen growled playfully. Their eyes met in intense attraction.

"My stealth girlfriend," Owen boasted.

Jade grabbed Owen's shirt roughly, almost kissing him. "As long as there's no other girl," she demanded.

Overly smitten by this, Owen made a growling big cat

sound, then put on his charming smile and shook his head "no," insisting there was no other girl but Jade for him.

Jade let go of Owen's shirt. "Just checking," she snarled.

Owen was even more smitten—which is when he noticed Bee watching them from her cool red Chevy. "Shoot! Little Neighbor With The Car!" Owen exclaimed.

Jade saw Bee too. "Run," Jade instructed. "Don't let her see us!"

Owen ducked and exited Jade's purple Cabrio.

Jade peeled out.

Bee saw Owen sneak down the block as Jade zoomed past her with her "T" and "Thunderbird Cheer Squad Does It Loud" decals on her car.

"A Thunderbird! What?!" Bee was shocked. She recognized Jade from the Thunderbird cheer squad from when she and Kate went to games. But she didn't know the cheerleader's name. "How could he be hanging out with a Thunderbird?" Bee cried about Owen.

Confused, Bee started driving after Owen, who was trying to ditch her. Bee rolled down the driver-side window and called after him, "Hey! Owen! Wait up! You okay?" She could tell that he was worried about being caught with a Thunderbird. "But he doesn't have to be," Bee told herself. "I understand...right?" But Bee wasn't sure that she did.

And Bee's calls for Owen to stop were futile. Owen couldn't hear her at all. He was too focused on his getaway. He ducked behind a hedge and into an alley.

Bee followed, driving slowly, yelling out the window, "Did you need a ride...?!"

Owen jumped several fences and ducked behind some bushes in the front yard of one of the neighborhood houses to hide.

"Shoot," Bee muttered, then shouted to Owen in desperation. "Owen! Wait! That's the house...! With the bees!"

Bee slowed. A car behind Bee honked. The bush Owen was hiding in started to shake and swarm. Bee waved the annoyed driver behind her around, just as—

Owen flew out of the bush, bees attacking, Owen crying out in fear and pain.

The driver swerved past Bee, not seeing Owen dart out and—BAM!—hit Owen.

Bee gasped and scrambled out of her car. "Owen, no!!!! You said, *Why not?...!* You said, *Why not?...!*"

The bees attacked Owen, who was clutching a purple and orange Thunderbird scarf.

Bee grabbed a fire extinguisher and sprayed it to stop the bees.

# 4 THE LIONS THINK BEE IS OWEN'S SECRET GIRLFRIEND

Owen, out cold on major meds, lay in a hospital bed in a waist-up body cast and right-leg cast, bee stings on his face.

Bee stood awkwardly by Owen's parents, Gloria and Jim Fleet, and Owen's eleven-year-old sister, Claire. Claire had an annoyed, judge-y, distrusting look on her face as she watched Bee's every move.

A doctor was just leaving.

"Thank you, again, doctor," Mrs. Fleet gushed.

"Thank the gal that got him here so fast," the doctor replied, smiling at Bee—clearly the superhero gal he was referring to. "Your son got lucky," the doctor smiled warmly at Owen's mom and exited the room.

"We can't thank you enough, Bee," Mrs. Fleet gushed at Bee now.

Bee blushed. "It was just lucky that I was there," she managed, obviously a total lie.

Claire eyed Bee suspiciously, sensing something weird about this "Bee" girl who saved her brother from *the bees. Too bizarre*, Claire disparaged in her head.

"Will we see you tomorrow, Bee?" Mrs. Fleet asked, voice croaking with emotion, hope and perfect manners.

Bee smiled sympathetically and nodded.

"I'm sure Owen will appreciate that," Mrs. Fleet managed, on the edge of tears. "Everything. When he recovers." Mrs. Fleet started to cry, and Mr. Fleet ushered her and Claire out of Owen's hospital room, Claire shooting Bee a disdainful look as she exited.

Bee felt awful. She went over to Owen. *Still gorgeous*, she thought. *Criminy*. She tried to brush the hair out of his eye, gently, but it was stuck on bee-sting medication goop. "Oh, gosh. I'm sorry, Owen. I'm really, really sorry," she told him, even though he was totally out of it and couldn't hear or comprehend a word she said.

Bee watched Owen breathe for a moment, then whispered encouragingly, "But you're gonna be okay. And I got your friend's scarf!" And she discreetly "showed" him the purple and orange scarf that she had hiding in her tote bag—even though his eyes were shut—that she'd grabbed from the scene of the accident. "Kinda weird that you were hanging with a Thunderbird though," Bee admitted.

Owen groaned and a giant spit bubble formed on his lips. Bee popped the bubble and wiped it off with the scarf. She felt totally guilty.

Then, suddenly, she heard a ruckus in the hall.

And a deep voice bellowed out, "Alright, Lions, listen up!"

Bee panicked and looked for a place to hide—

—as the Lions' football team, over-confident cheerleaders and Coach Wells—ex all-star, beaten down by team drama, fund cutting and divorce—gathered right outside the open door.

Bee, trapped, watched, listened, heart racing.

"This isn't going to be pretty," Coach Wells continued with his loud, baritone voice, "but Owen's strong and he'll recover fast. A couple weeks of meds, intensive rehab, and he'll be back." Then, Coach Wells faltered and croaked under his breath, his distress escaping, "Next year."

But no one seemed to hear his worry.

And everyone cheered.

Coach Wells tried to muster enthusiasm, "To win."

Everyone shouted, "To win!"

Coach Wells took a breath and entered the room.

Bee pressed against a wall at the side of the hospital room, hoping not to be seen but, for once, to be her usual invisible self.

Coach Wells froze when he saw Owen. They all did. A guttural sound emanated from Coach Wells.

Running back Glenn looked worried about their supposedly fearless leader and asked him, "You okay, Coach Wells?"

Coach Wells nodded, grabbed his inhaler and inhaled. "Fine," he managed unconvincingly, lungs full. "Perfectly fine!" He exhaled. "And we're all going to be fine!...Right, Lions?"

Owen groaned. Another bubble formed on his lips. *So not fine.*

Coach Wells frowned. "Because we got Lion spirit," he croaked, barely audibly, "and we..." He walked over to Owen, stared at the bubble, not sure what to do, about to fall apart. "...*were* gonna win the State Championship." He bit his hand.

Head Cheerleader Demi Steele—gorgeous, poised, born leader, micro-manager—whispered to running back Glenn in disbelief, repeating Coach Wells' words but with total disdain and disbelief, "'*Were* gonna win'...?! *Were*?!! Past tense?!!!!"

Coach Wells wanted to pop the bubble on Owen's lips but couldn't get himself to do it.

Bee stepped in to do the deed. "Here you go," she assured Coach Wells and popped Owen's mouth bubble. "See. Better already," she grinned, hoping to make Coach Wells feel better and wanting to ensure him that everything would be okay. Even though she had no idea if anything would ever be okay again.

All eyes were suddenly on Bee as she wiped the popped bubble off of Owen's face.

"Who are you?" Coach Wells asked Bee.

"Yeah, who are you?" chimed chirpy cheerleader Chrissie.

"Me?" Bee managed. "I'm, um...leaving." Bee waved and

bolted for the door.

Demi stepped in. "Wait," she demanded of Bee.

The linebackers closed together to support Demi's attempt at stopping Bee and blocked her from leaving.

Lion defense Drew-ster joked to Lion defense Trent, "Maybe she's the secret girlfriend."

"What?" Bee cried, stunned by this comment.

The guys laughed. Trent high-fived Drew-ster.

"Owen's girlfriend?" wondered cheerleader Chrissie.

"Me?!" cried Bee.

"No wonder he kept it a secret," joked Trent.

More laughs filled the room. Coach Wells groaned and thought—*Here we go again*. This Owen girlfriend drama was nothing new to him or the team.

"Yay! It's not Jade!" cheered Chrissie about Owen's secret girlfriend.

"Jade?" wondered Bee.

Demi sized up Bee then took control of the Jade-mention situation. "Jade was a summer fling," she informed the room. "Owen broke up with her as soon as he found out she was a Thunderbird. And actually, you make sense, in a totally unexpected Owen-esque way." Meaning Bee made sense as Owen's girlfriend.

"No, I don't make sense," insisted Bee. "I'm just, the neighbor, Bee. He was, I was...giving him a ride to school. In the carpool."

"Our school?" wondered running back Glenn.

"And there were bees," continued Bee desperately.

Demi instantly recognized the opportunity here. The wheels turned in lightning speed, and she exclaimed, "You're the one who saved him!"—playing it up to hit it home for everyone in the room that Bee was the superhero in this situation and, of course, Owen's girlfriend.

Cheerleader Chrissie bought it instantly, "She's the girlfriend! Bee's the girlfriend! The secret one!"

"No," Bee defended.

"Told-ya he had someone on the sly," Drew-ster boasted,

and he and Trent high-fived.

"Wait, you're the girlfriend?" Coach Wells blurted out at Bee, equally shocked.

"Yes!" Demi cheered. "And any girlfriend of Owen's is a friend of ours."

Everyone enveloped Bee in a group hug.

Overwhelmed, Bee laughed nervously and bolted from the room, instantly relieved to be out and able to breathe.

Coach Wells was right behind her, exiting Owen's hospital room door into the hallway.

Coach Wells and Bee both caught their breaths, and Demi stepped over just inside the door to eavesdrop, where they couldn't see her.

"It can get overwhelming," Coach Wells consoled Bee knowingly. "All that spirit all the time. But what can you do?" He poured two cups of water at the water cooler—one for her, one for him. He downed one, but then got lost in thought and pounded the cup of water meant for Bee before he could give it to her. Then, he realized he'd forgotten her and poured her another cup of water and handed it to her. "At least you're a nice girl," he told Bee kindly as he poured himself a third cup, "not a distraction for Owen. Gives me some hope. For next year." He toasted his water cup to Bee.

Bee toasted back and drank, relieved by Coach Wells' comment.

"And this year, our baby quarterback Reno gets slaughtered," Coach Wells added, downing his third water, suddenly miserable again.

Bee felt unbearably guilty. "Well, I'm sure it's not that bad," she attempted.

Coach Wells' look said it was more than bad.

"Like, uh...," Bee continued, searching her mind for a solution, then tried to help with, "maybe he'll surprise you. Reno. Or...or...maybe everyone else will play so amazingly it won't matter!"

Coach Wells stopped, considering this possibility.

"See, there is a little hope," Bee added. She smiled nervously and awkwardly patted Coach Wells' arm—

—as Demi's voice chimed from the door, and she stepped out from her hiding spot, cheering, "Hope!"

The team was right behind her and crammed in the doorway. Demi pushed timid, giraffe-skinny, fifteen-year-old second-string quarterback Reno forward toward Coach Wells.

Cheerleader Chrissie cheered, "Go, Reno!"

Everyone joined in, "Go, Reno!"

Reno turned bright red.

"Someone shoot me," groaned Coach Wells under his breath.

"And go Lions!" Demi shouted and got in there with the team and cheer squad. "Let's show Reno how it's done! Woooooo!"

The team ran out from Owen's hospital room, surrounded Reno and lifted him up.

The Lion football team and cheerleaders chanted, "Reno! Reno! Reno!"

Demi beamed at Coach Wells.

Bee was paralyzed with horror—*How on earth is this happening?*

Coach Wells glanced at Bee and hit his inhaler.

And Bee knew this was the most awful day of her life and there was nothing she could do to fix it.

# 5 LION DEMI AND THUNDERBIRD JADE KEEP BEE IN CHECK

Shortly after the Reno pep rally, Demi escorted a still-in-panic-and-shock Bee down the hospital hallway to the elevator and hugged her way too tight. "You totally saved us," Demi rejoiced to Bee. "I swear, if you hadn't showed up, Coach Wells was 'gonna walk. Or suffocate." She smirked.

"Actually, Demi...," Bee tried to cut her off before she got too excited.

"Seriously," Demi deftly shut Bee down, "Owen's the only thing that's kept Coach Wells going since his ex bailed on him. And Nick."

*Nick?* Bee wondered to herself. *Who's Nick?* Clearly, she hadn't heard Owen mention Nick's name after she bumped into him in the stage curtains that night at the talent show.

Demi fixed Bee's hair, and a loving smile came over her. "You actually remind me of Owen. Totally positive. I seriously see you two together, and I have no idea why he kept you a secret."

"Actually, I think...," Bee tried again to stop Demi before this secret girlfriend thing got out of hand.

"Don't think. Just be happy," Demi insisted, playing it perfectly. "Owen's gonna pull through. And we are so lucky you were there." Demi pumped up some calculated teary emotion, then deftly reigned it in to assure Bee that she was strong and courageous, and then, she hugged Bee.

Bee was paralyzed, tongue-tied, overwhelmed. She laughed nervously, nodded and bolted, leaving Demi with a satisfied grin on her face. "Touché," Demi told herself. "For the win."

***

Bee hurried into the hospital parking garage after escaping Demi. She just wanted to get out of there and go home, away from her guilt about causing this disaster with Owen and this stupid lie about being his secret girlfriend. She had to think. She had to find a solution. She had to come up with a new plan.

Suddenly, out of nowhere, a loud HONK! reverberated through the garage.

Bee screamed and jumped. Then, she heard a screeching voice—

"Pssst! Get in the friggin car!" It was Jade in the purple Cabrio with orange Thunderbird stickers, sunk low, hiding.

*What the...?* Bee recognized the car from earlier that day.

Jade honked again. Bee nervously looked around, wanting this Thunderbird nut to shut up. *Please just stop*, she thought. *No more attention.*

One more honk, and Bee ran over and hopped in Jade's car shotgun.

The doors locked. Bee was trapped.

And Jade was instantly up in Bee's face with a purple spray-paint can. "Betray me and I'll go Thunderbird ballistic on you," Jade threatened.

"What? No. What do you mean?" Bee pulled back, turning her face away to avoid the spray paint.

Jade did a tiny spray, purple spray paint shooting out onto Bee's hair on the side of her head. "You're just a freaky stalker aren't you?" Jade sneered.

Bee was confused. "Stalker?"

"Just tell me he's really okay," Jade demanded about Owen's health status and pushed the spray paint closer to Bee's face. "Tell me Owen's okay!"

"He's okay! Will be okay!" Bee cried, trying to placate this ballistic Thunderbird.

"Then, tell me what they know!" Jade insisted.

"Who?"

"The Lions! About the accident!"

"Nothing. He was attacked by bees. And got hit by a car," Bee recounted to Jade.

"Nothing about me?" Jade demanded.

"No," Bee insisted.

Jade wasn't convinced. "So Little Neighbor With The Car didn't tell them I was there?" she interrogated.

"Little Neighbor?" Bee asked. "What the heck are you talking about?"

Jade did another tiny spray of purple paint.

This one hit Bee's face, right on the nose and mug. Bee grimaced, trying not to show any emotion, not wiping it off, as if it didn't faze her at all.

"And you're not going to tell, are you?" Jade threatened. "Because you're a pathetic Owen groupie. And Owen'd hate you if you told his secret. Just like I hate that he can't tell them about me!!!"

"You?" Bee wondered, totally in the dark here.

"We're best friends," Jade lied then smiled and reached back for Owen's sports bag and slammed it on Bee's lap. Her smile turned contemptuous. "And Thunderbirds and Lions can't be friends." Then, Jade abruptly ripped open the sports bag and produced the blue Italian glass earrings in the gift box with a crazed look, like she was gonna blow. "Friendship earrings from Owen that I can't wear," Jade told Bee about what was in the gift box. "In case I forget and wear them, and Nick sees, or anyone." She opened the box quickly and showed Bee the gorgeous blue glass earrings.

"Nick?" Bee wondered aloud and thought, *Again with this Nick person.*

"As if I would forget to not wear them and give away our secret!!!" Jade cried, not even registering the Nick comment. She shut the earring gift box and squeezed it, crushing it, getting madder and madder. Then, she threw it in the back seat and smiled, maniacally, fishing for answers, "Or maybe there's another reason Owen's hiding me...like another girl! Friend!" She grabbed Bee's shirt, fisting it into a bunch by the collar, pulling Bee close so they were nose to nose.

"What other girl?! Friend?" Bee cried, innocently oblivious to this drama.

"There'd better not be another girl!" Jade threatened.

"He doesn't even talk to me!" Bee defended. "Or like me! But look, here! He was clutching it—when he went down." Jade let go of Bee's shirt as Bee pulled out the purple and orange scarf.

Jade took the scarf, her scarf, smelled it, trying to detect any bit of Owen's perfect scent, suddenly looking totally vulnerable. Then, she pressed the scarf to her face and inhaled like it was a bouquet of glorious Owen. Then, she slammed it down and rallied with a vengeance in defense of her love, "If you tell anyone that Owen and I are friends, I will take you and his star-boy reputation down."

Bee laughed nervously and bolted out of the car.

# 6 BEST FRIEND KATE AND ENAMORED EXCHANGE STUDENT DIEGO ARE NO HELP AT ALL

Bee sat in the Strawberry Firecracker Bomb Mobile in front of her house clutching Owen's gym bag as she watched Kate and Torian do a "trust" exercise on Kate's front lawn across the street: Torian standing behind Kate who was standing plank-straight, ready to fall back and have him catch her. Bee had called Kate from the hospital parking lot right after the Jade incident. She desperately wanted to tell Kate what had happened with Owen and Jade. But Kate hadn't picked up. Instead, Kate texted Bee that she didn't have time to talk. So, Bee had texted Kate all the details about the whole situation and then also left a voice message for full emotional effect. And now, Bee was hoping to get help from her best friend about what to do with this disaster even though she didn't want to deal with any of it at all.

"C'mon, you got this," Bee told herself, pumping herself up, encouraging herself to go and get Kate's advice, even though Kate clearly hadn't had time to talk to her but had tons of time for this falling-trust thing with Torian, which was super annoying and discouraging to Bee.

Bee got out of the car anyway and walked across the street.

"Hey, there," she said as Kate stood still as a plank, getting ready to fall back but still trying to reposition herself in just the perfect spot.

"Wow, you're in it," Kate said as she inched to the left.

"You read the text?" Bee asked.

"Yup," Kate smirked. "And heard the message."

"What's so funny?" Bee was annoyed, even though she knew that the mischievous look on Kate's face meant Kate was intrigued and cared and had an opinion and, therefore, maybe advice. Still, Bee was pissed. "This is a mess!"

"So, Jade's his jealous secret friend and the team thinks he has a secret girlfriend?" Kate grinned, repeating what Bee had just told her in the text and voice message. "Wow."

"It's weird," Bee replied, feeling more and more defeated by the minute.

Kate had a different take. "Totally unbelievable actually, but lucky! For you—Owen's 'girlfriend'! It's awesome!" Kate chimed then nodded to Torian and fell back plank-straight. Torian caught her. She smiled up at him.

"It's not awesome," Bee countered.

"You totally went along with it!" Kate reminded Bee of this reality.

"Because they're so desperate!" Bee defended as she watched Torian push Kate back up to a standing position. Bee deflated. "And they're kind of nice, and I feel so guilty." Bee frowned.

"Well then it's a total win-win," Kate beamed. "You save Owen's reputation and get him to notice you, and they get something good to focus on." Kate handed Bee her phone to video them doing another plank-trust fall.

"You're just saying that so I'll have something to focus on," Bee accused Kate as she started to film her and Torian as they switched positions.

"Exactly!" Kate cheered as she went and stood behind Torian. "Helping Owen's team win! Your poet soul mate, like you said." Kate caught Torian as he fell back, and she beamed down at him. They cooed like pigeons in love.

Bee stopped filming. "I can't do it, Kate; it's too weird," Bee insisted about the Owen-fake-girlfriend thing.

Kate took her phone back from Bee and played back the video as she continued consulting Bee on her dilemma, "Okay, let's play devil's advocate. Say you take away the only bright spot on the team's horizon, and they find out about Jade, and the Lions tank the rest of the season and don't make State. And all Owen's hard work goes to waste. Could you live with that? When all you have to do is pretend to be his girlfriend for a little while?" Kate smiled at Bee and praised her for the video, "Excellent framing, Bee. JYM!"

*Crud*, thought Bee. *Even Kate isn't helping.* And she moped home feeling even worse, with Kate calling after her, "It's gonna be fine. Just be patient!" Which didn't help at all.

***

Back in her room after the exchange with Kate, Bee threw Owen's bag down and flopped on her bed, miserable, feeling more guilty than ever and feeling the weight of the Lions' chances at the State Championship on her shoulders. She looked at her Owen news photo. *That smile*, she thought.

Then, out of nowhere, there was a KNOCK, KNOCK on her bedroom door.

"Who is it?" Bee called out.

Diego's cheerful voice came through the door, "Your favorite Diego. Future mathematician fantastico."

Bee groaned. "I know who you are, Diego," she replied as calmly as possible, determined not to open the door. She just couldn't deal with him in her current pool of misery and guilt.

"I have brought you another Friday afternoon delight," Diego continued through the door. "Made by me!"

Bee caved, dragged herself over and opened the door.

A FLASH of light blinded her as Diego snapped a Polaroid and offered her paella on a plate, his special dish that, apparently, his mother taught him to make back in Spain when he was just ten.

Bee slammed the door in Diego's face.

Suddenly, a shrimp came sliding under the door.

Bee stared at the pink sea creature in Diego's yummy paella sauce, then turned and took in Owen's news-photo smile and deflated. She was at a complete loss as to what to do.

# 7 BEE CONFESSES HER TRUTH TO OUT-OF-IT OWEN

Bee walked through the hospital hallway, slowly approaching Owen's hospital room. She was filled with dread and in her own world and didn't see Demi by the nurse's station. But Demi definitely noticed Bee and went on high alert. *What is she doing here?!* Demi wondered.

Bee entered Owen's hospital room slowly.

Demi followed but stopped at the door and positioned herself just so to eavesdrop and peek in.

As Bee stepped forward, she saw that Owen was sleeping. *He looks so peaceful too*, she thought and wished that she felt that peaceful.

Then, Bee sat down in a chair next to Owen's bed and listened to him breathing for a few minutes. She knew she had to say something. She'd been thinking about it nonstop—ever since Kate reminded her of how much the Lions' football team needed to believe in Owen if they wanted to get to the State Championship, let alone win it—like they had been poised to do before this Owen-in-a-body-cast disaster. And Bee had decided that she just needed to see Owen in person. She thought that maybe seeing him would give her insight about what to do. Which is why she was there now at the hospital by his bedside—hoping that seeing him would help her figure it out. Help her be her true self. Bee knew she had to be her true self to find a solution. She had to listen to her heart and do the right thing.

Owen stirred.

Bee leaned close. "Hi, it's me again—Bee," she began. "The one who created this mess."

Owen drifted back to sleep, still totally out of it from the meds.

Demi quietly peeked in the door, quickly, to suss out the situation, then pulled back so as not to be seen.

"And look, I brought you this," Bee continued. She pulled out a handmade Owen collage from her bag and held it up as if Owen could see it.

The collage was made up entirely of close-up photos of Owen and Owen getting accolades in football.

"Okay, so I've been stalking you since kindergarten," Bee admitted to Owen, laughing at herself, then quickly hiding the collage on her lap.

"I also brought this," Bee said. "I was gonna sing it at the rally." She pulled out a crumpled paper with handwritten lyrics and whisper-sang them, "We are Lions; Hear us...soar; Bears, Falcons, Thunderbirds, bring it, more; No match for Fleet; Rise above; Champions are we; Roar and love." Bee looked up at Owen and blushed. "Okay, even more embarrassing."

She shoved the paper with lyrics back in her bag then smiled at Owen, nervously psyching herself up to say what she had to admit next. "And now you're going to hate me. Because they think I'm your girlfriend, and you don't even know my name."

Bee started to get emotional, unable to hold her embarrassment and guilt in as she continued, "Which is super humiliating. Because I actually thought you liked me. I mean..."

She "showed" him the Owen collage again and pointed to his smile. "You've been smiling at me like that since first grade. What else was I supposed to think?"

Bee held back tears and watched a bubble form on Owen's lips.

"You see? Even when you're foaming at the mouth, I love you," Bee cried and popped Owen's mouth bubble. "I can't help it. You're the only one that ever made me feel okay. Even if it was just a stupid fantasy."

Bee looked down at one of Owen's photo smiles on the collage and touched it, feeling terribly miserable, not noticing Demi's "oh crud" look as she peeked in from the hospital hallway around the doorjamb.

# 8 BEE GETS A CHEER SQUAD GIRLFRIEND ASSIGNMENT

After her exhausting revelation of bittersweet heartfelt honesty to her heartthrob crush Owen and the resulting sense of relief that came with the truth expressed out loud, even though Owen couldn't understand a word of what Bee had said since he was totally out of it from the painkillers, Bee had curled up on an armchair in Owen's hospital room and fell asleep on top of her Owen collage and Owen's collage-photo smile like a pillow. The last thing she expected as she drifted off was for anyone to come in, but shortly after she began snoring lightly, a chorus of song echoed through the halls outside Owen's room, "The Lions go marching four by four, hoorah, hoorah...," as the Lions' football team and cheerleaders marched in.

Bee popped up.

The cheer squad did a jump-spin-thingy and launched cheerleader Chrissie right over Bee.

Bee ducked. "Ohmigosh, what are you doing?!" she cried.

Cheerleader Chrissie called out to Bee with glee, "You're here! Yay! Just in time for our pep rally!"

Bee quickly hid the Owen-crush-revealing collage.

Luckily, cheerleader Chrissie turned her attention to

sleeping Owen and talked to him as if he weren't totally out of it. "And look! Owen! We found it!" she cheered as she grabbed a life-size, stand-up cardboard-backed photo image of Owen from blushing Reno and presented it to Owen as if he could see it. "So you can be with us! In spirit! When we beat the Bears tonight!"

Cheerleader Chrissie frowned when Owen didn't react to the life-size cardboard replica of himself then turned to Bee, desperation cracking through her cheer. "I think he wants to be with Bee," she cried—meaning that she thought Cardboard Owen should hang with Bee as if he were real and had real feelings.

"Uh, actually, I've gotta go," Bee managed. "Maybe, someone else can...?"

Demi stepped in to protect cheerleader Chrissie's feelings. "It's okay, Chrissie, I'll do it," she comforted then shot Bee a wicked glare.

*What the heck?* Bee shuddered from Demi's look.

"No," cheerleader Chrissie insisted to Demi, unwilling to even hand over the cardboard Owen stand-up to her. "He wants to be with Bee! She can bring him to the game tonight! Her official girlfriend cheer job!" Chrissie jutted stand-up Cardboard Owen out at Bee.

Bee stared at Owen's likeness.

"And then you can come to the party after!" Chrissie continued to Bee. "It's my birthday! And Nick'll be there. Back from his mom's wedding. Please." Chrissie looked desperate.

*Nick?* Bee wondered.

Demi looked tense.

All eyes were on Bee.

She caved. "You know what?" Bee said. "Why not? For now." Bee smiled, grabbed stand-up Cardboard Owen and took off.

And the team and cheer squad broke out in mega cheers behind her.

***

Bee sat in her upstairs window, poetry notebook in her lap. The Lions vs Bears game was starting soon, and she had no intention of going, even with her new Cardboard Owen cheer squad/girlfriend assignment.

Instead, she watched Kate and Torian head out clad in green, blue and gold, the Lion school colors. *Definitely going to the game*, Bee thought about Kate. Kate had asked her to hang with them that night, but Bee hadn't replied to Kate's text. Everything was just too emotional, and right now, she didn't think even Kate would help, even if Kate paid attention to Bee, which she hadn't been much lately.

Kate and Torian saw Bee in the window and waved. *Ugh.*

Bee shot them an unenthusiastic hand-up-and-not-waving wave-type signal then looked out at Diego working on his Bee installation on the front lawn. *Double ugh.*

Then, Bee turned to stand-up Cardboard Owen and his cheeky grin. "See, we are going to have a nice evening in, complete with poetry reciting," she told her cardboard friend. "And hot chocolate."

Bee toasted her mug to Cardboard Owen—then looked back out at Diego and deflated. "Seriously pathetic and alone," she added about her reality, half to herself, half to Cardboard Owen. "But with integrity. And real. Me being real. Like my true self. Like not wanting to go to the game and pretend I'm the real you's secret girlfriend, which I don't want to do. Which is why we're not going."

Bee looked back at Cardboard Owen's frozen grin, hoping for encouragement. It didn't come, especially because she knew that telling the real Owen her truth when he was out cold didn't count and the fact that she even had taken Cardboard Owen from cheerleader Chrissie meant that she was perpetuating the lie and making it worse. And losing all self-respect.

All she could do was sigh back at the stand-up's grin, knowing she'd have to go to the game if she didn't want to let Owen or herself down.

***

The Lions vs. Bears football game was in full swing as Bee walked along the bleachers towards the Lions' bench holding Cardboard Owen, trying to appear brave.

"Just a quick hello. No big deal," Bee justified to herself and her stand-up friend, trying to muster up more courage and positivity.

Bee saw the scoreboard: BEARS 7, LIONS 7.

"Tied," she uttered, feeling the nerves jump around in her stomach. The pressure was on.

Suddenly, she saw Reno blast wildly through two Bear defense guys.

The crowd went nuts.

Reno braved a mad-giraffe-esque touchdown attempt, weaving, ducking, until BAM!—he was down.

Demi screamed in frustration from the Lions' cheerleader-squad lineup, trying to keep up their spirits on the Lions' sideline. Crosstown Thunderbirds sitting with Bears on the visitor bleachers waved signs to intimidate their rivals: "LOSER LIONS! MEOW!"

"That's okay! You guys are awesome!" Coach Wells shouted to the team, but he didn't sound like he believed it.

The cheer squad stepped in, going nuts, pumping up Reno. "Reee-no! Reee-no!"

Bee saw Coach Wells turn and hit his inhaler.

Demi saw it too and deflated.

"Okay, maybe now's not the time for us to make an appearance," Bee told herself and Cardboard Owen, then quickly turned and started to go.

Demi spotted Bee and bolted after her. "Hey! Bee! Wait!" Demi called out, knowing Bee was their saving grace.

Bee pretended she didn't hear Demi.

But Demi was fast and determined. And caught up to her. "Hey! Bee! Yay! You're here!"

Bee stopped and plastered a fake smile on her face. "Oh hi!

Yeah, I, uh, forgot my jacket. I was just going back to get it," she fibbed, hoping to avert disappointment.

Demi looked at Bee's jacket tie-wrapped around her waist. Clearly, there was no forgotten jacket.

"But here! He totally wants to go with you!" Bee deflected, waving stand-up Cardboard Owen around. "Go Lions, go Lions!"

Demi wasn't buying it and grabbed Cardboard Owen in order to stop this waving insanity from Bee. "He wants to stay with you," Demi insisted with a fiery glare. "And you owe it to us to help us win."

Bee saw that Demi meant business.

"We like you, Bee," Demi added. "Deal with it." And she grabbed Bee's arm and dragged her and Cardboard Owen over to the team bench and cheer squad. "Look who's here!" Demi called out, bringing back her positive cheer vibes with renewed intensity and Lion pride. "Wooooooo!"

The Lion cheer squad enveloped Bee and Cardboard Owen. "Bee!!!" they cheered.

Coach Wells couldn't believe his luck. He and Reno both groan-exhaled with relief when they saw Bee.

Bee felt a wave of relief too. Finally, her guilt over this whole stupid situation lessened, even if it was just the tiniest bit.

And then, miraculously, with this smallest bit of positivity and hope on Bee's part, things started to get better.

Demi gave Bee her cheer Varsity letter jacket to wear and pushed Bee over to the cheer squad line, forcing her to fit in. "Just do what we do. Be enthusiastic and get Cardboard Owen in there! Loud and proud!" Then, Demi mimed waving an imaginary stand-up Owen to show Bee what to do, yelling, "Lion Pride, on our side! Goooo, Reno!"

Bee nodded and hesitantly waved Cardboard Owen around. "Gooo Lions!"

"Yeah!" Demi shouted encouragingly. "Bigger! Louder! You got this!"

Bee started waving Cardboard Owen around more, bigger,

shouting, "Lion Pride! On our side! Lion Pride! On our side!"

"That's it!" Demi cheered.

"Go, Bee! Go, Bee!" cheerleader Chrissie chimed in.

And the whole cheer squad joined in, "Go, Bee! Go, Owen! Go, Lions!!! Lion Pride! On our side!"

The timing was perfect. The players hit the field again, each high-fiving Cardboard Owen on the way out.

And each time Cardboard Owen got a high-five, Bee grinned from ear to ear at the player and felt a jolt of energy and Lion pride. She couldn't believe it. She was actually helping pump up the team. *Because they see me*, she chimed to herself. Now that she had Cardboard Owen and his vibe with her, it was as if she and the real Owen were one. And she was part of something, *part of this team! Finally!*

And everything changed. The Lion team energy was suddenly high.

They all felt it.

They huddled on the field and did a huge Lion-pride roar. The electricity filled the field and bleachers.

And it continued as play began. Quickly, Reno got the ball and threw it to running back Glenn, and Glenn scored! The Lions went nuts.

Demi pointed to Bee, and on cue, she held up Cardboard Owen.

The crowd roared with Lion pride.

And all the cheering at Bee all at once gave her a rush of pure joy.

And it continued. The rest of the game was a Lion success, and Bee got more and more caught up in it, feeling quick blasts of happiness as Reno and Glenn rocked it, Bee and the squad cheering and egging on every Lion in the stands.

And as the clock counted down the last seconds of the game, Glenn ran a final touchdown. And the buzzer rang. And the Lions won!

Bee screamed with joy.

Coach Wells fell to his knees in disbelief.

Demi and Chrissie hugged Bee.

And the team lifted Reno, Bee and Cardboard Owen on their shoulders and paraded them around with pride and glee, everyone cheering, "Lions! Lions! Lions!"—

—while from the other side of the bleachers amongst the Bears fans and dressed in her Thunderbird cheer-squad letter jacket over a cute purple and orange mini-dress, Jade seethed. She was beyond pissed at this development.

# 9 THREE CHEERS FOR GIRAFFE-SKINNY-AWESOME RENO AND THE GREAT PRETENDER BEE

The celebration of the Lions' big win over the Bears, even without Owen playing, continued after the game at cheerleader Chrissie's house. Even though the weather was getting cold, Chrissie's parents had decided to heat the pool in the backyard one last time for this party. Pools weren't too common in the Flathead so this was a real treat.

The Lions' took advantage of this and the chanting continued as some of the football players carried Reno and Bee overhead around the pool. "Lions! Lions! Lions!"

"Initiation!" Demi shouted.

And the players launched Reno and Bee into the pool, both screaming as they sailed towards the water, "AHHH!"—then, splashed in and surfaced, laughing.

"Our good luck charms!" cheered Demi. "On the road to the State Championship! Falcons in fourteen days then Thunderbirds the next Friday!"

Coach Wells stood with Chrissie's parents and beamed.

Suddenly, all the football guys pushed the cheerleaders into the pool and jumped in as well.

Chrissie's brother started DJ-ing, blasting music over huge

speakers.

Drew-ster put Cardboard Owen on a raft.

There was tons of splashing, dancing and joy.

And everything went into slow motion for Bee as she watched the celebration, awed by how happy everyone was in this moment—including herself.

***

Bee managed to relax and enjoy the start of the party. Really, she had no choice but to look happy, given the ruse, but this time, she didn't have to fake it. Everyone was buying that she was Owen's secret girlfriend and they had won! *What a relief.* Plus, watching everyone get wild and being part of it all—being carried around like a superhero—was pretty awesome, she had to admit.

But as the night wore on, Bee felt reality set in again, namely that she didn't really fit in here. Eventually, everyone at this party would probably find her weird and she'd find them boring, and then, her fake relationship with Owen would fake break up. Bee laughed at her own absurd thoughts as she got out of the pool and stood watching the others and tried to come up with a good reason for her escape.

Semi-dry, in a towel over her drenched jeans and favorite daisy-covered shirt, she thought, *Thank goodness I didn't wear a skirt*, and she found a good spot near the dance floor, with Cardboard Owen standing next to her, to pass some more time and think. After a while, everyone was out of the pool, and together, she and Cardboard Owen watched Demi and Glenn slow dance. On the other side of the dance floor, Chrissie flirted with Reno. And pretty much everyone was paired up.

Bee awkwardly talked in their direction as they danced and chatted, "Hey, guys. I'm going."

No one noticed.

*Good*, thought Bee, and she subtly walked backwards away from the dance floor then turned quickly to go and bumped right into Nick Wells, knocking a present out of his hand. "Oh,

43

shoot, sorry...," Bee said and hustled to pick up the gift and hand it back to him, which is when she saw his face.

"Well, if it isn't Curtain and Lighting Girl," Nick teased, smiling warmly, his deep brown eyes flashing as he recalled their little run-in during the talent show in the curtains.

*Dang, he's cute*, thought Bee, not knowing who he was but recognizing him from the curtains.

And clearly, Nick thought she was cute, too.

"Actually, I was just...," stammered Bee, "...leaving."

"Me, too. Not really my scene," Nick said and put the birthday present for Chrissie down on the sofa side table.

"Didn't you just get here?" Bee asked, suddenly, weirdly bold. No shyness around this guy.

"I did," he replied and waved at Coach Wells, who was still on the patio with Chrissie's parents.

"Yeah, no, it's uh...gotta go before midnight," Bee chirped. "Gonna turn into a sherpa otherwise." She gestured playfully with her head at Cardboard Owen to nail the sherpa joke home.

Nick's eyes flashed, amused by this giant replica of his best friend, and he grinned, clearly getting Bee's humor.

Bee was intrigued—

—which is when Coach Wells came over and guy-hug-back-slapped Nick warmly. "Nick my man, you made it out alive!" he teased.

*Nick?!* thought Bee. *This is the infamous Nick?!*

"No wedding injuries I see," Coach Wells continued. "That's good. Your mother's off the hook for making you be in her new wedding." Coach Wells hugged Nick again.

Nick feigned "choking" for Bee, then pulled back and looked at Coach Wells, scrutinizing. Nick was surprised by what he saw. "What happened?" Nick asked him. "You're happy."

"Scrawny giraffe boy rallied!" Coach Wells exclaimed, still in shock.

Nick did an over-the-top fist pump.

"And Vinchenzo! Two field goals!" Coach Wells added.

"Dad, Vinny always rallies; he's better than me. Always play Vinny!" Nick insisted.

*Dad?!* cried Bee in her head. *This is Coach Wells' son?!*

Coach Wells continued, blatantly ignoring Nick's demand that he play Vinny instead of him, "And you know our new cheer gal, Bee, Owen's new girlfriend."

Nick couldn't hide his shock—*Girlfriend?!!*

Bee smiled nervously.

"You guys haven't met?" Coach Wells was surprised. "Bee, this is my boy, Nick. Finally transferred in this year after I lured him away from the enemy: his mother." Coach Wells knuckle-rubbed Nick's head playfully. "And he's gonna be our star kicker for the next two games."

"Yeah, hi, welcome. And thank you," Bee said awkwardly to Nick as she handed Coach Wells her towel. "It was a blast," she added and ran out, banging Cardboard Owen's head on the front door of Chrissie's house, then hurrying away, trying to fix Cardboard Owen's bent head as she bolted.

Nick followed her out, "Hey! Lighting Girl! Wait up!"

Bee stopped. Nervous. Heart racing. This Nick guy saw her. Got her. *But what if he gets my lie about Owen too?!* she worried in her head.

"I'm glad Owen's gonna be okay," Nick said, totally genuine, and pushed Cardboard Owen's head up for Bee, fixing it so it stayed.

Bee laughed, more nerves, and waited, pretty much paralyzed and expecting him to call her out about the "Owen's girlfriend" lie.

But Nick just smiled.

"That's it?" Bee said, unable to hide her surprise.

"Should there be more?" Nick wondered with a cheeky grin.

"No! Perfect!" Bee chimed nervously, grinning back, trying to look calm and cool. "Me too. Super-duper glad he's gonna be okay." Then, she did a corny thumbs up and took off with Cardboard Owen.

Which is when Nick called after her, "Actually...!"

She stopped.

"I'm curious...," he continued. "When did you guys start dating? 'Cuz when I left, Owen was..."

—"...with Jade," Bee admitted just as Nick said, "...not dating," both finishing the first part of Nick's sentence at the same time.

Bee wanted to take back the dating-Jade mention instantly. It was obvious that Nick didn't even know about Jade. Clearly, Owen was amazing at keeping secrets, even from his best friend, Nick, who looked totally confused by Bee's Jade comment, which, unfortunately, he did hear, just like Bee heard what Nick said about Owen "not dating," which solidified to Bee Owen's lie of omission to Nick.

"It just happened," Bee quickly quipped, covering up Owen's secret and leaning into the dreaded lie that she was Owen's girlfriend. "We were friends. In the hood," she shrugged as if it were obvious and the most normal thing ever.

"Oh, right...cool," Nick deflected his surprise, thrown off by this comment but rallying with as much charm as he could muster.

Nick's warm smile caught Bee off-guard. But at least he seemed to buy the Owen-girlfriend lie, she thought. Bee shrugged and bolted awkwardly but totally relieved that she got away with that. She grinned at Cardboard Owen. "Okay, maybe there is some hope for us."

Then, Bee looked back at Nick watching her go. He was both confused and utterly intrigued. And Bee felt oddly inspired. Which is when that favorite R&B song of hers started playing in her head—"September," by Earth, Wind & Fire— which was a sign that good things were on the horizon. "And me," she told herself and Cardboard Owen, "maybe there's some hope for me."

# 10 BEE STEPS OUT IN TRUE AWESOME-BEE FORM

After the party at Chrissie's house, Bee's taste of hope turned into a surge of confidence. If she could pull the wool over Owen's best friend Nick's eyes, surely she could keep the ruse going long enough for the Lions to win against the Falcons in two weeks and then the Thunderbirds a week later so they could get to the State Championship and win.

And so, Bee dove into Owen's world in full force—as herself, the real Beatrix Plumb, even if she was also masquerading as Owen's fake secret girlfriend.

"Debutante girlfriend extraordinaire," Bee boasted to Cardboard Owen, as she now had "someone" to optimistically narrate her life to.

Bee didn't tell Kate about the escalation of the ruse immediately. She figured Kate would be pleased. After all, Kate was the one that had told her to double down and go for it. But Bee didn't want any distractions. She just needed to stay focused. And Kate could definitely be a distraction.

Besides, there was a good chance Kate would quickly figure out about Bee's stepped-up involvement with the cheer squad through her keen observation skills even if she was too distracted by Torian to say anything.

*Yeah, Kate wasn't born yesterday*, Bee thought and assumed she didn't need to have a conversation with Kate about the team, cheer squad or her run-in with the infamous Nick. This was a relief. Mostly. And so, she shut down the little voice inside that said, *But she's your best friend and you tell her every little tiny thing and this one is big. It's a big thing.* And instead, Bee forgot about Kate and decided to be all-in as Owen's girlfriend...starting with going straight out and washing the SFB Mobile at the self coin wash.

Then, Bee pulled out all her cutest clothes and accessories—the ones that she was usually too shy to wear because she didn't want all that attention. "What was I thinking?" Bee told Cardboard Owen as she admired her cool lime-green beret in the mirror and her light-blue dress with tiny white flowers and her polka-dot tights, "Why wouldn't I want people to see this cuteness?" Then, she strutted out the front door of her house, all put together to start the week as her new self.

Diego and Paige were waiting by the SFB Mobile for carpool to school when Bee came out. Diego's eyes lit up as soon as he saw her in her new look. He immediately snapped a Polaroid. "What is this, my Bee? You are radiating," he gushed.

For a change, Bee didn't cringe at Diego's admiration. Instead, she just continued strutting, tripped on the uneven spot on the driveway where it hit the sidewalk, then immediately recovered like a well-coordinated, captivating, football-player-adoring goddess warrior of cheerleading love and continued to the SFB parked curbside in front of their house.

Bee unlocked the car door with her key. She was beaming, with a slight breeze gently blowing her bobbed hair as she got in. She started the engine then honked long and loud for Kate, who came running over instantly and said, "Torian's waiting out at the corner," with a smile and hopped in back next to Diego. Bee didn't even ask why the heck Torian was at the corner when his car was parked right in front of the house next to Bee's where he parked every day. No, the new Bee miraculously wasn't annoyed by Torian's weirdness and couldn't be bothered even to mention it.

Paige sat in her usual spot shotgun and studied her sister for a moment, noting this odd change in her behavior—until she got a text from her boyfriend, Tommy, and forgot about Bee, as usual.

Bee turned on her favorite playlist, mostly R&B, and pulled out onto the road while Kate and Paige looked at their phones; Torian hopped in at the corner, kissed Kate and looked at his phone; and Diego danced in the back seat "discretely," only snapping Polaroids of this newly enchanting Bee every once in a while.

Bee rejoiced in her mood, not shying away from anything—namely her music and her feeling of confidence and bliss.

"So, yeah, this was the start of the new me," Bee narrated to herself as they drove.

And the next few days were a blur of more confidence and bliss as Bee strutted—

—dropping off Kate and Torian at Kate's house after school that day, after Entertainment Club, and heading over to the hospital to decorate Owen's hospital room with indie movie posters and Feynman physics posters—some of her favorite things from her own room. She also put up cool wall-decor stickers that she'd bought online but that had been hiding in her craft drawer for months—namely, she arranged pine trees and a giant sun rising on one wall and "Here comes the sun," lyrics by The Beatles on another. Then, she hung a "Go, Lions!" banner that she'd taken from the Entertainment Club storage closet.

Owen snored away the entire time Bee was decorating, and when she was done, she stood back and said, "So much better," aloud. "Right?" She smiled at Owen and heard a voice from the door behind her.

"Looks great!" It was Nick. He weirdly blushed when Bee turned to look at him, and he shoved his hands in his pockets and nodded as he took in the new decor, surprised by her choices. "All things...Owen now loves?" he teased. "Clearly, you have a much better influence on him than me. Feynman?!"

Bee blushed. This made her nervous. *Nick must really know Owen well*, she thought. He seemed observant. And if she were honest, she knew Owen probably wasn't into these things either. But no one else would know.

And luckily, Nick didn't stay long. He said "hi" to Owen, going over to the bed, nodding at him and bro-teasing him, "Dude, what the heck? You'd better get better quick, my bud." Nick seemed shaken by the casts and the fact that his buddy was so out of it. Then, he smiled at Bee, gave her a quick wave and rushed out.

Leaving Bee with another win.

***

The next day at lunch, Bee had yet another victory. As usual, she was sitting with Kate and Torian, who were kissing nonstop—*Gross!* Bee was trying really hard to ignore them. Which is when Demi and cheerleader Chrissie passed their table and invited Bee to the jock table. Bee's heart started racing, and Kate nudged her mid-kiss to go, which was a win for Bee in and of itself.

*See, Kate's got my back, in spite of Torian Borian*, Bee mused. *And she IS being observant, so I don't have to feel guilty about NOT filling her in on everything.* There was that little voice inside Bee's head again missing her friend and it was nice to have solid defense about why she was right in shutting it down. *Justified!* she bragged to herself, feeling energized and vindicated, and glanced over at Nick—then quickly looked away.

Bee avoided Nick's stare as she went over to the jock table, head held high, and pumped herself up inside her head. "Yes!" she cheered, which made her feel even more confident when she joined Demi and Chrissie and the football guys. Demi greeted her with a huge smile and a "Hey! Nice hat," about her super cute lime-green beret, and it felt to Bee like a cherry on top of an already incredibly sweet ice-cream sundae of confidence.

Everyone smiled at Bee as she sat down at the table, and miraculously, she fit right in, listening to them mostly because she wasn't exactly sure what to say. But that seemed like the cool thing to do anyway.

The only issue happened when Bee looked over at Nick again, and their eyes met. Something felt off inside Bee—like, even though she was being true to herself, she was also being fake. *Yuck*, she thought. The meeting of eyes also seemed to arouse suspicion in Nick. Somehow. *Darn*, she thought and told herself to work on that—*Why did I ever have to talk to him?* she reprimanded.

Nick's suspicion was confirmed later that afternoon when Bee was on the bleachers at football and cheer practice with Cardboard Owen. At lunch, Demi had invited her to come out and suggested she join the cheer squad for the rest of the season at least. "It'd be super helpful," Demi told her.

Bee wasn't sure that joining the cheer squad was such a good idea. She had no clue how to be a cheerleader, but when she caught Nick staring at her with furrowed brow from the field with his hands on his hips—as if he were thinking, "Huh, what the heck is she doing here?"—Bee got super nervous again that he might be onto her, so she ran down and told Demi, "Okay, I'm in," meaning, *Yes, I'll be on your stupid squad even though it freaks me the heck out and you all seem so overly enthusiastic! Like are you even real?*

But the cheer squad squealed with glee when she stepped onto the grass, and they lifted her overhead.

Bee surprised herself by enjoying it, and she even laughed. *Maybe this isn't so bad after all*, she thought—until they almost dropped her. Which is when her eyes instantly went to Nick and she saw him gasp. Which is when she knew that at least he cared about her well-being and that maybe helping the team was the right thing to do after all. Bee beamed with Lion pride until Nick gave her that furrowed-brow look again when she tripped and wasn't exactly a natural with the cheers, as if he were thinking—*What the heck is she doing?*

And then, doubt set in again for Bee. It was getting tiring having all these emotions, like it was making her seasick going back and forth between confidence and doubt. And she thought, *Hmmm, Nick may care about me, but clearly, he's not buying the girlfriend-cheerleader thing.* Which was a conundrum.

So, to mitigate Nick's doubt further, Bee stayed after cheer practice, which ended earlier than football practice, and she looked at football plays with Coach Wells on the sidelines on his laptop.

Bee pretended to understand what was going on as Coach Wells explained his thoughts about the plays to her. She was attentive and made over-exaggerated nods so that ever-more suspicious Nick could see.

It didn't work perfectly—Nick still looked suspicious, but afterwards, Bee drove over to the hospital and read to Owen and that helped build her confidence all over again. Owen looked so peaceful. And that just made her so happy, and she felt like everything would be okay.

Bee's confidence must have been palpable, because the next couple of days, as she happily walked down the school hall between classes, head held high, a bounce in her step, everyone smiled and nodded at her. Yes, for the first time in her life, people actually were noticing Bee. And on top of that, they were all happy to see her, even the teachers.

*This never happens,* Bee thought. And when she passed Demi and Chrissie sporting green hats the same exact color as hers but with brims—as if she, Beatrix Plumb, were starting a fashion color trend—and they tipped their hats to her in acknowledgement, she knew something big was happening here.

Maybe even something bigger than herself.

Because Bee was truly no longer invisible. Instead, she was being seen. Like she'd set out to do in her Junior Year Manifesto—to be seen by Owen. Had she reached her goal—*sort of?* Bee wondered. And as Bee contemplated this, she felt a rush of love in her heart and beamed and cheered to herself with glee, "Gooooo, Bee! JYM! JYM!!!"

# 11 BEE DEFTLY DITCHES SUSPICIONS ABOUT HER FAKE-GIRLFRIEND MOVES

After just a few days of her new self, Bee's joy was becoming part of every fiber of her being. She'd even had the nerve to suggest to Demi that she be more like an adjunct satellite or guest cheerleader, just coming in with Cardboard Owen for special cheers and lifts, like at halftime or when they needed an extra cheer punch to support the team.

Demi agreed, and they arranged it so that Bee just showed up and hung out in the bleachers doing homework next to Cardboard Owen while the football team and cheer squad practiced on the field.

"Amazing what a boyfriend can do to your self-esteem," Bee told Cardboard Owen, relishing in her situation and waiting for Demi to call her down for her cheerleading part again if needed, basking in her bliss—

—until she caught Nick watching her again from the field as he did drills with back-up punter Vincenzo.

"But what's up with Mr. Judgey?" Bee demanded from Cardboard Owen about Nick. "How is he your best friend?"

Out on the field, Coach Wells shouted, "Last push!" Then,

after they finished their drills, he shouted, "Water break!"

The guys headed to the bench, and Coach Wells went over and slapped Nick's back. "Lookin' great out there, Wells."

"Vincenzo's your kicker, Dad, not me," Nick replied with a grin, knowing his dad didn't want to hear it. Coach Wells truly wanted Nick to be the main punter.

"Right now, I'm focused on Reno and beating the Falcons a week from tomorrow," Coach Wells told Nick, diverting the conversation away from his choice of punter and turning to yell at the team, "and Thunderbird tail-kicking in fifteen days!"

The players and cheer squad shouted back, "Fifteen days!"

Coach Wells noticed Bee in the stands waving Cardboard Owen around and joining in the "Fifteen days!" pep cheer. He waved to her.

Bee smiled and waved back.

"Finally, your friend picks someone good, and actually nice," Coach Wells told Nick. "Who won't distract him."

"Something's weird," said Nick about Bee as he watched Bee in the stands.

"Don't knock nice," Coach Wells insisted then turned to the players finishing up their water break. "All right guys!" he shouted.

Everyone looked over.

"We need Owen's playbook for next Friday!" he continued. "Who's gonna get it?"

Off Nick's judgey look, Bee jumped up and eagerly pumped her hand, while Nick and Bee's voices rang out simultaneously. "I'll do it!" shouted Bee while Nick exclaimed, "Right here!"

"Bee! You're on!" said Coach Wells. "Nick, you've got some more practicing to do."

Relieved to get away from Nick, Bee booked it off the field and out of there.

***

Bee took her time driving over to Owen's house, realizing as she got closer that she might have to deal with Owen's family and that meant possibly lying.

She parked the Strawberry Firecracker Bomb Mobile on the street in front of his house and told herself, "You got this, Beatrix Plumb. You are rockin' it. JYM." It didn't sound too convincing. She took a deep breath and got out then walked up to the front door and stood there for a moment, heart racing.

Finally, she knocked firmly on Owen's front door.

Owen's little sister, Claire, opened the door, looked Bee up and down, super judgey, then called off to her mom in the house, "It's that Bee girl!"

Mrs. Fleet appeared in the door. "Hey! Bee! Is everything okay?" Owen's mom asked with a smile that also had a twinge of worry behind it, before glancing up at something behind Bee moving on the street.

Bee glanced back and saw Jade's purple Cabrio with Thunderbird-orange stickers pass slowly. *What the...?* she thought and quickly turned back to Mrs. Fleet with a smile that said "everything's fine" while her heart pounded like crazy in her chest. "I just came to get Owen's playbook," Bee chirped to Mrs. Fleet, trying to divert her attention while being as cheerful and worry-free as she could.

Claire's eyes narrowed into an uber-suspicious glare at Bee. "You are so not his type," she accused Bee.

"Claire!" reprimanded Mrs. Fleet.

"What?!" Claire defended to her mom. "Owen is so not into those super old black-and-white movies. Or science...?!"

Mrs. Fleet's lips pursed at her daughter, even though she knew Claire was right about how Bee had decorated Owen's hospital room. Then, Mrs. Fleet deftly turned her lips into a warm, diplomatic smile for Bee. "It's very nice what you did with his hospital room, Bee," she complimented. "Owen could do with a little more culture. Come in."

"You're letting her into his room?!" Claire cried out at her mom in disbelief—

—as Bee edged past Claire in the front door well.

And Claire watched Bee like a psycho sister.

Mrs. Fleet led Bee down the hallway, which was lined with Owen and Claire's yearly school photos all the way up from kindergarten. When they got to Owen's door, Mrs. Fleet opened it and told Bee, "Go right on in. I'm not sure where he keeps his playbook, but I trust you might have a clue."

Bee smiled then nodded with a nervous laugh.

Mrs. Fleet seemed to sense something weird now too but, clearly, decided to just ignore it and not get involved. "Or not," Mrs. Fleet said to Bee with a smile and a twinkle in her eye and left down the hall.

Bee saw Claire glaring at her from the other end of the hall and went into Owen's room and shut the door so it was just ajar—hopefully just enough privacy without looking like she had something to hide, like how she had absolutely no clue as to where Owen's playbook might reside.

Owen's room looked like Bee had imagined—full of everything football: photos, posters, trophies and framed news articles of himself and the team, like when the Lions won the State Championship the year before.

"Yup, got that one," Bee whispered to herself about the news clipping and blushed and laughed at herself. "Okay, carry on," she instructed the image of Owen in the photo and kept perusing.

When she got to Owen's green Lions' jersey, she touched it, took it in her hands and squeezed and smelled it, breathing in deep in hopes of getting a sense of Owen close up. *Nothing.* Only some kind of light citrusy scent. Clearly, someone in the Fleet house was on top of the laundry.

Bee moved on to a bookshelf and peered into some scrap books. More news-article clippings, a few that she didn't have. And school notebooks, which she flipped through—*nothing interesting.* Finally, she moved on to Owen's desk—

—and his computer with a giant screen. *It has to be in here,* she thought about the playbook and sat down in his worn black desk chair. It looked like an office chair, and Bee wondered if it came from Owen's dad's office. She didn't actually know what his job was, but he seemed like someone that would have a proper office and a desk chair.

Then, Bee saw a laptop on the side of the bigger screen, hidden under a notebook. She perused the notebook quickly: nothing but a few pages with notes from a history class. *But maybe the laptop*, she thought. That seemed like a more likely location for the playbook than the bigger computer, which looked more like a gaming station. Bee looked around nervously—over her shoulder and at the door, as if someone were watching—before flipping up Owen's laptop lid and turning the laptop on. After all, it felt like she was about to enter his most private space, maybe even more private than his phone because it was hidden here in his room.

The screen lit up, and Bee saw Owen's screensaver—an Owen photo collage. Bee laughed. "Hey, just like mine," she chimed to herself.

Next, Bee grabbed the headphones that were plugged into the bigger computer and put them on—gamer headphones, she assumed because they looked pretty fancy—and she turned on Owen's music on the big computer. Loud metal blasted. She turned it down. "Yuck," she muttered in a whisper under her breath. She perused his playlist. Nothing good. Then, she found another list called "Kickster" filled with all kinds of interesting stuff, including one song she really liked. "Earth, Wind and Fire! I love that. I knew you had some soul in you," she mused to "Owen" in a whisper and blasted the song and left it at that, grooving out and singing along—which is when Bee spotted a folder on Owen's laptop called "HOT."

Bee opened the folder and found a trove of Owen and Jade photos. Every single one featured the two of them in some kind of high-adrenaline activity—paintball, forest laser tag, snowboarding, water-skiing, cliff jumping into a lake and all kinds of things.

Bee clicked on the forest laser-tag one and made it bigger so she could get a better look. The location looked familiar. Yeah, she'd definitely hiked in that area before with Kate. In fact, it looked exactly like the spot where they used to go and make forts and play spy with Paige and her friends. It was like hide-and-go-seek but the seekers were James Bond and friends, and the hiders were Russian agents or rogue MI6. Kate and Bee were always the hiders and would climb high up in the trees and Paige and friends could never find them. Kate and Bee would laugh and sit up in the tree till the James Bonds gave up and went home. *Good times*, thought Bee, missing Kate and then forcing herself to move on.

She minimized the photo and moved on to the one of Owen and Jade mid-air cliff jumping into a lake. She wondered who took the photo and then noticed a tattoo on Jade's leg, just above the ankle. She zoomed in to get a better look. *A bird? Thunderbird maybe?* Bee wondered and thought, *Probably*, just as she heard a deep voice coming from right outside Owen's bedroom door—

"How's it going?" the voice boomed.

Bee screamed and jumped.

It was Nick.

"Nick!" she cried and slammed off the headphones, looking at him leaning against the doorjamb nonchalantly with a grin on his face. Clearly, he'd quietly pushed the door open and had been watching her.

*How long has he been there?* Bee panicked, feeling caught, and stammered, "What're you...?! You're supposed to be at practice."

Nick started over to Bee.

Bee quickly closed as many windows as possible on Owen's screen as another classic disco soul song blasted out of the headphones.

"He hates that song," Nick laughed and unplugged the headphones so he could hear better. "That's my playlist."

"I hate it too," Bee lied.

Nick studied her eyes, her hair.

*This is weird*, she thought

And Nick thought the same about Bee, *Weird. But intriguing.*

*And awkward*, thought Bee, her heart racing, a fake smile plastered on her face as she tried with all her might to keep it there, hoping Nick wouldn't see through her ruse.

"I figured you may need some help," Nick told her.

"I'm totally fine," Bee chimed, sitting tall, abruptly turning to the laptop screen and quickly grabbing the mouse. *Luckily, there's a mouse*, she thought and said, "See..."

Bee scoured the screen, heart pounding along with the disco. Until she saw it—a folder called "Football." *Yes!* she cheered in her head then smiled up at Nick as confidently as possible. "Right here," she said and quickly opened it. "See."

Luckily, it was all videos of Owen's football plays.

"So, he didn't use his playbook-under-the-pillow romance tactic with you?" Nick teased, half razzing Bee, half trying to figure out what the heck was going on. Then, he went over and pulled the prized playbook out from under Owen's pillow. "Guess not," he grinned and held it up as evidence as if he were a detective.

*Crud*, thought Bee. "What are you talking about?" she scoffed.

"Well," Nick began with a cheeky smile as if narrating a story. "Romantic quarterback, dreams the plays, writes them down, wins the hearts of many a fair maiden with his passionate football acumen."

"He does not do that," Bee laughed, quite sure of herself. "That is totally not possible."

"Witnessed it with my own two ears, in fact," Nick declared. "And Amy Geary's heart." He smirked, again cheeky, totally enjoying this.

"Amy Geary?" Bee wondered.

"Summer camp, ninth grade," Nick informed her. "I couldn't compete with the playbook or Mr. Romantic's chivalrous charm, aka Owen. Even the earrings I got for Amy couldn't win her heart after Mr. Wonderful's passion for football acumen."

"Earrings?" Bee wondered.

"Blue Italian glass, a stab at originality. My only hope," Nick admitted with a lightly pained laugh and handed Bee the playbook.

*Oh, crud.* Bee couldn't believe it. *Italian glass.* Jade's earrings were Italian glass. The ones from Owen. The gift from Owen that Jade loved and wanted to wear but couldn't because she was Owen's actual secret girlfriend. The earrings Jade shoved at Bee in her purple Cabrio in the hospital garage. Beautiful blue. *So, does that mean Owen didn't even buy them? But Nick did?!* Bee wondered. "So what happened to the earrings?" she asked, doing her best to maintain composure.

"Uh...well, being the upstanding friend that I am, I gave 'em to Owen," Nick told her. "For Amy. Better she have 'em than no one, I thought, young pup that I was. The only problem then was that Amy dumped Owen first. Karma, I guess."

*Oh, gosh*, thought Bee. *Definitely the same earrings as Jade's!* "So, where are they now?" Bee asked Nick about the earrings.

"You are a strange...inquisitor," he teased. "Maybe Owen'll give 'em to you."

Bee turned scarlet. Then, abruptly turned to the laptop and shut it. "So, you came here to tell me this?" she asked, still facing the desk, afraid to look at Nick.

He waited.

Bee turned to him, hoping that if her cheeks were red, he'd think she was angry—not embarrassed about her feelings and panicking all at once.

"I came over because...," Nick said and paused, checking out Bee's dress and how cute she was. "...To do what Owen does every Thursday."

*Uh, oh*, Bee thought. She had no idea what that was. And Nick was looking at her so weirdly, like maybe he was expecting her to know what Owen did on Thursdays and this was a test. Bee grabbed her stuff and stood up, facing Nick. "Well, I don't know what that is, so maybe Owen just doesn't like me that much," she said, blushing again, but luckily, definitely sounding quite angry. And maybe even hurt—*Darn*, she thought and added, "As you seem to be implying."

"Touchy!" Nick teased but noticed that her discomfort was growing so he backed off. "I just came to take Granny Fleet for a walk and bring her pie. That's what Mr. Chivalry does on Thursdays."

"Oh, right, Granny Fleet," Bee rallied. "Of course. She's so sweet."

"Sweet?!" Nick exclaimed. Clearly, he didn't think "sweet" was the right adjective to describe Granny Fleet—

—just as Mrs. Fleet came into Owen's bedroom with a huckleberry pie, followed by Claire. "Nick, are you sure about this?" Mrs. Fleet asked. "Claire and I can go. Or maybe Bee wants to go. Or both of you can go together."

Claire glared suspiciously at Bee.

Nick shrugged at Mrs. Fleet's suggestion and nodded to Bee.

"I'll go!" Bee chimed with the biggest cheerleader-esque smile she could muster. "By myself. No problem." She smirked at Claire and took the pie out of Mrs. Fleet's hands before anyone could protest and left, hurrying down the hall, glancing and nodding at Owen's cute kindergarten smile in the photo on the wall, which gave her a rush of confidence—she was definitely doing this for all the right reasons; she loved Owen and he deserved this—and she strutted out the front door.

But Bee's confidence got a little shaky as she approached the SFB Mobile with the Granny Fleet pie and got in, realizing she had no idea where to find Granny Fleet. She put the pie on the seat next to her, then moved it to the floor so it wouldn't fly off if, by chance, she had to make a quick stop and slam on the brakes—

—which is when, suddenly, Jade popped up in the back seat next to Cardboard Owen, purple spray paint pointed at Bee. "You said there was no one!" Jade shouted. "And now, posters all over his room! In the hospital!"

Jade climbed into the front seat, pushing the purple spray paint in Bee's face.

"What the...?" Bee managed, pulling back from the spray paint can pointed right at her.

"If you don't tell me who she is right now—this new poster-hanger-slash-probable-girlfriend—purple and orange will be all over your boring, old car." Jade pressed her finger down deftly. A tiny spray of purple misted out on Bee's face.

Which is when Bee lost it. She'd had enough and couldn't take it anymore. She grabbed onto the spray paint can above Jade's hand and attempted to wrestle it down. "Me! It's me! I decorated Owen's room!" Bee shouted with all her might, sick of this whole shebang.

"You?!" Jade shouted back in total disbelief as they wrestled.

"To keep your secret!" Bee continued. "They think Owen has a secret girlfriend! Okay?!! And they think it's me!"

"Owen would never date you!!!" Jade screamed and pressed down on the spray paint can sprayer.

Purple sprayed out onto the car and Bee's knee.

Bee fought with all her might to get the can away and screamed, "And he's gonna hate you if you blow it and let your secret out and ruin mine 'cuz I'm just trying to help!!" Bee slammed Jade's arm down and came face to face with her adversary—noticing immediately that Jade was wearing the blue Italian glass earrings.

Jade pulled her hands away, letting go of the spray paint can, and quickly covered the earrings, embarrassed. "I deserve these earrings," she cried, her desperation seeping out in spite of herself.

Bee was confused—it showed. Her brow furrowed. *Why is Jade suddenly looking so hopelessly sad?* she wondered.

Jade couldn't stand Bee seeing her vulnerable truth and frantically ripped off the blue Italian glass earrings and shoved them at Bee then seethed, "I'll be watching you," trying her best to somehow rally with at least a semblance of pride. "Thunderbirds have pride too, you know," she screeched then quickly turned to get out of the car on the passenger side—

—which is when she saw the pie for Granny Fleet at her feet. It was a stab to her heart. She gasped, the pain of betrayal and disloyalty by Owen radiating through her being. And this time, Jade really couldn't hide it. "You're going to Granny Fleet's?!" Jade cried, voice trembling.

Bee stared. What was happening?

And Jade scrambled to get out, carefully maneuvering

around the pie as she bolted out the passenger door, leaving it wide open.

Bee turned and watched Jade storm back to her purple Cabrio parked a half a block away, and she heard Jade cry out to Bee, "I hate you!"

Bee looked at Cardboard Owen and his gleaming smile in the back seat. "What did you do to her?" Bee asked and groaned at her predicament, not at all sure what to make of any of this. Clearly, Owen's relationship with Jade carried a lot of weight for the annoying Thunderbird. Bee shook her head at Cardboard Owen, sighed in annoyed acceptance, got out, went around the car, shut the passenger door, got back in and drove off.

And quickly, she remembered that she had no idea at all where Granny Fleet lived or where she was going.

# 12 A VISIT TO GRANNY FLEET

Once Bee got far enough from Owen's house, she pulled over to the side of the road and just sat there staring out, trying to brainstorm how she could possibly figure out where Granny Fleet lived.

"Where? Where does she live?" she asked Cardboard Owen out loud without looking back at him. "Of course, you're not going to tell me," she snarked. "You're just going to sit back there with your hot smile as if everything's fine and your stupid girlfriend isn't about to blow this for everyone...or as if I'm not going to blow it if I can't figure out where Granny Fleet lives!"

Bee looked down at her phone as if it would give her the answer. It didn't. She went to Owen's socials. Scrolled through. Nothing. Just football shots. But luckily, she kept scrolling because when she went back far enough, she found a photo of Owen and Demi. "Demi!" Bee exclaimed. "That's it." After all, Owen and Demi had dated for a hot minute, and since Demi was so on it with everything, she probably knew all there was to know about Granny Fleet.

Bee quickly wrote a text to Demi: *Hey there! Any chance you have the address for Owen's grandma? I can't remember how to get there and promised him I'd go by. I guess I wasn't paying attention the other times really. Owen was driving. I'm so bad with directions.*

Bee hesitated before sending the text, reread it and then went for it.

Luckily.

Because Demi texted back right away: *Ten Acres, over near that one field, just south of Owen's. Like it's really pretty close. In that other neighborhood there.*

"Yes!" Bee exclaimed with a fist pump and grinned back at Cardboard Owen. "We totally got this." Then, Bee quickly looked up the address and directions to Ten Acres. *Bingo!*

Another text came in from Demi: *I hope she's nice to you! Don't let her give you any lip. I know from experience. She's only nice when Owen's there. Brace yourself!*

***

Bee pulled up to Ten Acres Senior Living Apartments. It looked like a nice place. She parked the SFB Mobile in the spacious parking lot and went in. Anastasia and Wyatt greeted her kindly at the front desk—they wore nametags, which is how she knew their names. They were over-the-top friendly until Bee said she was there to see Granny Fleet and they saw the pie. That's when a weird look of tension crossed both of their faces.

*Or maybe it's an "I'm sorry you have to be here" look?* Bee thought.

"She's right down that hallway," Anastasia said with a forced sweet voice.

*Definitely an "I'm sorry" look from Anastasia*, Bee noted.

"She's sitting right in front of her apartment door," Wyatt added, forcing a smile. "You can't miss her."

"Ready for her walk," Anastasia chimed. "Which she won't want to go on."

"Unless it's Owen," clarified Wyatt. "She loves Owen. And you are?"

"His girlfriend," Bee replied.

Anastasia and Wyatt looked at each other in surprise but

covered quickly. Bee guessed that they were used to dealing with lots of family drama with the Fleets.

"She usually calms down once she gets outside," comforted Anastasia.

"And I'm sure Mrs. Fleet, Gloria, is grateful that you're here," added Wyatt.

"How is Owen?" asked Anastasia. "We heard about the accident. What a terrible ordeal."

"Good! He's good!" Bee exclaimed way too enthusiastically then toned it down. "I mean, better. Owen is better. And he's going to be fine." She beamed but felt her distress escaping—as if it were shooting out of every taut pore on her fakely smiling face.

It must've shown. "Well, don't worry. You'll do great. And the pie will help," encouraged Anastasia. "You can bribe her."

"Bribe?" Bee wondered.

"It may work," Wyatt agreed. "To keep her quiet. And if it doesn't, just push. The wheelchair. Hopefully, she'll calm down once you get her outside."

Anastasia shot Bee a smile that said, *We really are sorry*, and told Bee, "You look fit. It'll go fast."

"The faster you push, the less painful it'll be," Wyatt chimed.

*Not helpful*, thought Bee but said, "Thank you," then, made her way over to the hallway where she supposedly would find Granny Fleet.

And she did.

Bee instantly spotted Granny Fleet sitting in her wheelchair several doors down the hallway. It had to be her. She was the only one in the hall, just like Anastasia and Wyatt had said.

Bee's heart started to race as she got closer to Owen's grandma. She sized Granny Fleet up, figuring she was in her mid 80s—which was older than her Nana Jana, who was super fit in her 70s. Owen's dad seemed to be older than Owen's mom so that sort of made sense. Maybe Granny Fleet had Owen's dad when she was older. Or Owen's dad was older than he looked. Or Granny Fleet was younger than she looked.

Even from down the hall, Granny Fleet looked wiry and feisty, fists clenched, feet on the ground moving her chair back and forth, unable to hold still, as if she were a young kid.

Granny Fleet glared at Bee as Bee approached.

*Roberto Benigni meets Carol Burnett*, thought Bee. *That's definitely what Granny Fleet looks like.* Bee was drawing on her film and TV acumen and the fact that seeing Owen's grandma made her think of her own nana. She and Nana Jana had probably watched every movie ever made. Nana Jana had been an actress in Hollywood at some point before becoming a makeup person. And since her grandpa, Papa Robbie, was a film editor in the movies—someone that put together the different angles and shots that were filmed, found the best bits and set the pacing of the movie—both of Bee's grandparents were super well versed in film and knew the best movies going back to the start of the talkies.

Mostly, Bee watched movies with Nana Jana at their house in Whitefish because they had a giant fireplace and an enormous screen. Bee's mom and dad had moved to nearby Kalispell shortly after Bee was born and their house wasn't as big—no extra-large screen either.

Watching movies was a Saturday-night ritual when Nana Jana was in town. Nana Jana would cuddle up with Bee and Paige on the sofa, and the three of them would drink hot cocoa while they watched the oldies as well as new films and TV too. They also always made popcorn, slathered it in butter and watched Nana Jana's favorites. They'd watched *Life Is Beautiful* a bunch of times, starring Roberto Benigni. And also *Down By Law*. Both Nana Jana and Bee agreed that Roberto Benigni was hilarious in person when they watched him on interviews and amazing as an actor. *The Carol Burnett Show* was a staple too, and Carol Burnett was even funnier than Roberto Benigni. *And together, they're the perfect mashup for Granny Fleet*, Bee thought and couldn't wait to tell Nana Jana about it. She'd have to find a way to get a photo of Granny Fleet to see if Nana Jana agreed with her description.

"Who are you?" Granny Fleet barked as Bee approached.

"Hi," Bee replied with her sweetest voice possible. "I'm Beatrix Plumb, Owen's...friend?" She stopped a couple yards from the old lady, feeling the "stay away" vibes shooting out at her.

Granny Fleet sized her up. "You don't know if you're his friend or not?" she scoffed.

"No, yes, I mean, yes. I am definitely his friend, girl, girlfriend, and I brought you a pie, from Mrs. Fleet," Bee defended and smiled, "which I'll just put in your apartment so we can have it after we go for a walk."

"I'm not going for a walk with you," Granny Fleet barked. "Where's Owen?"

Bee ignored the question, laughed nervously and went into what she assumed was Granny Fleet's apartment. "I'll just put the pie in here."

The entry of the apartment was covered in photos of Owen and Claire and their parents, so it definitely was Granny Fleet's place.

"What the heck are you doing in there?!" Granny Fleet growled from the hall.

Bee put the pie down on the kitchen counter and came running back out. "Okay, ready."

"I'm not going!" bellowed Granny Fleet.

"It'll be fun," Bee encouraged as she got behind Granny Fleet's wheelchair and grabbed the handles. "Owen asked me to bring you."

"I thought he couldn't talk!" shouted Granny Fleet.

"Just in general," Bee waffled as she tried to push the wheelchair. It wouldn't budge. She kept trying to make it go. "I think he can hear—I mean, through the fog from the meds, in the hospital, and he'll be so happy when I tell him I took you for your walk," Bee added and finally looked down, saw the wheelchair brake and undid it.

"Where's the other one?! The other girlfriend?!" Granny Fleet complained. "I don't like you!"

"Shhh, shhhh, let's just go outside and everything will be better," Bee insisted, trying to calm her down, not at all knowing if it'd get better. Then, she just started pushing the wheelchair down the hall. *Please make her stop*, she thought—

—which is when Granny Fleet started to yell, over and over again, "Help! She's kidnapping me!"

The cafeteria staff, Anastasia and Wyatt waved as they passed, obviously encouraging Bee to get the screaming biddy out.

***

Granny Fleet stopped screaming for help and to alert Ten Acres residents and staff of her alleged "kidnapping" as soon as Bee got her outside, but she hardly stopped screaming at all—just that now the screaming was more like barking orders as if she were a staff Sergeant and Bee were her lowly newly enlisted recruit.

"Can't you go faster?!" bellowed Granny Fleet as Bee pushed her and her wheelchair up the hilly road behind Ten Acres.

Bee was out of breath and sweating profusely halfway up the first hill. *How does Granny Fleet weigh so much?* she wondered. "Please, Granny Fleet, I'm just helping Owen, your chivalrous grandson!" she defended in between pants.

"Owen would never leave me with you!" Granny Fleet insulted Bee.

Which is when Bee's phone rang. *Thank goodness*, she thought and turned the wheelchair sideways so it was facing the sidewalk curb instead of up the hill so it wouldn't roll back at her. She let go of the wheelchair handles for a second to grab her phone out of her tote bag and answer the call, but before she could—

—in a flash, Granny Fleet started "walking" the chair towards the sidewalk, and it took off rolling fast in the direction of the curb.

"Wha...noooo! Grannyyyy!!!" Bee shouted, trying to catch the wheelchair—

But...BAM! It hit the curb. Granny Fleet flew out, Judo

rolled, and landed flat on her back on the sidewalk, the wheelchair bouncing back upright on the street.

"Omigosh! Granny Fleet, are you okay?" Bee cried as she bolted over to the old lady lying prone on the concrete sidewalk.

"No! Help! Call 911!" Granny Fleet screamed with all her vigor, seemingly unscathed.

Bee tried to lift Granny Fleet.

Granny Fleet shouted more, "Where's Owen?! Get Owen!"

*Crud, crud, crud*, thought Bee, still trying to lift Granny Fleet with all her might—

—which is when, suddenly, Nick appeared on a long-board skateboard riding up to Ten Acres.

Granny Fleet, as if hearing a choir of angels, cried, "Nicholas! My savior! Hellllpp!!!!"

Bee instinctively ducked to hide behind the wheelchair as—

Nick skateboarded over. "Granny Fleet?" he wondered, concerned to see her lying there flat on her back. "What's going on?"

"Save me from *her!*" Granny Fleet cried out with desperation.

"Who?" Nick asked, seeing no one—

—until Bee smiled up at him from her hiding spot behind the wheelchair, laughing nervously and eked out a, "Me."

# 13 NICK RESCUES BEE AND GRANNY FLEET FROM THE GREAT WHEELCHAIR ESCAPE

Nick easily lifted Granny Fleet off the sidewalk and sat her back in her wheelchair, unscathed, and then immediately started diverting Granny Fleet's attention from Bee, talking to her about how he was glad to be on the Lions' football team as the kicker—*which was a lie*, Bee assumed. And he told Granny Fleet that his dad, Coach Wells, was super happy to have him on the team—*which wasn't a lie, for sure.*

Nick asked Bee to hold his skateboard and then he run-pushed Granny Fleet in her wheelchair to the top of the hill, zooming back and forth, crisscrossing the seemingly untraveled street, and back down, with Granny Fleet laughing and thoroughly enjoying every minute of it.

When they got back inside the senior apartment building, Anastasia and Wyatt were over-the-top relieved to see Nick's smile and Granny Fleet's grin. They waved, and then Nick, Granny Fleet and Bee continued on to Granny Fleet's apartment.

Once inside, Nick got out plates and utensils from the

kitchen, and he and Bee sat in chairs in the family room area while Granny Fleet stayed in her wheelchair and the three of them ate pie.

Silence filled the room as they savored the amazing huckleberry pie, made from scratch by Owen's mom. Granny Fleet seemed abundantly happy. She swallowed a bite, relishing the taste, then paused for a moment to squeeze Nick's hand before digging back into the pie.

"So, what do you usually talk about?" Nick asked Granny Fleet and Bee, smiling at Bee, totally fishing.

"Uh, football? Weather? The usual," Bee replied with only a smidgeon of eye contact, staying focused on her slice of deliciousness in hopes that he wouldn't detect the lie.

Granny Fleet ignored Bee. "Did I tell you, Nicholas, about when I was downhill skiing champion at the Olympics?"

"Yes, Granny Fleet, faster than most," Nick assured her.

"What about *her*?" Granny Fleet asked Nick about Bee, as if Bee weren't there, sitting there eating pie with them. "What's her talent? Cheer dance like the other one?"

"I don't know," Nick replied, relishing this opportunity to turn to Bee with a grin and ask, "So, Bee, do you dance?"

Bee studied Nick's amused, prying look.

"Owen really loved that Jade," Granny Fleet asserted and took another bite of pie.

"Jade?" Nick asked.

"Of course, I dance," Bee interjected, standing up tall and deftly diverting Nick off the Jade trail. She  quickly  assessed the room then moved her chair over to give herself space to dance, looked at her audience of two—Nick waiting with a this-should-be-good grin on his face and Granny Fleet scowling with a "what-now?" look. Bee exhaled and did some Appalachian flatfoot moves.

Granny Fleet frowned. "Reminds me of Kentucky," she grumbled critically.

Nick laughed.

Bee started a turn, forcing herself to continue her flatfoot dance, and as she pivoted to face the back wall and window, she spotted her nemesis right there outside the window pane in a tree. Yes, it was Jade, positioned on a branch, spying on them.

Bee leapt over to the window and slammed down the blind before Nick and Granny Fleet could see Jade—then grinned as if slamming the blind shut were the most normal thing ever. "Just remembered!" Bee exclaimed in a panic. "We gotta go...!" Bee looked at Nick's shocked face. She hoped for an answer...as to what to do. But there was nothing.

Then, Bee looked around the room for an answer. Also nothing—

—until she spotted a framed photo of Owen and Granny Fleet next to Owen's suped-up blue mustang.

"...get Owen's car!" cried Bee. "Nick, we gotta go get Owen's car! In the shop! From before! I promised him! Them. Before it closes. Bye, Granny Fleet, so good to see you. I'll win you over yet." Bee went to kiss Granny Fleet—

—but she turned her head away in disgust and crowed, "Don't you dare."

—as Bee pulled out a confused Nick before he knew what was happening.

# 14 BEE GETS CAUGHT AS THE APPALACHIAN FLATFOOT POET ON THE SLY

Bee peeled out of the Ten Acres parking lot, spotting Jade in the rearview mirror walking to her purple Cabrio with orange Thunderbird stickers *crying!*—

*Why is she crying!* Bee wondered. *What the heck is wrong with her?*

Nick rode shotgun in the SFB Mobile—clutching the door handle as Bee swerved right—trying to keep himself from leaning into the middle.

"Is that Jade?" Nick asked, now noticing Bee's nemesis too in the side-view mirror.

"Jade?!" Bee exclaimed. "I mean, no, of course not," she added, cleverly rallying like the deceptive goddess that she currently was, then made a sharp left turn, slamming Nick against the SFB Mobile passenger door.

Nick braced himself again as Bee gunned it and continued as if her driving and this whole situation were normal, "...Why would Jade be here?" Bee asked as calmly as possible.

In the rearview mirror, Bee saw Jade, now deflated, wailing, opening her purple car door.

Bee made a sharp right—then a sharp left.

"What're you doing?!" Nick cried, still holding on for dear life.

"Shortcut," Bee explained, still acting as if these shenanigans were normal as she continued "escaping" until she hit a throughway and gunned it. *Phew*, she thought, finally able to relax and smiled at Nick. He looked really stressed out. "You okay?" she asked him.

"Oh, yeah, sure, nothing like a 'lil high-speed afternoon pick-me-up," he joked, with a what-the-heck look for sarcastic effect, and then he exhale-laughed like he was okay in this moment—while also knowing that this crazy driving and Bee's behavior were not at all normal in any world.

Bee laughed.

"Not to mention the Scottish tap dance clogging," Nick teased. "You're just full of surprises, aren't you?"

"Actually, it's Appalachian," Bee corrected. "Not Scottish."

"Sure, who wouldn't know that?" Nick grinned.

Bee laughed again, taken off guard by his genuine smile.

"And how did you come to learn this strange back-mountain dance?" Nick inquired.

"My sister," Bee retorted.

"Your sister?!" Nick exclaimed, truly surprised.

"The ballerina," Bee replied. "Paige. She got the graceful, doe-like, adorable genes. And I got rhythmic timing. Uses the same part of the brain as math." Bee shrugged, suddenly feeling a little cheeky.

Nick couldn't help but be amused. And charmed.

"I'm serious," Bee defended playfully. "It's an art form. My parents sent me to Tennessee when I was nine to stay with Aunt Becky and learn flatfoot."

"Wait, Appalachian flatfoot?" Nick demanded, putting it all together, suddenly realizing. "You're the flatfoot poet!"

*Uh, oh*, Bee cringed. "Uh...nope—not me," she defended with a cute smile while turning bright red—*omigosh*—and turned on the radio and blasted the music. Another of her favorite songs was on, "Boogie Shoes," by KC and the Sunshine Band.

"You're the friggin' flatfoot poet!" Nick exclaimed.

Bee deflected, singing, pretending to not hear him, "I want to put on, my my my my my boogie shoes. Just to boogie with you," and did a few dance moves as she drove on. Then, she stopped singing and hit search on the radio dial. "Yuck, hate that song, gross," she declared and hit the dial again—*hit, hit, hit*.

Nick reached over and turned the music all the way down, looking at Bee intensely as their hands touched. "I like that song," he told her.

"Okay...," Bee replied and quickly brought her hand back to clutch the steering wheel, not sure what to make of this.

"But Owen would hate it," Nick continued. "*AND* he didn't know your name at the talent show and pep rally, Flatfoot Poet. Why is that?"

"He was faking it," Bee scoffed.

"Are you sure?" Nick inquired teasingly, suspicion growing exponentially.

Bee suddenly swerved to the side of the road, no mechanic in sight, only fields. "Can we talk about this later?" she asked rhetorically and got out of the car.

Nick got out too, totally confused by Bee's move.

"And can you step back off the road? By the grass? Away from the SFB?" Bee asked calmly over the top of the car but with a certain directness, as if he didn't have a choice.

"What?!" Nick replied, "SFB?"—not at all getting this insanity but stepping back anyway, away from the car just as Bee had requested.

"Perfect!" Bee chimed. "Safety first! The mechanic is just around the corner." Which is when Bee jumped back in the car, reached over and locked his door and yelled out the window at him. "If you could just get Owen's car! 'Gotta tutor math! Thanks...! Byyyyeee....!"

And Bee peeled out, leaving Nick in the dust.

# 15 NICK, DIEGO AND DIEGO'S BEATRIX PLUMB INSTALLATION OF LOVE

Bee went straight home after the whole Granny Fleet, Nick and Jade ordeal. She knew that Nick was seeing tons of holes in her fake story about being Owen's secret girlfriend, and she wasn't sure how long she would be able to keep him at bay.

The "we have to get Owen's car" save at Granny Fleet's and on the roadside had been brilliant, but somehow, she just couldn't help feeling anything but awful about pulling one over on Nick, especially when he was so cute and funny and helpful. She told herself to let it go and get out of the car and move on.

No one was downstairs when Bee went in the house, *thank goodness*. They were probably all on their phones somewhere, she figured. She went up to her room, locked the door and tried to forget everything by focusing on homework, sitting on her bench with the cute, red polka dot cushion in the bay window. Bee loved that window. And she loved sitting there on the bench. It was her cozy, chill place, where she could think and write songs and just be herself.

It worked for a while until Kate and Torian came out of Kate's house across the street and sat on her front lawn talking, laughing and cuddling. *Gross.*

Then, Diego came home and immediately went outside and started working on his Beatrix Plumb installation on their front lawn. He seemed to be adding new elements in the "sky"—some planets or stars or something.

*At least, he wasn't here to see me come in*, Bee thought, trying her best to maintain even the smallest modicum of positivity.

And then, Nick drove up in Owen's blue suped-up Mustang. It was fast. And loud.

And Bee knew—as her stomach clutched and her throat seized up—that this was not good. She ducked down behind the windowsill. *Crud, this can't be happening*, she thought, her heart pounding out of her chest in a panic. *What do I do?*

She peeked up and saw Nick get out of Owen's Mustang, his eyes going straight to Diego as he was trying to attach a comet in the "sky" of his installation. Bee saw Nick's brow furrow in confusion at this odd sight. A giant sun crashed down.

And then, Bee saw the realization on Nick's face as he took in what stood before him amidst the constellation of stars at the top, the snapshots of Bee hanging down from wires, the carefully placed mini spotlights and other shiny and hilariously bizarre items of celebration and loving homage, namely: the giant clay statue of Bee.

"What the...?" Nick uttered in shock and awe, Bee easily deciphering the words on his lips as he moved closer and took in this elaborate Beatrix Plumb installation. Nick inspected the newly added snapshots of Bee in little planet-esque stars orbiting the statue, each featuring Bee with an annoyed or shocked look on her face.

"You like?" Diego asked Nick with his Spanish accent. "It is a soul homage."

Bee quietly cracked open her window so she could hear better.

"Excuse me?" Nick managed, trying to hide his laugh and process the situation.

Diego beamed, admiring his heartfelt work, "An homage to

my art-meets-life soulmate."

"Bee?" Nick wondered in surprise.

"Yes!" Diego chimed. "You know her?"

"Recognized her even," Nick smiled. "You said she's your soulmate?"

"Yes," Diego told him with sudden and serious deeply emotional sincerity. "Beautiful, like an eclipse. Shadow and light. At once."

"But your *soulmate*?" Nick asked again, trying to understand this odd confession. "As in...?"

"As in love at first sight," Diego clarified, as if it should be obvious. "Between a fresh young heart. And a simple Spanish boy. She is my muse." Diego smiled proudly.

Nick took a closer look at the photos. "Well, you might want to get more of the light in there," he told Diego. "I don't see her smile anywhere. Best part."

Bee's heart leapt at this weird but ultra-sweet admission by Nick.

And Diego frowned, knowing Nick was right—

—just as the front door to the Plumb house opened and Paige and Bee's mom, Judy, exited.

*Crud*, thought Bee. *Now?! They have to come out now?!* And she quickly hoofed it downstairs to try to make sure the situation didn't get worse.

"Hi! Can we help you?" Judy asked Nick with a friendly smile.

Nick smiled back and walked over to Mrs. Plumb.

Bee arrived at the front door, which was ajar, stealthily peeking out one of the little windows in the door just in time to see and hear Nick respond to her mom—

"Yeah, I'm a friend of Bee's," he told Mrs. Plumb. "Just came to tell her I got Owen's car."

"Owen?" wondered Bee's mom.

"Her boyfriend?" Nick replied to Mrs. Plumb, Diego and Paige as if this should be obvious.

The three responded all together in shock, "Boyfriend?!"

"You sure you have the right Bee?" asked Paige.

"Uh...yeah," Nick said and gestured to Diego's Beatrix Plumb installation. "That's the Bee I'm talking about."

Paige and her mom stared at Nick in disbelief.

Diego emitted a muffled cry then fell to his knees. "She has insulted my honor and love. And misled me!" he cried with desperation about Bee, looking from Judy to Paige then back to Nick.

"C'mon, Barcelona Boy," Paige encouraged, trying to diffuse the situation. "Owen doesn't even know who Bee is. You're the only one for Bee."

"Bee?!!!" Judy yelled back at the house, up towards Bee's bay window.

Bee popped out from her hiding spot behind the front door. "Hey, Nick! Diego! Nick!! Thank you! Keep the car. I'm good," she grinned as hugely as possible, as if this were totally normal behavior, then turned to Diego. "Diego, Mi Amore, let's make paella."

Bee grabbed Diego by the arm and started to lead him towards the house.

Diego melted instantly, leaving Nick standing there in shock.

Bee waved back to Nick with a totally cheeky smile and saw Jade pass in the purple Cabrio, going super slowly.

Nick noticed Jade pass too, noticing Jade's look of utter dismay as she saw Owen's car in front of Bee's house and Nick too.

Bee turned and pulled Diego along faster, hurrying to the house. She looked back with a glance—a quick peek but enough to see that Nick looked like he was now very confused and likely very suspicious about Bee being Owen's secret girlfriend. Clearly, it wasn't adding up for him.

*Crud*, Bee thought and went inside, pulling Diego along, closing the door on Nick, Paige and her mom and hoping Nick would just leave and not talk to her mom or Paige. *This has to end soon*, she thought to herself and pulled Diego into the kitchen.

# 16 ANNOYANCE AND PANIC IN THE LUNCHROOM

Bee was a ball of nerves. Ever since Nick drove away in Owen's car the night before, she just couldn't relax. Obviously, he'd gotten a gazillion times more suspicious thanks to stupid Diego and her mom and Paige looking so shocked about Owen being her boyfriend. *Why did they have to be so surprised? And why did Jade have to drive by? Right at that moment!* All of which was just going to make her life that much worse.

No, luck had not been on Bee's side the night before, but she had her JYM and she knew she had to keep going to help Owen.

But as she ate lunch with Kate and Torian in the school cafeteria, Bee noticed Nick. He was sitting at his own table near the jock table with his earbuds in. It was strange that he wasn't at the jock table and awkward because he kept watching her.

"He knows," Bee said in a deadpan low whisper to Kate without taking her eyes off Nick as she hid behind Torian's big puffy hair so Nick wouldn't see her watching him. "Nick knows and I'm in way over my head."

Kate giggled, distracted as Torian fed her the crinkly, salted

Kettle chips that she had packed in her lunch at home and put in her hand-sewn lunch bag that matched Bee's hand-sewn lunch bag because they had made the lunch bags together. Kate ate the same thing every day: a cheese sandwich with mayo, lettuce and tomato on home-baked sourdough bread. "Everyone is in over their heads," Kate responded to Bee as soon as she chewed and swallowed the chip. "That's how you take it to the next level: You jump in and swim. Because...," she sang.

"The secret of getting ahead is getting started. Mark Twain," the two friends recited the end of their favorite quote together—Kate spirited, Bee deadpan.

"And you're started!" Kate chimed. "And noticed, taking risks! It looks desperate now, but then, it'll be awesome."

Torian frisky growled into Kate's ear as Kate looked at Bee.

Kate turned and growled back at Torian playfully.

"I just told you that Nick knows I'm not Owen's girlfriend and you completely ignored me," Bee scoffed at Kate in spite of the fact that it wasn't true: Kate had not completely ignored her. Instead, Kate had given her a crumb of advice. And they'd recited their favorite quote. But Bee couldn't get past her annoyance with Torian. *When will he go away?!*

A text came in on Bee's phone from Demi: *PLAYBOOK?*

Bee leaned forward and glanced at Demi at the jock table.

Demi waved at Bee.

"How could he possibly know?" Kate said about Nick, turning away from her boyfriend and back to her friend.

"Because he's annoying and nosey," Bee said, feeling more and more dejected by the situation with Nick.

"Maybe he likes you," Kate suggested.

Torian mauled Kate's ear.

Kate giggled.

Bee considered Kate's suggestion. *Nope, Nick liking me is not a thing,* she thought, unsure why, and told Kate, "Impossible."

"Better reign that in then," Kate advised Bee about Nick's suspicion about Bee's Owen-girlfriend lie, and then, she turned and went for Torian's neck, mauling him like a toothless, playful, snarly lioness.

Bee watched this insanity, snarled at Torian, grabbed her phone and untouched lunch in her cute handmade lunch bag that matched Kate's—once upon a time a sign of their immutable best-friendship and now a reminder of how much she hated Torian getting in between them. She huffed at this miserable thought and left the table. She had to get out of there.

"Bee?" Kate called after her.

But Bee ignored Kate in spite of the fact that ignoring Kate always made her heart squeeze with sadness, and she left the lunchroom. At least her sadness about Kate and her super annoyance with Torian fueled her mission: Help Owen and the team!

Once, she escaped the lunchroom and got away from all those eyes and attention, Bee stopped and texted Demi back: *Got playbook. Will bring to practice later.*

Demi texted back immediately with a thumbs-up and cheer megaphone and wrote: *Meeting at hospital first. Right after school. 3:30 PM! See you there!*

# 17 BEE'S WILY SAVE AT THE HOSPITAL AND OWEN'S GURLPLE LOVE POEM TO JADE

Bee heard the cheer squad cheering from Owen's hospital room as she walked down the hospital hallway and up to Owen's hospital room door.

She peered in.

Coach Wells and the football team stood round Owen's bed as the cheer squad was just finishing the cheer. "Win. For. Owen! Yaaaaaay!"

Cheerleader Chrissie did a flip thingy.

Everyone in the room cheered loudly.

Bee took a breath and entered, pulling Owen's playbook out of her handmade bag, another bag she and Kate had made together. This one was a tote that served as both a book bag and a purse. It was made mostly of jeans material and had some red and white flowery fabric for accents and the handles. Bee loved this bag, and at that moment, about to be faced by all the Lion team and cheerleader faces, it did the opposite of the lunch bag earlier—it gave her confidence. Thinking of Kate gave her confidence. For five seconds.

Then, she thought of Torian. *Yuck.* And smiled as everyone noticed her. "Hi!" Bee said and handed the playbook to Coach Wells, beaming with now fake confidence.

"We knew you'd come through," Coach Wells told Bee, beaming back at her as he took the playbook.

Bee high-fived Coach Wells, and as they moved apart, Bee noticed a girl's white sneaker under the bed. It had a little purple hand-drawn Sharpie "T" and an orange bird with outstretched wings drawn on the side and was clearly attached to a foot and a leg. Someone was under the bed, and Bee instantly knew it had to be Jade. *Yes, that's Jade's shoe*, Bee confirmed to herself and stepped over in front of the shoe to hide it, in case someone else noticed it too.

Which is when Bee spotted Nick studying her suspiciously. *When will this end?!* she groaned in her head and smiled to everyone in the room as if everything were just perfect.

"Well done, Owen," Coach Wells said to Owen about choosing Bee as his girlfriend. "You picked well. She got us the playbook. She's responsible. We love Bee."

Owen stirred, his head moving slightly as he made an attempt to open his eyes, then drowsily muttered his own name, "Owen..."

Bee smiled at Owen as if he'd be happy to see her, "Owen. Hi."

But Owen was super loopy and didn't notice at all as he drifted back into his over-pain-medicated stupor.

"He's still totally drugged up," Demi stepped in to clarify for Bee. "Doesn't remember the accident. But the doctor says it's normal."

"Oh, sure, totally," said Bee, trying her best to maintain composure.

"Owen!" cheerleader Chrissie yelled, trying to inspire Owen to feel hope now that Bee was there. "It's Bee. Your girlfriend."

Owen stirred again, his eyes opening in shock at Chrissie's loud and desperate plea. He peered drowsily at Bee and laughed, dozing back off. "Girlfriend," he managed.

Bee fake laughed at him lovingly, tickling his blanket.

"Don't worry," Coach Wells said half to Bee and the group and half for himself. "It'll all come back to him. He'll remember everything. Apparently, he's doing great and they're starting to taper off the meds." Coach Wells looked at Bee with a forced smile.

"What a relief," Bee told him with as much optimism as she could muster because this tapering-off-the-meds thing was a problem worth panicking over but she couldn't let them see.

"And then maybe he'll want to know about your other boyfriend," Nick interjected from the back of the room.

Bee froze.

The players standing in front of Nick parted so everyone could see him.

"What other boyfriend?" cheerleader Chrissie demanded.

"Gimme a D, Diego!" Nick cheered. "Go, go, Diego!"

"Diego is not my boyfriend," Bee defended.

"Sorry, 'Art meets life soulmate'?" Nick added with a grin.

Bee gasped under her breath at Nick's disclosure. Her heart started pounding.

"I thought Owen was your soulmate," cheerleader Chrissie said to Bee, disturbed by this intel about Diego and totally buying it.

Bee knew she had to do something and turned to Nick. "What are you talking about?" she scoffed as if he were insane.

"I think someone's got us fooled," Nick said about Bee to the group without taking his eyes off Bee's.

"Fooled?" Coach Wells croaked as if his world were about to fall apart again.

"Either that or she's two-timing Owen," Nick observed, eyes still piercing Bee's and her stare.

Cheerleader Chrissie gasped.

Bee's heart pounded out of her chest. She just hoped no one could hear it or see her body pulsating with fear—terrified that her lie would be found out.

Coach Wells couldn't help but laugh nervously. The tension was high, and he was losing it.

Everyone turned to look at him.

"Sorry, sorry!" Coach Wells rallied and awkwardly told Nick and Bee. "Go on."

"That's not true," Bee told Nick, insisting she wasn't two-timing Owen.

"Well, then what is?" Nick challenged her.

"What're ya thinking, Thunderbird spy?" Drew-ster joked, enjoying the game. He and his football buddies laughed at the thought of Bee being a spy for their rivals.

"Maybe," Nick said, still not taking his eyes off Bee, not giving her a break.

"He's an exchange student!" Bee insisted about Diego, deftly defending her position. "Diego is an exchange student who thinks he's in love with me. But it's all in his head."

"Ohhhhhh, yay!" cheerleader Chrissie cheered in relief.

"Yeah, artsy guy's got a crush on her, Nick!" Demi jumped in to defend Bee. "Who cares? Let it go."

Nick didn't let it go. "And Jade?" he jabbed at Bee. "Showing up and Bee pretending she doesn't know her?"

"Jade's crazy," Demi scoffed at Nick. "You know that. And you know nothing about Bee." Demi's gaslighting skills were on fire.

"Like I said, Thunderbird spy," Drew-ster interjected, followed by more laughter from the peanut gallery.

"All right, guys, we're 'gonna let this lie for now, for Owen," Coach Wells stepped in.

But no one was ready to let it lie, especially cheerleader Chrissie. "I'm sure Bee can prove she's Owen's girlfriend," Chrissie insisted defensively to Nick then turned to Bee with innocent hope and defiance on her face. "Right, Bee? Just tell us how you and Owen met. And show us a photo or something."

The cheer squad cheered, "Beeeee-eeee!"

Cheerleader Chrissie gave Nick a "you see" look as if this cheer solidified her notion as fact.

All eyes turned to Bee.

Bee panicked, eyelids involuntarily fluttering. Short breaths. She looked at the ground searching as if an answer would magically appear there on the tiled floor. "Uh, well, I always...," Bee managed, shaking her head, trying to decide what to do, what to say. "...liked him, liked Owen," escaped from her lips. Her heart pounded like a drum. She looked up from the tiles. All eyes were still on her.

And then, it happened. Bee felt a rush of confidence—brightness filled her heart. Because she'd spoken the truth: She'd always liked Owen.

She glanced at Demi who nodded for her to continue. This helped too.

And so, Bee continued, "And so, I took the initiative." *Also true.*

The football team cheered, "Woot, woot!"

"My kinda girl!" Drew-ster shouted.

Coach Wells shushed them.

"And, um...," Bee managed but then was suddenly at a loss again. She looked at her phone, panicked some more, thinking about the truth, the past few weeks passing before her eyes—the accident, Jade and Owen in the car, the reality, feeling like she was about to throw in the towel, Jade in the car, in her backseat, spraying her with purple spray paint, Jade hiding under Owen's hospital bed right then and there.

And then, Bee remembered—*the earrings!* The blue Italian glass earrings that were in her pocket! The ones that Nick had bought for some girl named Amy, who was smitten with Owen, that Nick had given to Owen for said girl, who Nick had moved on from, and who broke up with Owen—the earrings that Owen had then given to Jade but that Jade couldn't wear because she was a secret, so she'd given them to Bee in anger and frustration and due to her own guilt.

A choir of angels chimed in Bee's ears and a rush of adrenaline shot through her body. "Well, he did give me these," Bee said nonchalantly as she pulled the beautiful and now-glorious gleaming blue Italian glass earrings out of her jacket pocket.

The cheerleaders gasped.

Nick paled.

Bee put the earrings on. They sparkled gorgeously.

"What the...?" Demi whispered under her breath because she wasn't exactly expecting Bee to come up with anything. But then, she rallied as if it were a given that Bee had those earrings. "See!" Demi chimed, as if anyone that didn't believe Bee was Owen's secret girlfriend now was insane.

Bee's heart pounded again in a panic because of the lie, brightness disappearing—but she hid it well.

"Actually, no, I don't get it," Coach Wells admitted to Demi about the earrings, brow furrowed, feeling like he was melting into a puddle of incompetence, wishing he understood things that he didn't understand, then doing his best to rally. "But that's okay. They're beautiful. Beautiful earrings. Good choice, Owen. Shoulda' got some for Nick's mom. Maybe she woulda stuck around."

Coach Wells looked up at Nick with desperate eyes.

Nick shot his dad a "what the heck?" look, like—why would his dad ever bring his mom and their relationship into this?!

"I'm joking," Coach Wells told his son.

Nick clenched his jaw, trying to hold in his frustration.

Coach Wells couldn't win and muttered, "Not really joking," as he looked away, shaking his head at himself, rubbing his brow, just wishing this was over or he knew what to do.

"I don't get it either," said Drew-ster about the earrings.

"They're from Owen," Nick informed the room for those that didn't know. "The earrings are a gift from Owen to Bee."

Four cheerleaders and Demi clearly did know something about the earrings and simultaneously added to Nick's story with utter glee, "His Italian grandmother's."

Which, obviously, was untrue.

"What?!" Nick exclaimed, knowing that the Italian grandmother was a stealth Owen-girlfriend-luring lie.

"I still don't get it," said Drew-ster.

"No one gets it," added running back Glenn.

"He's in love with Bee!" Demi clarified. "Owen is in love with Bee. That's what those earrings mean. That's why he gave them to her. Owen was waiting for The One."

Cheerleader Chrissie burst into tears. "Because they're an airboom," she cried with joy and turned to Bee, opening her arms for a hug.

Bee hugged cheerleader Chrissie, amused that she'd said "airboom" instead of "heirloom," while also feeling totally done and totally relieved that her lie worked even though it was also creating a pit in her stomach. If she hadn't remembered the earrings, her fake Owen-secret-girlfriend lie and the Lions' chance at getting to the State Championship and alleviating her guilt would've been dust.

Nick looked at Bee, defeated.

Bee's eyes met his.

Nick looked hurt.

And then, he left.

Demi watched the whole eye-look exchange between Bee and Nick, worried about Bee and her secret getting found out in spite of this luck. Because Bee looked done.

Demi's wheels turned. "All right everybody, let's get to practice and let Owen get some rest." She high-fived Bee and made a lasso move as if she were rounding up the team and cheerleaders.

Coach Wells shot Demi a look of gratitude, high-fived Bee and left, still in shock and relieved that things were still moving in a good direction, relatively. "As good as they can," he muttered to himself as he walked out.

Bee waved as cheerfully as possible as Demi herded the team out of Owen's hospital room to go back to the school for cheer and football practice.

As soon as she was sure they were gone, Bee closed the door until it was ajar—and, unbeknownst to her, enough for Demi to come back and eavesdrop again. Then, Bee whispered loudly towards the bottom of the bed, "Okay, it's safe."

Jade stuck her head out from her under-the-bed hiding spot, pissed, then jutted a piece of paper out at Bee. "To remind you who Owen really loves, because you're pushing it," Jade snarked at Bee.

"And you're lucky I'm doing this," Bee snarked back as she yanked the paper away. "Protecting your lie! And Owen's status!"

Jade slid back under the bed, being stealth in case any of the Lions returned, while keeping her eager and pissed face out enough to watch Bee's reaction to her precious treasure.

The piece of paper was folded and partially crumpled, as if Jade had been clutching it for dear life. Bee unfolded it. It was a handwritten love poem, or at least she figured as much because it had little hearts drawn around on it and it was written in poem format.

Bee read aloud, "Roses are white (sometimes). Violets are purple. Chili is spicy hot. And so are you, my...Gurl-ple." *What the heck is a Gurlple?* Bee wondered. "Gurlple?" She looked at Jade for an answer.

Owen shifted in his dozing sleep and muttered, "Gurlple."

Bee flipped the paper over and read, "To Jade. Love Owen," written in a mix of Thunderbird purple and orange and Lion blue and green.

*Worst poem ever*, Bee thought.

But clearly this homage of love meant something to Jade.

Jade stuck her head out further from under the bed, proud, with a beaming smile and said, "See! It's me. Owen loves me!"

# 18 DEMI'S SURPRISE VISIT TO BEE'S HOUSE

Bee went straight home after the hospital. She didn't go to practice. There was no way she could face any Lions right now, especially Nick. She didn't say hi to Kate sitting outside on the lawn with Torian, their now everyday spot.

She didn't try to do anything.

She was exhausted. And luckily, the house was quiet when she went in the front door. She figured no one was home. Or maybe her mom was holing up in her office working or taking a break or binge watching a show. That was definitely a thing. Her mom was good at creating balance.

*Thank goodness*, Bee thought. *Finally, a stroke of luck. Of privacy. Maybe it's the blue Italian glass earrings*, she joked to herself. And flopped down on the couch in the family room.

Suddenly, there was a blinding FLASH in her eyes as Diego snapped a photo with his old-school film camera.

*Wrong again!*

"What the...? No! Go away!" Bee cried out and covered her face with a couch pillow. "I can't do this right now!"

"No problem. I'll wait," Diego declared with his Spanish

accent. "My mother, she sent me my special camera from Barcelona. The photos will be more sharp. So your eyes will sparkle and so will your spirit. That boy in Owen's azul automobile was correct. We need your smile!" Then, Diego climbed onto the couch arm and stood above Bee waiting with the camera pointed at her.

Bee pulled the pillow down to see what he was doing.

Another FLASH blinded her as he snapped another photo.

Bee growled, "Stop!" And furrowed her brow into the meanest, angriest scowl she could muster.

"Just one little smile?" Diego begged with a pouty "please" face, as if this would help.

Bee had had enough. She lunged for the camera.

Diego jumped down off the sofa arm.

Bee rolled swiftly from the sofa, jumping to her feet faster than she knew she was capable of, and flew at Diego.

Diego took off running around the couch.

A chase ensued—

"Give me that stupid camera!" Bee shouted as she pursued him around and around the sofa.

"I just need a shot of your smile. To get the light side of you," Diego cried as he hightailed it about the side table for another lap.

"Do I look like I'm light right now?" Bee shouted back as she suddenly bounded over and across the sofa to catch Diego on the other side and pounced. "I'd say I'm more like a dark friggin' abyss!" *Success!* She blocked Diego from escaping and lunged for the camera.

But just as she got her hands on it and yanked the camera away from Diego, there was a knock at the front door. *What?!* Bee wondered and said out loud, "Everythings's weird," as she went over and peeked out the peephole in the door.

The view was a fish-eye distortion on Demi, who looked weirdly and uncharacteristically nervous.

*Criminy!* thought Bee. *What now?* Then, she shouted through the door to Demi, "Just a minute! Be right there!" Then, she turned to Diego as she clutched his beloved camera and whispered sharply, "You need to go to your room. If you ever want to see your camera again!"

"Why?" Diego wondered, completely flummoxed by her ire.

"Because I can't deal with you right now! And her! At the same time!" Bee whisper-yelled, unable to contain herself as she shoved the camera at Diego, caving on her bargaining tactic. "I'll do the smile photo when she leaves. I'll let you take it. Okay? You and me together. Now go!"

Diego shot Bee a truly annoying flirty smile. "Anything to help, Mi Amore," he whispered with a grin and dorky passion in his eyes, then left, bounding upstairs, two steps at a time, heart aloft with impossible dreams about Bee.

"Omigosh," Bee whispered under her breath and turned and opened the front door.

Demi quickly hid her worry and stood tall, beaming at Bee, "Hi! Beatrix! I was just in the hood and decided to come by, old-school style. To make sure you're okay."

From inside the house, Bee's mom's voice rang out, "Honey...?"

*She is home*, Bee thought and realized that she must've been utterly exhausted not to have noticed that her mom was there.

Bee's mom walked out from the kitchen on her way upstairs. She was on the phone and stopped mid-walk when she saw Demi, surprised that anyone would be there to visit Bee, then continued to Bee, "I need you to take Paige to ballet practice, okay? Ten minutes," and disappeared upstairs.

Bee stepped out the front door and shut it behind her, now standing weirdly and awkwardly close to Demi, almost nose-to-nose on the front-door porch because it wasn't that big. She tried to smile, tried to act normal.

Kate and Torian, still on Kate's front lawn, waved.

Demi tensed, looking more awkward than Bee felt. She took a deep breath, held it, exhaled and smiled.

Bee knew in that instant that Demi was gearing up to say something big.

And she did. "I know you're not Owen's girlfriend," Demi

admitted to Bee in a serious whisper, as if their entire existence depended on her saying this. "And Jade is," she continued. "Jade is Owen's secret girlfriend."

Bee gasped and felt herself crumble inside.

"But it's okay!" Demi continued, deftly mitigating any damage. "I spied on you in the hospital, a few times, including today, with Jade and the weird 'gurlple' letter-slash-poem, and I saw it all, the desperation, the love; and I wasn't going to say anything because your performance's been, well, perfect. But today, with Nick, there were cracks."

"Omigosh, I'm so sorry," Bee cried in a whisper.

"Don't be sorry," Demi told Bee, desperately trying to regain her own usual Demi-entrepreneur-goddess-clad self-assurance. "You totally saved us. And I want to help you."

"What?" Bee uttered, confused. *Demi wants to help me?* This was almost too unbelievable.

Demi put her hands on Bee's shoulders, one on each, and smiled, ready to crack herself but holding it together almost perfectly. "I want to help you. Till we win. That's why I'm here."

"But he's gonna come off the meds and know I'm not his girlfriend," Bee reminded Demi.

"Not till after the game next Friday," Demi insisted. "And then, I'll make it all okay, okay?"

Bee glanced at Kate, who was across the street watching this whole exchange like a hawk. *That's weird too*, she thought, then sighed. Clearly, there was nothing she could do. Truth was surfacing on all fronts. "Okay...that sounds great," Bee told Demi, resigned to this fate, looking Demi in the eye and nodding her commitment to the plan—

—just as Paige and her boyfriend, Tommy, barreled up the sidewalk, up the front walkway and to the front door, not stopping. "I'll be ready in five," Paige barked at Bee, pushing open the door and going in.

Bee was annoyed with her sister. And then, the upstairs window to Diego's room opened and out he popped with his camera and—FLASH!—Diego snapped a photo of Bee and

Demi looking up in wonder and surprise from the front step.

Diego smiled down at them.

*So weird*, thought Bee.

"That's weird," said Demi out loud, then continued on, looking back at Bee, without the flash ruffling her at all. "I knew I could count on you," she said and smiled encouragingly, hugged Bee and left, bounding off the front porch with a spring back in her step.

Bee looked over across the street at Kate on her lawn with Torian, both had been watching the events closely. Bee and Kate's eyes met, and Bee knew Kate knew her well enough to read her body language and see that she was stressed out. And Bee knew that Kate would be wondering what was up with Demi. And Bee knew that she hated Torian in that moment because if he and Kate hadn't started dating, none of this would be happening.

Bee turned away, took a deep breath in and stepped inside.

# 19 NICK SHOWS UP TOO

Bee walked in the house slowly after her encounter with Demi and shut the front door, taking it all in and recommitting to pulling off this secret-Owen-girlfriend lie as she had just worked out with Demi—but doubtful that it was going to work. And also doubtful about how she was ever going to feel okay again without Kate by her side as her forever teammate, the person that made her feel like the best version of herself, all-powerful and full of courage and hope and knowing that everything would be okay. The person that made her know that she was and would be okay. Instead of the current situation, namely—just feeling bad and worried all the time.

Bee only got two steps in the house before Diego bounded down the stairs with his camera—a fancy digital camera this time—and a determined smile and flashing, passionate eyes aimed right at her. He leapt off the bottom stair. "Okay, beautiful lady," he said moving towards Bee. "Shall we?"

*Ugh*, Bee thought, remembering the fact that she'd promised him a photo with a smile earlier in exchange for him disappearing upstairs when Demi showed up.

Diego put his hand on Bee's shoulder and moved her over

to the light at the front window.

And then, there was a knock at the front door. *Again!*

"What now?" Bee wondered. *What was happening here? Was Demi back?*

Diego bounded over to the front door.

Bee groaned.

"Yes?!" Diego chimed playfully as he threw open the door.

And there stood Nick.

Bee paled when she saw him and her heart sank.

Nick noticed, "Now, there's a welcome if I ever saw one," teasing Bee with a smile.

"Nick! My man," Diego declared. "We can use you."

"Like an underpaid muse, I hope," Nick joked, not sure if Diego got the Beatrix Plumb obsessively over-the-top lawn installation muse reference but going for it anyway.

Diego did not get the reference. "For the photo," Diego explained in all seriousness. "You have a good eye." And then, he ushered Nick in.

Bee couldn't believe this was happening.

Nick nodded to Diego and shot Bee an amused grin.

"And then everyone will be leaving," Bee insisted and shot eye-daggers at Diego as she stepped closer to the window for the photo. "Is this okay?" she asked, annoyed, and plastered a big, fake smile on her face.

"Yes, perfect," Diego said, then handed Nick the camera and ran over to Bee's side to pose with her and her plastic smile.

Nick was amused by Bee's annoyance and lifted the camera then began to frame Diego, Bee and Bee's fake smile in the giant fancy over-the-top lens. Nick chuckled.

"Just take it already," Bee chided.

Nick toyed with them, "Um, there's something not quite right here. Let me see..." He moved camera angles, trying different positions. "No, it's you, Miss Plumb," Nick said with all the fake earnestness he could muster. "Can we get a little more Appalachian?" Nick looked up at Bee, over the camera, with happy eyes and his hot smile.

Their eyes met.

Bee's stomach flipped.

FLASH! Nick snapped the shot.

"Wait," Bee said.

FLASH again! Another shot.

"That's not fair," Bee cried. "I wasn't...smiling!"

Nick grinned, amused, and shrugged.

This made Bee laugh. She shook her head. Nick was funny.

FLASH! Nick took a shot of Bee laughing.

"And bingo!" Nick cheered with joy and grinned at Bee as he handed the camera back to Diego.

Diego looked at the photos in the camera and stopped when he saw the last one of Bee laughing. He deflated. "He sees you," Diego said to Bee about Nick. "The man sees you. Better than me. He captured your smile. Your laugh. Your spirit. Perfectly." Wounded, Diego hung his head and walked off upstairs like a hurt Eeyore.

Nick playfully gestured to Bee with I-see-you fingers from his eyes to hers.

Bee laughed.

"I knew Appalachian girl was in there somewhere," Nick beamed.

"Honey...?" Bee's mom called out to Bee, coming down the stairs into the living room, still on the phone. "Liv needs a ride too. She and Paige. And they can't be late! Important dance rehearsal." Bee's mom looked at Nick, once again surprised that Bee would have a visitor—a sudden abundance, no less—as she continued on, never breaking stride or pausing her phone conversation. And then, she disappeared into the kitchen.

"Wow, Grand Central in here Appalachia," Nick mused to Bee. "I'd better be quick. And I, um..." Nick stopped when he looked at Bee and their eyes met. Then, he rallied, "... I...I'm sorry about before. At the hospital. With the earrings. And the weirdness. Which is why my dad sent me to ask you to dinner. I mean, he wants to invite you to dinner, his idea. Not that I wouldn't want to...invite you to dinner. Or even have dinner...with you. It'd be great, but wow, this is coming out bad." Nick laughed, embarrassed by his awkwardness, and turned a crimson red. "...but yeah, dinner, for a simple thank you. At my uncle's fish taco place. With music. If you want to. Uh... " Nick paused, looking for words, then downplaying the whole suggestion, "I mean, or not, if you don't want to, no big deal; but if you do, just say so, whenever, we'll do it. You can text me. Or tell me at school."

Nick looked so nervous, Bee thought. But it was nice.

Which is when Paige suddenly came barreling downstairs in her ballet gear on the phone. "Mom!" she bellowed out towards the kitchen as she ran through the living room, "Tommy's coming too, and we're going to Jess's movie night after!" Then, Paige was out the front door, expecting Bee to follow and be her ride.

Bee jumped as the door slammed, exasperated with the idea of being Paige's chauffeur. Then, she turned to Nick. "Sounds great," she told him with a smile. "I'd love to hang out sometime. Like now. How about now?"

Nick laughed nervously at this unexpected turn. *"Right now?"*

"Yes!" Bee chimed.

Bee sure was full of surprises, Nick thought. "Uh, sure," he said, pleased.

"Great," Bee replied, then turned and yelled to her mom in the kitchen, "I'm going out, Mom! You'll have to take Paige." She grinned at Nick.

He was amused and laughed out loud, getting what she was up to—

—just as Paige poked her head back in the front door, still on her phone, and barked at Bee, "We have to go! What are you waiting for?"

—just as their mom came out from the kitchen, also still on the phone, surprised by Bee telling her she had to take Paige. "What's going on?" their mom asked. "You can't take Paige?"

"No. Gotta run. Plans," Bee grinned at her mom then turned to Paige. "I'll see you all later." Then, she gestured to

Nick to follow her out the front door. "Probably, like, a lot later, like I won't be home for dinner," Bee added, calling back to her mom and grinning at Paige's look of disbelief as she and Nick squeezed past Paige, through the front door, and kept walking.

They heard Paige cry out behind them, "Mommm! What am I supposed to do?!"

"Just get in the car and stop shouting!" their mom shouted.

Bee laughed with joy at her sudden courage. She'd never had the courage to tell them "no." Maybe her luck really had changed.

Nick threw his skateboard down on the sidewalk. "Well, how about a cliff jump? We've got some time to kill before tacos."

"Now?!" Bee wondered. "I mean, isn't it gonna be cold?"

"Part of the point," he grinned. "Right?"

*What?!* Bee thought and panicked. She'd never cliff jumped before. Unlike Owen and Jade in the photos on Owen's computer, Bee was even almost too chicken just to bridge jump. She had done it though, but only because Kate had convinced her to. They'd gone to Old Belton Bridge and jumped off together, holding hands. Bee had only jumped because she'd done it with Kate. And then, they'd gone back to Old Belton over and over, especially this past summer when they did a lot of hiking. *BT*, Bee thought in the moment as she stood there with Nick. *Before Torian. And everything was so perfect BT.* She'd drive her and Kate in the SFB Mobile. They'd park in West Glacier, do their hike and end at the bridge. Sometimes they'd do a float and then pull over and jump into the water, but only from very low points.

Bee wondered what it'd be like next summer. Would Torian still be around? Would she be forced to float and hike and jump with him if she wanted to hang out with Kate? Would Kate and Torian go without her?

*Whatever*, she told herself. *That was then, and this is now.* And now, she was there with Owen's best friend, Nick. Heart pounding. And the water, wherever they went, whether the river or lake, would be way too cold. And a cliff would be scary! "Yeah, of course," she told Nick in spite of all that panic, trying to sound cheerful. "You're right."

Nick nodded. "I'm sure you're used to it with Owen. How 'bout his favorite spot?"

"Great," Bee chimed as if she had a clue where that was and had gone with Owen a million times.

"You don't sound like it's great," Nick observed.

"No, no, I'm just...," Bee looked for an excuse just as her mom came out of the house to take Paige to ballet and gave Bee a weird look.

"What's wrong with her?" Paige scoffed to her mom about Bee.

Mrs. Plumb looked at Bee, like, *What are you doing?*

Bee laughed and turned to Nick. His eyes laughed too at her predicament. "They're just distracting me," Bee retorted to deflect his suspicion about her lie about wanting to go cliff jumping.

"I see," Nick said, totally understanding. "And this will be good for you then. We can take the long hike in."

"Sure," Bee said as convincingly and enthusiastically as was fakely possible. "Do we, uh, should we take the Strawberry Bomb?"

"Excuse me?"

"The car. My Nana Jana named it. Strawberry Firecracker Bomb Mobile, or SFB for short. It was a gift from my grandpa to her and now to me, on loan."

"Ah, right, you called it that when you dropped me off at the side of the road mysteriously," he grinned.

Bee laughed nervously, not sure how to deflect or explain that away.

"How 'bout I drive?" Nick suggested. "We ride over to my house, and I take the Dude Mobile. So, you can chill and just relax for a change. And I can drive slowly and not feel like my life is in your reckless-driver hands."

Bee laughed. "Dude Mobile sounds perfect."

Nick nodded and put his right foot on the skateboard,

waiting. "All right, c'mon," he told her, gesturing for Bee to get on behind him.

Bee's heart raced in a panic all over again, but she covered it with a smile and stepped on the back of his longboard skateboard, grabbing onto him for dear life.

"You sure about this?" Nick teased.

"Yeah, yeah, of course. Owen and I do that jump all the time. And I love that hike!" Bee squeezed Nick tighter in a panic and realized she was getting way too good at this fibbing thing. The question was: When would her tower of lies collapse?

# 20 CLIFF JUMPING INTO THE FREEZING COLD LAKE WITH NICK

Bee clutched Nick's waist, holding on tight as they skated on his longboard skateboard through the Kalispell burbs from her house to his.

"So glad you're into this," he yelled back. "You're 'gonna love the jump even more in the cold!"

"Great!" Bee shouted up to him. "Nothing like a high-octane time killer!"

They skated over a bump. Bee clutched harder, squeezing her eyes shut, looking forward to this ending and sitting in the Dude Mobile as she wondered what the Dude Mobile was like, while at the same time kicking herself for agreeing to this excursion so quickly.

Nick laughed, sensing her panic but assuming it was about riding on the board. Clearly, she'd never done this before.

Once they reached Nick's house, they climbed into his truck, an old, blue Ford F150.

"So, Dude Mobile huh?" Bee laughed.

"Well, not exactly. I call him Truck," Nick admitted. "And my mom called him Ferdinand Ford when we first got him."

"For the cow?" Bee wondered. "Ferdinand the cow?"

"Steer," Nick corrected, amused. "That Ferdinand is a steer."

"We're kind of more city folk," Bee defended.

"Clearly," Nick laughed.

"I mean, we were. Until we moved here."

"When was that?"

"Right after I was born," Bee told him.

"Where were you born?" Nick asked.

"Thousand Oaks. California."

"Well, Ferdinand is actually named after the band. Which you may have heard of in your city vibe life?"

"What band?" Bee wondered. She had no clue.

"Franz Ferdinand," Nick told her. "That's the band's name and they're named after the guy that was shot in Sarajevo."

"Oh, maybe I've heard about that," Bee admitted.

"The band?"

"The Archduke."

"That was shot in Sarajevo, very good," Nick laughed, pleased that she knew this. "Who are you?"

"Total nerd," Bee chimed playfully.

"No kidding," Nick teased and checked out Bee's hair, then started the truck. "It was my mom's truck first. She got it when my folks split. But it wasn't really her style. So, she named it Ferdinand so she'd like it better."

"There you go," Bee mused.

"And then, she gave Ferdinand to me. And I call him Truck."

Bee saw a bit of sadness flash across Nick's eyes. She didn't know why. "Where is she? Your mom."

"Seattle," Nick told her.

"Oh," Bee managed.

"It's a bit of a bummer, but I'll go back next summer. And now, I get to hang with coach. Coach Wells."

"He seems so happy you're back," Bee said.

"He is," Nick agreed and put the manual transmission in reverse.

"So, why not Fordinand?" Bee mused.

"Huh?" Nick wondered.

"It's a Ford, right? Your truck?"

Nick laughed. "Fordinand! I should've thought of that."

Clearly, he was amused by Bee's clever suggestion and their eyes met.

Bee nodded and turned forward quickly, pleased that he got her suggestion.

Nick backed up, turned the truck so they were facing the road and sped out onto it.

Bee grabbed on for dear life, not expecting this. "What the heck?"

Nick laughed, "Just kidding," and he started driving at a normal, relaxed speed. Then, he put on his playlist, and the song "The Weight" blasted out.

This was unexpected too. Bee pretended not to like it even though she did, realizing she'd better pick up her Owen's-secret-girlfriend game before she lost ground after the earring win and Nick got suspicious again—because Owen probably wouldn't be into this song.

***

Bee huffed uphill behind Nick. They were on the hiking trail that Bee supposedly had done with Owen a bunch of times, and Bee was having a hard time keeping up.

Nick looked back at her. He seemed happy and in his element.

Bee gave him a thumbs up and kept trudging. Nick was definitely going faster than she was used to when she hiked with Kate. Although Kate did walk faster than Bee and got annoyed sometimes when she had to wait for Bee to catch up. But this was something else, as in Bee was really struggling to keep up.

Bee wondered if Torian was a fast hiker and if Kate would get annoyed with him if he were slow. He seemed like he'd be slow. And Bee was annoyed with Torian just thinking about him being a slow walker and the idea of having to wait up for him. Like, what if she was faster than him? She wouldn't be able to handle it. She was already impatient enough just waiting for Torian to go away so she could have her best friend back. And that was annoying enough. *What if he never goes away?* Bee thought and then told herself to stop thinking about Torian and enjoy this stupid hike. Maybe it'd be surprisingly awesome, and then, Kate and Torian would break up, and then next summer, she could bring Kate here and they could jump the cliff. And Bee would be the expert this time and get to coax Kate into jumping. That'd be good, though her being the braver cliff jumper would probably never be the case since Kate was kind of fearless that way.

But at least thinking about showing Kate this hike and cliff jump gave Bee courage and a jolt of energy, and she picked up her pace to try to keep up with Nick a little better.

***

Finally, Bee and Nick reached the top of the cliff overlooking the lake. The view of the water with the Rockies in the background was stunning. It never ceased to amaze Bee.

But this jump thing was suddenly getting too real.

Nick took a giant step up onto the ledge rock that was the last bit of land before the cliff drop and the lake below. He moved right to the edge and looked down and then out, taking in the beauty and majesty too. "Can't ever get enough of that," he grinned.

It felt like a cue, like Bee had to step forward to the cliff's edge too or else she wouldn't be agreeing with his comment about this majestic work of wonder. She forced herself to go at least up to the rock just before the ledge rock that ended in the cliff, taking a solid step with her right foot and bringing her left up to stand firm in her pretend joy while her heart pounded in panic. If she looked to the left or right, she'd be able to see how high up they were exactly—and it felt pretty darn high— so she kept her eyes forward, looking out at the lake in the distance and the Rockies, not looking over and down. *Crud, how far is it?* she couldn't help but panic some more inside about how high up they were and how far down the jump to the water would be.

Nick looked back at Bee and helped her up onto the ledge rock, taking her hand and pulling her up.

*Double crud*, she thought, realizing she may not be getting out of this.

Nick seemed proud to show her the view, as if he'd created it or something. This was weird, she thought, but somehow nice. She clutched his arm, nervously, as she moved to the very edge. She didn't have a choice now but to notice the height. The cool wind was stronger even just a few feet closer to the water. She peered out and then down at the water beneath them—a good twenty feet down. "Oh, heck no," came flying out of Bee's mouth in spite of herself. And then, she managed, "I mean, woo, love it!"

Nick lifted an eyebrow.

"Okay, fine. I admit it! Mr. Romance didn't share this with me either, just like he didn't share the stupid playbook hiding spot. But don't rub it in. Or ever try to get me near that itty bitty jumping target down there."

Nick laughed.

And Bee turned and jumped down from the ledge rock and sat on another part of the rocks further from the edge where it was nice and flat and safe.

"I like your honesty, Appalachia," Nick teased, "but if you change your mind...," and he held out his hand to Bee as if he'd be ready at any time to help her back up onto the ledge right next to the drop-off, but then, he began to lean toward the water, keeping his body straight as a board, and he fell off the cliff. Clearly on purpose!

Bee screamed and jumped up, scrambling up the ledge rock, cautiously, and maintaining a safe distance from the drop as she peered over and watched Nick diving into the lake below.

Nick quickly surfaced, half laughing half crying at the shock of the cold. "Woooo!" he cheered with joy.

"Omigosh," Bee yelled down. "You're crazy."

Then, Bee watched him swim over to the shore and climb out, yelling, "It's friggin' freezing." Then, he ran over to a spot where the rocks dipped down and ran up a trail that looked like it was heading up to the top again.

Finally, he made it up, his T-shirt and jeans drenched, his shirt sticking to his body. He grabbed an extra set of clothes out of his backpack. "Good thing, I brought these," he managed, teeth chattering, and ran behind a tree, then reemerged with dry jeans and a T-shirt on. He grabbed his jacket and zipped it up to the very top.

"You're nuts," Bee told him.

"It was great. Amazing. But no pressure at all," Nick toyed. "But I do have a few more sets of dry clothes and a blanket if you change your mind."

"I'm just 'gonna sit here till you take me back the way we came," Bee clarified playfully.

"Great," Nick replied. "Let's sit. We've got tons of time before dinner, and you can tell me all about Appalachia." He sat down next to Bee on the flat rock, just back from the ledge rock. "Who are you Appalachia? And what do you like to do if you don't like jumping into gorgeous cold lakes?"

Bee laughed at Nick's exaggerated inquisitive grin. "Actually, I'd rather jump than talk about Appalachia."

"Aw, shy Appalachia; I want to hear about her," Nick continued toying playfully. "I mean, she's into physics and indie film...?"

"Huh?" Bee wondered.

"The posters? In the hospital?" Nick reminded her. "Nick Wells is paying attention here."

Bee felt her cheeks get hot and hoped Nick didn't notice. "True, yes, she'd be into those things," Bee managed, playing along.

"And hillbilly dancing. And poetry! And why were you hiding in the curtains at the talent show, Appalachia?" Nick tilted his head inquisitively, exaggerating his grin.

Bee laughed again, taking in Nick's disarming smile.

"Appalachia gets chicken sometimes," she admitted, and her cheeks got hotter. In fact, her entire face did. *Maybe he'll think I'm cold*, she hoped.

"Chicken? The Appalachian Flatfoot Poet is chicken? What's up with that?" Nick asked. "Because we could always use a good poet."

"No one could use a good poet," Bee joked.

"I could use a good poet!" Nick admitted and his eyes flashed with a spark she hadn't seen yet. "To help me write a decent song."

"You write songs?" she wondered. This was totally unexpected.

"Nick Wells writes amazing songs in a world called rock star fantasy planet," he joked self-deprecatingly, and now, his cheeks seemed to crimson too.

"So, he likes music," Bee played along. "Nick Wells."

"Don't go off topic, Appalachia," Nick insisted, "which is you. The topic is you. And if it's not, Nick Wells will seriously bore you to tears."

*Humble, funny*, Bee thought. "Not possible," she told him.

"Possible!" Nick chimed playfully with another self-deprecating grin. "I mean, the guy's got no dreams except to write a song."

Bee laughed, charmed by his unassuming wit.

"Immensely lame," Nick continued describing himself humbly. "And plays ball so he won't let his dad down even though he hates it."

"Really? You hate football? I kinda guessed that."

"Not to mention writing pseudo-poetic suburban-rap lyrics for his best friend, Owen," he continued, ignoring her inquiry into the football situation, "even though he hates writing them, 'cuz it's the only way for Nick-ster to get his buddy to sing."

*What?!* Bee wondered. This was a shocker. And she blurted out, "Wait, you wrote those songs? At the talent show? I thought that was Owen."

"Owen is the chivalry guy," Nick reminded Bee and glanced up at her quickly, then away. "Nick Wells: five percent poet, ninety-five percent boring normal guy. And why were you hiding in the curtains again?" Now, his eyes met Bee's and sparkled. "And why was there no chicken when you were manning those lights?" he teased.

Bee laughed again, even more charmed. And surprised that he was so observant, even back then at the talent show, and so disarming. "Well...Appalachia had her best friend Kate at the talent show," Bee admitted. "Kate takes away the chicken."

"So, where is this Kate when we need her?" Nick wondered.

"With her new boyfriend, Torian Bore-ian," Bee ranted playfully, "who stole Kate from Kate's best friend, Bee—I mean, Appalachia. You are in no way as boring as Torian is by the way." *Omigosh*, Bee thought as soon as that flew out of her mouth, *did I really just say that?*

"Finally, some good news!" Nick cheered.

*Thank goodness!* Bee thought.

They laughed.

And then, Bee felt her heart do a thing. Somehow, she'd let her true feelings out of the vice grip that she'd been holding them in. *Darn him*, she thought, and said, "Yeah I guess Appalachia just misses her friend. And now, she doesn't know where she fits anymore." And Bee felt more vulnerable than ever. Because it was the truth.

"You fit here," Nick said, totally sincere, and his eyes sparkled at Bee even more.

Bee's stomach flipped. Nick was hitting way too close to home regarding everything she wanted. *Like, he sees me*, she thought and weirdly panicked.

"I mean...," Nick continued, clearly feeling the connection too.

"Let's jump," Bee suggested, standing up quickly to hide her feelings.

Nick stood up too and cheered, "For Owen!"

"Perfect," Bee agreed and jumped up onto the ledge rock and peered down at the lake. *Yikes!* she thought, panicking inside again, but now, she was panicking because of the ridiculous distance down to the water—not because of how good Nick made her feel when he saw through her to her true self. "Yeah, I'm suddenly feeling super courageous just thinking about Owen," she chimed out the lie with ease. *Not.*

But Nick didn't see through the cover-up fib and smiled and held out his hand. "I'm no Owen, but I do provide wicked jump support."

Bee hesitated, then took Nick's hand, squeezed it, and they jumped.

Bee silent-screamed in terror and bliss as they flew through the air, clutching Nick's hand tighter and tighter until they smashed into the water.

It was friggin' cold!

But Bee felt a rush of joy anyways and let go of Nick's hand and swam to the surface. She couldn't help laughing, her breath creating little puffs of ice crystals.

And Nick beamed.

# 21 BEE LOVIN' ON NICK ON THE UKE AT UNCLE AL'S BLUEGRASS CAFE & EATERY

Back on Nick's longboard skateboard, Bee hung onto Nick for dear life again as he skated out of his neighborhood towards the little downtown Main Street area and his uncle's taco establishment.

Bee was wearing a T-shirt of Nick's and jeans. He'd found an old belt in his closet from when he was just a kid to help hold up the jeans. She looked weird in his clothes that were totally baggy on her, but she was glad he'd brought them to the lake so she could get out of her drenched clothes after the jump.

Bee replayed the whole afternoon in her mind as she squeezed Nick's waist tightly so she wouldn't fly off the skateboard. It had taken a while to get warmed up after the jump, but ultimately, Bee was super excited that she'd done it in spite of the freezing cold water. After they'd climbed back up to the top of the cliff and changed, they'd hiked back, jumped in Nick's truck, now officially called Fordinand, and then drove home to his house blasting country rock for half the drive and some hip hop for the rest. They barely talked except about music and the songs and musicians they liked. And Bee admitted that her taste in music differed from Owen's but said that she was cool with that.

When they got back to Nick's house, they went inside, and Bee waited in the family room by the door looking at a few photos of Nick as a little kid. Coach Wells wasn't home, and Bee was glad about that.

After Nick found the belt and some dry socks for her and they drank some water, they took off to Uncle Al's. It was nearing sunset and Nick thought they should get to the taco place before it got totally dark.

They hit a bump in the road, jarring Bee out of her thoughts. She clutched onto Nick more tightly so as not to fall off the skateboard and, surprisingly, felt another surge of joy, just like she'd felt after coming up in the icy cold water. This day and hike and cliff-jumping adventure had been Kate-level fun. Nick had made her feel like herself. She'd totally been in the moment after the jump. And he'd made her feel like her best and real self.

***

Nick hummed, beaming as he zig-zagged up to a little restaurant just off the main drag in Kalispell. A bright sign shone in neon above the island-inspired-themed roof: AL'S BLUEGRASS CAFE & EATERY.

"This is it," Nick told Bee as he came to a skating stop in front of his uncle's place. "Tacos and music."

Bee got off the skateboard and peered through the front window.

She saw musicians playing on a tiny stage—jamming on bass, drums and fiddle. Coach Wells stood at the counter next to a guy in a Hawaiian shirt that turned out to be his brother and Nick's Uncle Al. Wooden tables and benches filled the room adorned with island decor, including amusing palm trees and beach shacks in the corners and white-sand beaches and sunsets painted on the walls.

Nick hesitated, then stammered, "Hey, so, um, before we go in, Nick Wells wanted to..."

Bee turned to Nick with a smile, loving this place already and excited to go in.

Nick stopped when he saw Bee's sparkling eyes, a lump growing in his throat. But he pushed through and began again, "Actually, I want to apologize...to Appalachia...that I didn't believe you. About Owen. Especially in the hospital room. I guess I just...hate that he didn't tell me about you." Nick smirked, embarrassed now. "So much for the best-friend blood pact me and Owen did in second grade. And that thing hurt! Ouch!" He grinned.

"Hey, you know, I don't think you can get out of a blood pact that easily," Bee teased.

"That's what I like about you, Appalachia—keepin' it real," Nick retorted.

Their eyes met in that moment, like they both knew they had a connection and that neither of them was going to mention it—

—just as Nick's jovial Uncle Al barged out, ukulele in hand. "Nick, my man!" he boomed. "Where've you been?" He went straight to Nick and bear-hugged him. "And your young lady— nice to meet you," he gushed at Bee, with a nod. "You are in for a real treat."

"We have a guest, Uncle Al," Nick scolded, obviously not loving how jolly and forthcoming his uncle was.

"All the more reason for me to show off my *favorite* and only nephew," Uncle Al boasted and playfully shoved the ukulele at Nick. "Cuz when you're here, you're mine!" he gloated playfully about his high-uncle status. "I give you tacos; you play."

Then, Uncle Al winked at Bee as he ushered her and an embarrassed Nick through the front door of the restaurant, bells ringing as they entered.

Uncle Al led Nick straight up to the small stage in the corner. The musicians beamed when they saw Nick and welcomed him up. Nick glanced at Bee, clearly still embarrassed about being up there and his uncle's magnanimous merriness but mostly because he was now going to play in front of her and was shy about being on stage.

But as soon as the musicians started up and Nick joined in playing the ukulele, he came alive and was amazing.

"Now, everything is as it should be," Uncle Al told Bee as he walked back from the stage and gestured for her to follow him over to the counter. "Come tell me what I can bring you."

But Bee didn't budge. She was mesmerized by Nick. Now, he was in his element and his playing gave her an unexpected thrill.

## 22 BEE LETS DOWN HER GUARD AND HANGS WITH NICK ALL WEEK

The night at Al's Bluegrass Cafe & Eatery changed everything for Bee, if not on the outside, definitely on the inside. Uncle Al and even Coach Wells made her feel so special, and they obviously just adored Nick.

Uncle Al made Bee his signature fish tacos and brought out both apple and blueberry pie. She tried both, and he piled on the homemade whipped cream. It was all super yummy.

Nick played with the band the whole time, and they even played a song he wrote.

On the way home, Bee clutched Nick as they rode on his skateboard. It was the same as before but different. She was hyper aware of everything around her—the air, the sounds, Nick's voice when he spoke. Her hands felt every sensation, the texture of his sweatshirt, every move of his muscles, how his whole being shook when he laughed. And she felt her heart opening. She also noticed that she was so relaxed and happy and in her own element as the real Beatrix Plumb—so much so that she didn't even bother to worry about any of her secret-Owen-girlfriend lies because she felt like the bright force that was beaming out of every part of her being was bigger than everything. It was her truth—which made everything else unimportant, as if it were the mere background to this magic she was feeling.

*Maybe Nick feels it too*, Bee thought. *After all, he was more talkative on our ride home from Uncle Al's taco place than before. He was totally animated.* And Bee had listened to him, unbelievably happy, in the moment and enamored with her life.

Bee hadn't felt this way since before Kate met Torian and fell in love. She hadn't felt this way since the last time she'd hung out with Kate like normal—in that place where she didn't even think about other people and could just be. When she belonged to the Kate-Beatrix best-friendship.

*Beatrix Plumb, as is*, Bee thought.

And that wonderful feeling of love and joy that she had with Nick at the lake and at Uncle Al's and riding on the skateboard stayed with her into the next week as she got to be herself on the inside and Owen's girlfriend on the outside—and Nick's friend both inside and out. And in all cases, she was part of this new thing that maybe could be her new life.

A magic life that was like a happy movie montage.

"A life full of unexpected fluttery butterfly feelings," Bee narrated to herself and Cardboard Owen with glee at Saturday cheer practice the next day as she waved Cardboard Owen around while watching Nick practice punting.

Nick didn't say much to her when they got there, except, "Hey," but once they started practice, he kept making funny faces at her, and she sensed that he was in his element too.

*And maybe*, Bee thought, *he's okay with it too and not worried about the fact that obviously we have a connection even though he thinks I'm dating Owen.* "And we can keep being friends," she told herself and Cardboard Owen.

And that's what Bee did from that moment on. She actually did her thing. Her real thing. She started seriously working on her poetry for the rest of the weekend and hung giant handwritten words around her room and stood back and looked at all the notes and words surrounding her on her room walls and happily acknowledged that, "Yes, Nick inspired me. And I think my thing might also be his thing."

On Sunday night, Bee and Nick went and helped the Lions TP the Thunderbird bleachers at the Thunderbirds' high school, and Bee felt like she was in some kind of amazing fantasy bubble—especially when the spotlights unexpectedly turned on, blasting them with light, and Nick grabbed her hand, and they ran. And Bee felt so happy.

And Bee continued on her focused trajectory, just hanging out in her room after school the next day, reworking her lyrics. And her lyrics actually got better. "Like suddenly I have courage," Bee narrated to herself as she stood looking in the mirror, trying on dresses to wear for the rest of the week, then turned to Cardboard Owen and told him, "Maybe because, deep down, I want to show Nick what I can do—like I want to write lyrics for him. Or maybe with him. Like as a team. I like being in a team. Kate and I were a team. Maybe I can be on this new team with Nick."

And Bee leaned into her newfound confidence the next afternoon at practice, cheering on the team while Coach Wells kept yelling, "Again, again," because Reno kept throwing and Glenn kept missing. But finally, they got it right. And Nick seemed amused that Bee was getting in there too. And Bee smiled at Nick while narrating to herself, "And maybe, I look weird or silly, but I don't care. I don't feel that way." Then, she turned to Cardboard Owen "standing" next to her on the grass. "I mean, right? Reno's gonna get this." She nodded to Cardboard Owen and then to herself, knowing in her heart that they were all going in the right direction here.

The next day at lunch, Bee dared to be extra bold when Nick was playing guitar on the front school lawn. She went over and heard him try some lyrics. They were really bad. *Oh, no,* she thought and hesitated but then felt that surge of confidence out of nowhere and yelled, "JYM! JYM!" in her head and offered Nick a word for his lyrics, as in she blurted it out. He jumped when she said it because she kind of snuck up on him and he was totally surprised, but then, he tried her word in his song, and it changed everything. The word was "synchronicity." And it made his song awesome—they both agreed. And Bee beamed. And then blushed. And laughed. And said, "Weirdo," to herself in her head.

"And I got even more bold today at practice," she told Cardboard Owen the next night in her room, "when Coach Wells yelled at Reno, and I yelled too. Maybe it was a bit much, but guess what? It was like a song all its own, a thing of beauty—*throw, catch, throw, catch, throw, catch. Yes!*" And it was obvious this was working. "Me and Coach Wells even hugged! And I just have a feeling they're gonna win! Even without you. I mean, of course, they'd win more easily with you, the real you, but we're good." She high-fived Cardboard Owen and he fell back. "Oops," she laughed picking him up.

"But seriously, Reno just has this sudden burst of newfound ability and cohesiveness with Glenn," Bee continued her story to Cardboard Owen, both sitting in the bay window and Bee occasionally looking out at Kate and Torian on the lawn as she replayed the whole week again in her mind, "and that just keeps inspiring me." And she told him that she supposed that that's what inspired her and Nick to sneak out onto the Thunderbirds' field and spray all the trees gold the previous night. "Without getting caught," she shrugged at Cardboard Owen and grinned cutely.

And Bee told him how they also took Granny Fleet "running," which Granny Fleet loved, and how Granny Fleet kept shouting, "Faster!" And at the end, Bee and Nick were so tired they fell on the grass, exhausted, laughing and looking up at the sky. And they even looked once quickly at each other. Which didn't last long. "Neither did lying there," she continued, "because Granny Fleet wouldn't let us. She's really impatient. To say the least." Bee laughed at the thought and smiled at Cardboard Owen.

"But guess whose steady patience is starting to pay off?" she added, then recounted how she thought she'd finally gotten her lyrics right and that she'd been flatfooting and singing them. "And they might be perfect!" Bee exclaimed.

"And also perfect was tonight," Bee said, remembering, getting the chills and feeling all dreamy. "At the hospital."

And she recounted how she and Nick watched old movies and ate popcorn while Owen dozed. "He's still totally out of it. The real you. Even though they said they're tapering the meds." She nodded and friend-punched Cardboard Owen in the "arm" to give him confidence too.

And she told him how she felt so utterly happy and smitten. Even though this time, she realized she wasn't smitten with him, meaning Owen. The real Owen. "I mean, I might be smitten with you," she teased Cardboard Owen then got serious, realizing the repercussions of her feelings. "But I wasn't smitten with Owen. Actual real-life Owen. Not in cardboard or my romantic fantasy mind. No, I wasn't." *Crud*, she thought and admitted, "I think I'm smitten with Nick." She looked at Cardboard Owen as if he could react and took in her undeniable acknowledgement of her feelings. "And tomorrow's the big game against the Falcons. And we have to win."

And she admitted that she felt a surge of hope. And melancholy. And more butterflies just thinking about it. Butterflies of good *and* worry. And she said, "I wish this week with Nick and awesomeness could continue forever. Can it?"

She looked at Cardboard Owen for an answer, but again, he just kept smiling his fake, gorgeous photo-poster-boy smile. And Bee knew he didn't have the answer. And she was going to have to find the answer deep in her heart and as this situation played out. *Crud. This blows*, Bee thought.

And then the surge of hope rose again. It seemed to have a life of its own, bigger than all her worries and pre-JYM insecurities. "JYM," she cheered under her breath, cheeks flushing, embarrassed that she cared so much about life and Nick and Owen and the team and friendship and love and all these things and doing the right thing.

Then, she turned to Cardboard Owen again and said it with emphasis. "J. Y. M." And did an air-high-five in his direction, totally satisfied.

# 23 THE BIG LIONS VS. FALCONS GAME AND KATE FIGURES OUT BEE LIKES NICK

Bee brought her newfound courage and hope and ongoing nerves with her to the Lions' football stadium Friday night.

It was a tense game, and the Lions were down almost the whole time. With two minutes left to go in the fourth quarter, it was Lions 5, Falcons 7. Coach Wells, Nick, Bee, Cardboard Owen and everyone else on the Lion sidelines kept yelling for Reno to pull it together and be awesome, really letting him have it, like at practice. They tried everything. And it was getting desperate.

Finally, Nick had an idea. He nodded to Bee, and she hopped on his back. He passed Cardboard Owen up to her, and then, they took off—running around, up and down the side of the field, over to the players, to the Lions in the bleachers, waving Cardboard Owen, cheering, "Go, Lions...!"

Then, the cheerleaders started following them in a line, like a parade, until the whole Lion side of the stadium was up on their feet joining in the chant—"Go, Lions! Go, Lions!" It was simple, and it worked.

The energy was high. And when the next play began, the

energy stayed high and the Lions on the field were pumped.

The clock counted down.

Reno went back for two.

He faked to Glenn.

And then, he mad-dashed through the line of burly Falcons—

"Go, Reno, go!" Bee shouted and everyone joined in with matching claps, "Go! Reno! Go!"

—until Reno barreled into the end zone for a touchdown.

The buzzer rang.

The Lions won.

And all the Lions went nuts. Bee, Nick, Coach Wells, Demi, the cheer squad, the players—everyone flew out of their seats and off the ground, jumping up and down, hugging and crying with joy.

And Coach Wells yelled to the heavens, "One more game and Championship here we come!"

***

After the game, Nick walked Bee out to the Strawberry Firecracker Bomb Mobile in their high school parking lot.

"Luck of the Owen," he said as he put Cardboard Owen in the back seat of the car, propping him up at a side angle so his "head" was on one window and his feet were by the other door.

"Definitely awesome," Bee agreed.

"And maybe you're helping too," Nick added with a smile. "At least my dad thinks so."

"Go Lions!" Bee cheered playfully.

Nick smirked—*gosh, she was cute*—and he slammed the backseat car door shut. "And then there's this unexpected awesomeness," he grinned as he pulled out a folded piece of paper and offered it to her. "In case you just happen to have some awesome lyrics lying around."

Bee took the paper, uncertain, looking at Nick, wondering what this could be. It felt special, like he was offering her an unbelievably extraordinary gift.

His eyes sparkled with anticipation.

She unfolded the paper and saw what it was: Music notes written in black ink. A song. It was a song he'd written. And he'd given it to her.

Bee felt a chill knowing that, *yes*, Nick had written these notes, and they were for her. She was speechless.

She looked up. "Thank you," Bee told Nick.

Nick beamed.

*It's the most extraordinary gift ever*, Bee thought. But didn't say that. She couldn't say it. And she hoped her eyes didn't give away how much this meant to her.

***

Bee drove home after the game. She took her time. She didn't even turn on music. She listened to the silence and let herself just experience the joy she was feeling about the folded piece of paper from Nick, full of music notes, on the seat next to her—as if the song were royalty and the SFB Mobile were a carriage or a limo, and the three of them were going for a ride together.

It gave Bee the chills thinking that Nick wrote this and asked her to be a part of it. To write lyrics for it. And him. And the hairs on her arms stood up as if they were dancing.

Bee drove around the neighborhood for a long time and all the way up the 93 to Big Mountain and back before going home. The night was clear, and the giant sky was full of stars. She swore they were sparkling brighter than usual.

When she drove up to her house and parked, she saw Kate sitting on her front lawn. Alone.

*Huh, that's weird*, she thought and parked in front of her house like she always did and walked across the street.

Bee smiled at Kate, who smiled back as Bee stepped up over the curb, strode up the lawn and sat down next to her best friend. Kate definitely looked rather pensive, which wasn't really her style. Usually, she just knew things right away. "Where's Torian?" Bee wondered.

"Brooding," Kate told Bee and gestured across the street at Torian's old blue Subaru parked in front of Bee's neighbor's house. "We had a fight."

Bee looked over at Torian brooding in his car across the street.

"I told him I needed personal space," Kate explained matter of factly.

"Finally!" Bee exclaimed. This was amazing news. Then, she backed down from her excitement. It was a bit much and she didn't want to hurt Kate's feelings. She toned it down and tried to exude a shred of empathy. "I mean, wow, look at you—communicating so honestly."

Kate saw through the fake empathy, and the friends laughed together.

"The cornerstone of every good relationship," Kate beamed.

Bee couldn't help but laugh more. Kate did too. Finally, a moment together.

"And you guys won!" Kate trilled about the game.

Bee couldn't help feel a bit of unexpected panic at these words. Her heart started racing. She forced a smile with a quiet, "Mmmhmmm."

"What's wrong?" Kate demanded. She knew Bee all too well.

Bee shrugged, not totally sure why she felt so nervous.

But Kate nailed it. "You like the kicker," she mused.

"How do you even know that?" Bee demanded.

"Because I'm your best friend," Kate gloated. "And you can't hide from me."

*Aw!* Bee's heart expanded. She missed her friend so much. Then, Bee teased, "And you need to reign that in."

"And you need to tell your kicker the truth," Kate instructed.

"Huh?" Bee uttered as if she had no clue what Kate meant, as if there were no massive lies being thrown about in her world.

"You need to tell him that you like him," Kate explained as

if this were a no-brainer. "And that you want a more authentic relationship with him than the fake one with Owen."

"That you pushed me into!" Bee defended.

"Things change," Kate insisted. More facts. "You 'gotta stay flexible to keep the relationship which you love."

Bee looked at Kate—like, *Now you change?!*

Kate grinned. "Like us."

"You and Torian?"

"You and me," Kate smirked.

*What?!* Bee thought as more friend love was flung her way.

Kate grabbed Bee and hugged her tight.

"He's gonna think I'm a fake," Bee cried, finally letting herself be vulnerable and truthful. "And he's 'gonna hate me."

"You are a fake, and you're rockin' it, that's why he likes you," Kate expounded with all certainty. "Confidence'll do that." Then, Kate stood up and looked over at Torian, still brooding in his old blue Subaru across the street. "Okay, he's suffered enough," she declared then fist-pumped to Bee. "Face your fear! JYM! Junior Year Manifesto!"

"I know what it means!" Bee chided.

Kate grinned at her best friend and started over across the street to her boyfriend—

—who instantly burst out of his car and ran over to Kate.

Bee watched Torian grovel chivalrously and Kate smile—like she really forgave Torian for whatever annoying thing he had done. And Bee mocked Kate's words in her head, *Face your fear.* This was so frustrating. *Easy for you to say*, she thought as she watched Kate and Torian hug. *You have a new best friend! Or at least an extra one. To help you walk through your fears and your problems. And my supposed new best friend, Nick, IS my problem.*

# 24 HEAVY METAL JADE LOVES OWEN AND HE'S GOING HOME

Bee left the house super early the next morning even though it was the weekend. She wanted to beat everyone else to Owen's hospital room to say hello and leave a little token to show that she'd been there. She knew Owen was going to be getting more and more alert as they tapered off his pain meds, and she wanted to stay vigilant with the girlfriend lie for when he eventually came to. At least for now.

She especially wanted to beat Nick to the hospital that morning and leave before he got there so she didn't run into him. She felt so weird after admitting to Kate, and basically herself, how much she liked Nick, and she wasn't ready to face him—even though to be true to the JYM she'd eventually have to come clean so she could maintain self-esteem and feel good about herself. She also knew Nick would be there by 9:00 a.m. It was 8:15 a.m., so she had about thirty minutes. And she thought she was good.

But as Bee rounded the corner into Owen's hospital room carrying a "FLEET 2 BEAT THUNDERBIRDS" banner and chiming, "Guess who won the game...?!"—she came face to face with a shocking sight, namely Jade decked out in a heavy metal groupie disguise, complete with a giant bouffy haired wig, white and yellow face makeup, black lips, black stars on her cheeks and yellow lightning bolts across her eyes, desperately performing a heavy metal love anthem for Owen, who was clearly out of it and hearing and seeing none of her performance. "Oh, oh, look what you've done to this rock 'n roll clown; oh, oh, look what you've done," she sang, doing a pretty good rendition of Def Leppard's "Photograph."

Bee gasped, "Omigosh, Jade! Hi! What's going on?"

Owen chuckled in his sleep, as if he were having a really great dream.

Jade didn't take her eyes off Owen, looking like she was about to cry. "It's all my fault," she confessed in desperation—first to Owen and then to Bee. "I told him to run when we saw you sitting in your car across the street. But I don't care anymore who sees us." Jade draped her whole body over Owen like a blanket, clutching him.

*Omigosh* was all Bee could manage in her head, *How is this happening? It can't possibly be real!*

"Because keeping love secret is never the right thing to do!" Jade declared. "Because our love is real! Me and Owen!"

Owen mumbled in his sleep.

Jade draped herself over him again. "But I'll do it for you, Owen. I'll keep it secret," she cried. "Anything for you."

Bee hesitated, speechless, frozen and really worried. "Jade please, Nick's 'gonna be here soon."

Jade popped up, Ninja-flying while spinning swiftly off of Owen and the bed. She got right up in Bee's face. "And as soon as he's off the meds, your girlfriend gig is up," Jade menaced. "You are way too freaky for Owen. And we're not breaking up. Ever!"

Then, Jade screech-cawed at Bee like an angry Thunderbird, claw-pawed the ground with her foot, flapped her arms like wings and turned and left.

Bee just stared after heavy metal Jade, trying not to feel intimidated but totally feeling intimated. And then, it got worse, her heart racing as she heard Nick in the hallway, singing, approaching, hoping with all hope that he didn't see Jade—

—which he didn't. Luckily.

Instead, Nick brought other problematic news as he entered carrying boxes, a bounce in his step, and announced with cheer in a playfully deep voice, "Guess who's goin' home early?" His eyes lit up when he saw Bee.

Bee gasped in shock. *What? No!!!* she cried in her head.

"And who's ready to party?!...," he crooned at Owen, voice full of amusement, winking at Bee.

Her heart flipped and sank all at once.

# 25 OWEN'S COMING HOME PARTY

Bee looked up at the "FLEET 2 BEAT THUNDERBIRDS" banner next to the "WELCOME HOME, OWEN!" banner on the wall by Owen's hospital bed in the living room of his house. She'd suggested they hang it as soon as she arrived, mostly because she needed something to do to avoid talking to anyone for as long as possible. Or even looking at anyone.

And now that the welcome home party was fully underway with Owen's friends, teammates, classmates and family filling the family room and spilling out into the backyard, the open sliding door letting in cold air and some smoke from the fire pit and BBQ, Bee didn't have too much to hide behind.

Owen's sister, Claire, kept shooting Bee glary, judgey, condescending eye daggers, while the cheerleaders were beaming at her and the team members kept nodding to her respectfully.

Owen was in a rented hospital bed situated on the edge of the living room right next to the sliding glass door—and Bee had been standing with Nick right next to it for the past forty-five minutes, watching the party goers celebrating and pinching her hand in an attempt to distract herself from her heart pounding in a panic. She hadn't expected Owen to come home this soon. Nick was just standing there pretty rigidly and awkwardly too, like he didn't know what to do or say either, which almost made it worse.

Owen, meanwhile, was on less meds than at the hospital—apparently, they'd been reducing them more than Bee knew for the past few days. But he was pretty loopy, just a bit more alert than he'd been that morning when heavy metal Jade had been dancing for him. His eyes would open, and he'd watch his friends laughing and chatting outside. Then, he'd turn his head on the pillow to watch the DJ—who happened to be Drew-ster for this party—who was mixing at the turntable just outside the sliding glass door. Then, Owen's lids would start to droop again, and he'd doze off. Then, his eyes would pop open again when someone would hoot or a new song would start.

It was all very unpredictable and made Bee nervous.

But this time, he'd dozed off for quite a while, which had given Bee the chance to regroup and feel a glimmer of relief. But not for long.

Demi nodded to Glenn, and Glenn whistled loudly.

Everyone stopped, Owen jolted awake, and DJ Drew-ster turned down the music.

"Okay," Demi began with her booming cheer voice as she strutted over to Owen's bedside. "Before it gets too Fleet-style wild, let's welcome Owen home."

The cheerleaders, football team and other guests whistled and cheered and gathered round the sliding glass door and Owen's bed.

Owen responded by roaring like a drunk Lion—

—which is right when Bee noticed Jade in a giant tree in the next yard, right at the back fence, disguised in a rainbow clown wig and Super Mario costume, spying on the party with a perfect bird's-eye view of Owen.

"What the...?" Bee sputtered under her breath.

"Starting with a few loving welcome-home words from his adorable girlfriend, Bee," Demi trumpeted.

Which was followed by a loud "No!" shout outside by the

back fence and a thud as Jade fell out of the tree.

"Bee?" Owen wondered, loopy and confused.

"Who he doesn't remember yet," Demi bubbled to the crowd with a laugh, covering the near blunder.

"I remember you, DEM-EEEE!" Owen called out with a giant smile.

Demi did her best fake laugh and gently patted and rubbed Owen's blanketed, non-casted leg, like "there, there."

Owen purred up at Demi, lovingly.

"And Bee, who he won't remember until he comes off the meds more tomorrow," Demi informed the party-goers like the expert that she wasn't. "Or not. Trauma'll do that." Then, she smiled like a politician and waved Bee closer for effect, even though Bee was already standing just a few feet behind Owen's bed and head.

Everyone shouted to Bee, "Speech! Speech! Speech!"

Which just made it worse, but Bee nervously stepped forward next to Demi, where Owen could now see her.

Owen roared at her, toying playfully.

And Bee laughed nervously and began, her voice going extra high with total panic, but no one seemed to notice, "Well, we are seriously happy you're home, Owen. You're totally inspiring, brave and loyal, like a Lion, right?"

Owen loopy-lion roared.

Everyone laughed.

Bee exhaled with relief, calmly, subtly so no one saw. *Phew.*

Coach Wells beamed at Bee, so relieved and proud of her. And proud of Owen. And everyone. Maybe even himself.

"And...," Bee continued, voice only slightly squeaking up at the end now

"And...," Owen joined in.

"We're gonna beat dem Thunderbirds!" Bee cheered. "In six days! Just for you, Owen!"

Everyone boomed out in response, "O-wen!" And then continued cheering his name, louder and louder until Owen brought it to a crescendo with a Lion Pride roar.

Demi nodded at Drew-ster to blast the music. And

everyone jumped right back into the party—dancing, chatting, celebrating Owen. The party was on!

"Woooooo!" Owen shouted and moved his head in sync with the beat and dancers, then stopped and cried out under his breath in pain. "Aaaaoooow!" He did little short breaths—*out, out, out, out*—like he'd learned in football to get himself to push through the pain and psych himself up.

"You okay, bud?" Nick asked Owen, worried about his buddy.

"Yeah, yeah, I'm good, good, it just...aaaow. More meds please!" Owen joked, clearly still in pain.

Bee felt herself shrinking into herself, wishing she could just disappear. She felt so guilty and awful about this whole debacle all over again, wishing none of this had ever happened.

"Your mom said you have to wait on the meds," Nick told Owen. "You're already too jacked up. Sorry, my man."

"Hey, Beatrix!" Demi called over. "Come help me with some drinks."

*Thank goodness*, Bee thought. *Momentary relief from the torment!* "I'll be right back," she told Nick and Owen with the best smile she could muster and followed Demi outside to the food table. The spread was amazing, and Owen's dad was grilling. He was definitely in his element with the BBQ.

Nick and Owen watched Bee and Demi maneuver through the dancing party-ers, past the fire pit and BBQ and over to the ice chest by the food table, where they began taking sodas out of shopping bags, pulling them out of the plastic holders and putting them into the ice.

"You lucky freak," Nick laughed, teasing his buddy about Bee. "How did you land her? Oh, wait! You're Owen. They all love you. Every single hot and even wildly cool Lion and not-Lion woman. Even in a body cast they love you." Nick lightly guy-punched Owen in the casted arm.

"Owwww," Owen cried out, laughing, razzing back at his friend. Clearly, it didn't hurt as much as before.

"Sorry, Dude," Nick scolded playfully, "but you deserve that."

"I do?" Owen wondered, suddenly seriously concerned.

Nick chuckled again at his clueless, loopy friend. "Maybe not," he offered, feeling bad, but just a little. "At least you gave her the earrings. Much better than Amy. I mean, what were we thinking?"

"Amy was hot," Owen hooted with joy.

*Right*, thought Nick, and he laughed to himself knowing his buddy, who he adored, was never going to change. Owen loved girls—*all* the girls—and he had no clue how that impacted anyone but himself.

Meanwhile, over by the drinks and food table, Demi and Bee were finishing restocking the ice chest with sodas.

"They're totally buying it," Demi boasted to Bee as she put the last soda in, shut the lid of the cooler and stood up tall with a smile of pride, handing Bee a soda. "They think you're his girlfriend."

"Who are you talking about exactly?" wondered Bee.

"Nick and Owen," Demi beamed, nodding over to the two guys who were still looking at them. She waved.

Nick waved back.

Bee's heart sank.

"I think we're good," Demi added.

"I think it's about to blow up in our faces," Bee groaned.

"You worry too much," Demi insisted. "We've got till tomorrow. That's when Owen really comes off the meds. By then, I'll have a plan." Demi watched Nick laugh, clearly enjoying hanging out with his best friend again. "Do you think we should tell Nick?"

"No!" Bee cried, then rallied with a calm, "I mean, no."

"Yeah, not Nick's style, this mischievous scheming thing," Demi agreed. "He'd hate it. He'd hate you. Although he does like you now." She looked at Bee, looked at the blue Italian glass earrings she was wearing, scheme-ingly scrutinizing. "Nah, he's gonna be pissed. Too serious. You know he bought those earrings for a girl they both liked. How'd you even get them anyway?"

*Oh, crud*, thought Bee, then admitted, "Jade."

"Mmmm," Demi took this in. "Yeah, we definitely have to pull this off. Without Nick."

Bee's heart sank all over again, and she felt the panic bubbling in her stomach.

"But I can't say I don't love the challenge," Demi chimed, smirking at Bee. "Owen will too. He loves this kind of stuff. So relax. Today we party. And tomorrow, you leave it to me." Then, Demi grabbed Bee's hand. "C'mon." And pulled her over to the dance area, calling out with her bossiest, surest, leader voice, "Glenn! Nick! Ask some girls to dance, already!" And she shot Glenn a playfully flirty smile.

Glenn swooped in to dance with Demi with a mischievous smile right back. "All right, miss bossy pants," he swaggered and pointed to other dancers. "Let's go." And he led Demi over to the dance space in front of where DJ Drew-ster was spinning—

—leaving Bee standing there super awkwardly. Bee glanced over at Nick quickly.

He was looking at her too, awkwardly, like he too was dreading this whole situation.

Bee darted her eyes away.

"C'mon, Nick!" Demi boomed loud enough for everyone to hear. "Man up for Owen."

Nick and Bee looked at each other.

Everyone looked at them.

*Oh, crud*, thought Bee. *Here we go.*

"Woooo!" crowed Owen.

Nick hesitated. He knew he had no choice but to dance with Bee *for* Owen now that Demi had suggested it, so he finally walked over to Bee.

Bee's heart pounded out of her chest.

Nick smiled, gentle and sweet and a little bit smirky—

—which made Bee laugh and relax.

And then, when Nick held out his hand to Bee like they were in a stupid Jane Austin novel or stupid *Bridgerton* at a stupid dance, she took it—warm, sure, sending sparks into her whole body—and she let him lead her out to the dance patio space.

And it was magic.

Awkward at first, but magic.

Nick did some dumb side-to-side step, and Bee mimicked him. Even though she loved to dance, this just felt weird, so she held back at first.

But then, another song came on. "A Drew-ster and Owen-ster and Lion Pride hip hop favorite," DJ Drew-ster trumpeted to the party crowd.

And everyone cheered and started bouncing to the beat, and Nick joined in and so did Bee, even though she didn't know the song, and suddenly all hesitation and awkwardness disappeared. And they were having fun.

And from that moment on, both Bee and Nick were just totally into the music, the dancing...and each other. At least, Bee felt it. And it seemed like the feeling was mutual for Nick.

And everything around Bee disappeared, and she let herself go into the moment, into herself, totally herself—*Beatrix Plumb dancing, dancing, dancing.*

And it was obvious to her that they fit—her and Nick were a good match.

And maybe it was obvious to anyone else who was paying attention, like clearly Owen was, because when there was a break in the music because Drew-ster was chatting up cheerleader Lacey and missed his change-over cue, Owen, in his totally groggy state and slurry-but-still-booming voice, sang out, "Nick-ster's got a girlfriend!"

Everyone laughed.

Bee panicked. Nick's heart sank, not wanting to hurt his buddy. Then, both Bee and Nick forced a laugh and played it off perfectly as if their love wasn't truly happening, while both knew inside that it was.

Demi nodded to Bee, acknowledging her brilliant acting and beaming with excitement that they were pulling off this ruse.

And Bee wanted to disappear.

And so, she did. This was too much to take.

# 26 BEE BAILS AND NICK WISHES SHE WERE HIS GIRLFRIEND

Bee hurried out of Owen's side gate into his quiet neighborhood. She'd decided she had to bolt as quickly as possible as soon as Owen blurted out the obvious—or what should be the obvious if there weren't a major lie happening—namely, that she and Nick really, really liked each other, and in a normal world, where Bee hadn't caused Owen to be stuck in a body cast on major meds, she and Nick might be dating and Owen would be correct that "Nickster's got a girlfriend"—namely Bee.

*Then, again*, Bee thought, *that probably wouldn't have happened either*, as she rushed over Owen's lawn to the street, realizing that if she and Nick had met in any other circumstance or point in time, she wouldn't have had her JYM, and she wouldn't be putting herself out there as herself to be noticed.

Nick followed, right on Bee's heels. "Bee, wait!" The side gate slammed behind him.

"I have to go! Tutor math," Bee lied. "Diego!" And she waved and kept walking.

"You did that this morning," Nick reminded her, catching

up. Clearly, he was paying attention and knew her schedule. And wasn't buying the lie.

"Please just leave me alone," Bee cried back at Nick.

"You know it's 'gonna get better tomorrow," he shouted. "He'll remember everything. Owen chivalry will abound."

Bee stopped, taking in Nick's beaming smile. It was honest even though he was totally crushing on her and pretending not to. "It's not gonna get better," she barked. "Stop being so cheerful!" She took off the blue Italian glass earrings and jutted them at him. "And stop following me!" she shouted with the angriest, meanest I-hate-you-so-leave-me-alone lying face that she could muster.

"I don't get it. Shouldn't I be the one upset here?" Nick insisted.

"No! Tomorrow you get your best friend back! And I get..."

"My best friend?" Nick interrupted her with this uncharacteristically sarcastic rhetorical question.

"At least you have a best friend," Bee snarked back.

"At least I know how to *be* a friend," Nick topped her.

*Ouch!* Nick's words stung. Bee stared, tears rising, doing her best to steel herself and keep them down while also looking angry. It was a tall order, but she pulled it off somehow.

Nick backed down, clearly feeling awful about his jabs.

Bee felt awful too about her mean barbs.

Nick shook his head, almost saying something, but not knowing what to say and not knowing why he felt so bad.

Bee didn't either. *This shouldn't feel so bad,* she thought.

And finally, Bee nodded and turned and walked away.

*****

Nick went back to the party in spite of himself—because all he really wanted to do was leave and go home and get away from everything he was feeling, especially his utter confusion about really crushing on Bee when she was totally off limits while knowing that Owen managed to steal the affection of everyone he was into.

Nick hung out with Owen until everyone left. Luckily, Demi ignored him once Bee was gone. And then, he helped Mr. and Mrs. Fleet clean up and told them that he'd hang out with Owen so they could chill a bit. This was a big day, and he could see that they were way more stressed out about Owen's condition than he was. He was just stressed out about Bee and figured the distraction of hanging with Owen would help...as long as he didn't think about Bee.

Nick suggested to Owen's parents that they move Owen's gaming computer into the living room, and he and Mr. Fleet moved the entire thing. Owen was getting off his meds the next day, and they were supposed to also start getting him up and into a wheelchair. Apparently, that'd get his blood flowing, which would speed up his healing. Which is why Nick suggested some gaming to pass the time until he could go back to school. And right now, it was a great distraction for Nick.

Owen fell asleep while they were setting it all up, so Nick just started playing. He got in, playing for both himself and Owen so that it was like they were playing against each other. Owen woke up a couple of times in the middle of some of the levels and got into it, watching from his bed over Nick's shoulder, cheering for himself even though Nick was playing for him.

It was a great escape from reality for Nick, as expected. He finally chilled out, and after a bunch of games, cheered, "Yes," when he scored for Owen, and joked, "You are kickin' my beehiney! In more ways than one," even though he knew Owen had dozed off again.

Nick looked over at his buddy who was snoring loudly, put down the control and stood up by the side of the bed. "Tomorrow'll be hell without meds," he told Owen even though Owen was out of it and not hearing a word. "But you'll be fine, oh Lucky One."

Nick smiled at his friend, glad he was getting better, and took the blue Italian glass earrings that he'd once bought for Amy Geary from his jeans pocket. "No worries, Stealth Dater," he teased sleeping Owen. "If you'd told me about Bee, I might've tried to steal her away. And failed! But if you mess this one up, I will not think twice. I will be the stealth one then." And he air-fist bumped one of Owen's casted hands, brought the earrings down the hallway to Owen's room, placed them on his dresser and left.

Once outside, Nick put on his playlist and skated home on his longboard, losing himself in the music, doing everything he could not to think about Bee and not to skate by her house.

***

Had Nick skated by Bee's house, he would have seen the light on in her room and maybe even seen her in the bay window, and he would've felt so much better. Well, if the window had been open so he could hear, that is—because she was playing his song on a recorder.

Bee had been practicing the song and was trying out a poem she'd written as lyrics. So, in between playing, Bee would sing and flatfoot out a hip hop beat to the poem up on her wooden dance board, a wooden box her Uncle Roy had made for her. It was about a half a foot high, which made her visible in the window to anyone that passed.

The whole song was coming together nicely. *And it's so fun*, Bee thought. Plus, it was a fabulous distraction from the mess at Owen's house with Nick.

She started again, rapping and flatfooting out the beat, "I hate my best friend; She hates me; But what she really hates is my poetry; That's okay 'cuz I hate her guy; And that's just how we're 'gonna fly."

Then Bee flatfooted out a bunch of beats and started the chorus, "Blood-pact sisters; Pride in the differences; 'Cuz she's just her; And I'm just me. Blood-pact sisters; Pride in the differences; Doin' our best to just keep it real."

Suddenly, Bee heard applause and "whoop, whoop, whoop" sounding from outside. She looked out the window and saw Kate and Torian across the street on Kate's lawn. At least they couldn't hear the lyrics, she thought and waved.

Kate waved back and simultaneously jumped up and did a silly side-to-side, jumping, turning dance thing, playfully making fun of her best friend like she usually did.

Normally, pre-Torian, Bee would've loved it. She would've run out, and they would've started silly-dancing on Kate's lawn, singing loudly, laughing, making up new lyrics until either they got called in by their parents or one of the neighbors complained.

Normally, Bee would've spewed every second of excitement and disappointment about Nick to Kate, giving Kate the play by play as everything went down. Kate would've been super excited about Bee getting to write lyrics for Nick, and Bee would've run them by Kate, even though she knew Kate really did hate poetry.

And in normal times, Bee never would've written anything even remotely disparaging about their friendship. She wouldn't have had to. At this moment, it was more of a song of where she wished she could get to inside. *Like aspirational*, she thought and laughed. The word aspirational sounded so ridiculous. Actually, she meant *inspirational* and laughed at herself again for getting the word wrong.

Bee also knew the song was good. And she knew it allowed her to express that she needed to accept that she felt so disconnected from Kate. Even though she wasn't fully there yet. And she especially liked the last line of the chorus, "Doin' our best to just keep it real." Even though she wasn't there yet either.

Bee looked at Cardboard Owen and told him, "My *real* is about to seriously stink."

# 27 OWEN DOESN'T REMEMBER BEE AND THE TRUTH GETS HARD TO CONTAIN FOR BEE AND IMPOSSIBLE FOR NICK

Bee headed over to Owen's straightaway the next morning. She peered in through the front window before going to the door and saw Owen sleeping in his hospital bed in the living room.

She waited for a while, dreading going in, but then, Claire passed from the hallway heading towards the kitchen with an empty cereal bowl and noticed her.

*Oh, crud,* Bee groaned to herself.

Claire glared at Bee, then shook her head and, resigned, came over and opened the front door to let Bee in. "Just keep it down with your stupid lies and weirdness, okay?" she snarked at Bee. "Our parents are still sleeping. They're exhausted from this nightmare, and you are not helping." Claire turned and left Bee standing at the door, shaking her head and muttering, "So annoying," before entering the kitchen.

Bee hesitantly came inside, shut the Fleets' front door quietly and tip-toed over to Owen's hospital bed.

"You don't need to be *that* quiet," Claire mocked Bee in a loud-but-whispering yell, startling Bee as she trounced back out of the kitchen and down the hall to her room.

Bee's heart pounded. "What a tool," she whispered to herself, then to sleeping Owen, "Your sister is a piece of work."

But Bee decided to let it go with a deep breath and heavy sigh, blowing out all the annoying negativity. Then, she smiled at Owen even though he was asleep and said, "Today is your big day," trying to get optimistic enough for both of them.

Owen mumbled something in his sleep.

And then, she saw him drool. And it sent her back over the edge. Her heart sunk and ominous dread and panic overtook her. *Ugh.*

She moved over on the other side of Owen's hospital bed, getting between the bed and the window next to the sliding glass door. She felt safe there and looked out into the backyard, remembering dancing with Nick and seeing Jade's desperate Mario-clown-outfit tree spying, realizing how strange love was and how it could make you do really stupid things. *Claire's right, I'm a friggin' weirdo, just like Jade*, Bee thought.

"I'm a friggin' weirdo, and I hate me," she rapped under her breath, tapping it out on the windowpane then doing a tiny flatfoot-tap move repeating the rhythmic beats.

Bee laughed, amused with herself, then shook her head, looking at Owen's restless reflection in the window. She rapped the rest of her thoughts to herself, tapping the beat out on the window again, "You're tellin' 'em who I am; and Nick's gonna know I'm a sham..."

"Hello?" Owen suddenly called out.

"Ahhh!" Bee screamed and jumped in shock—

—scaring Owen, who screamed and jumped in shock too, then screamed in pain, "Ahhhhhh! My leg. My leggg!"

Claire barreled out from her bedroom. "What are you doing?" she chastised Bee as she ran up to Owen. "Why are you here? You just make everything worse!"

Mr. and Mrs. Fleet were right behind Claire—Mr. Fleet unabashedly in boxers and a "Lion Pride" T-shirt and Mrs. Fleet in an elegant robe covering a posh nightgown.

"Call Dr. Grogan," Mr. Fleet told Claire and Mrs. Fleet.

Claire was on it as she glared at Bee.

Mrs. Fleet whispered to Bee, "You're fine. It's not your fault."

And Owen cried to his dad, "It hurts so much. Please make it stop."

***

Luckily for Owen and everyone who couldn't bear to see him suffer, the pain subsided thanks to time and a tiny bump of pain meds and expert assurance from Dr. Grogan, the team's main orthopedic surgeon, who stood by Owen's bed with Owen's main Lion Pride crew—Coach Wells, Demi, cheerleader Chrissie, Glenn, Drew-ster and, of course, Nick—who had all showed up for support.

The only one still in agony—well, plagued with panic would be more like it—was Bee, who stood behind all the others just wishing she could disappear.

"It's fine if I don't move," Owen told Dr. Grogan, trying to be optimistic.

Mrs. Fleet moved Owen's hair out of his eyes and cooed lovingly, "I'm so happy, honey. You're doing so well. And Dr. Grogan says the pain will ease up quickly, like it already has since earlier this morning..."

"Woo!" cheerleader Chrissie interjected with a mini-voiced cheer. "No pain. No pain."

"And this week," Mrs. Fleet continued, "You can be up and about to visit the team at practice. We're hiring a van and driver to take you around in the wheelchair. And next Friday, you can even go to the game with your friends and Bee."

"Bee?" Owen wondered, looking terribly confused.

Everyone that was gathered round Owen's bed parted like the Red Sea so Owen could see Bee.

His face brightened. "Little Neighbor With The Car!" he cheered. "Yeah, you were in here before. Thank you."

"And she's your girlfriend," cheerleader Chrissie reminded Owen.

"Who, Little Neighbor?" Owen chortled as if this were impossible.

"Uh, oh," Coach Wells muttered, foreseeing more grief in his future.

"Like I said earlier," Dr. Grogan assured them all, "sometimes amnesia comes up around trauma."

"Amnesia?" Owen scoffed. "I don't have amnesia." Then, he saw his mom's worry. "Mom!" Owen insisted, gesturing at her with his chin to prove his point. "You're Mom! And I don't have amnesia. And there's you, Nick, my main man," he jutted his chin at Nick then continued round the crew circling his bed. "And there's Claire, Coach Wells, Chrissie, Glenn, Demi...lookin' good. Dr. Grogin...looking tan..." He waited for laughs.

But they didn't come. Except from Dr. Grogan, who liked the tan joke because he'd just been on vacation and was much more tan than usual. Everyone else just looked very somber.

"C'mon!" Owen insisted. "Seriously, I'm all here. Dr. Grogan was just in St. Martinique. How was it?"

"Fantastic," Dr. Grogan replied.

"Dude, tell them," Owen turned to Nick. "Boogie Snoop, our next rap."

Nick nodded with a cheeky smile that this was impressively true: Boogie Snoop was, in fact, their next rap number.

"And seven zip!" he exclaimed to Coach Wells. "Our last Thunderbird trouncing."

"Yup," Coach Wells nodded.

"And you," Owen said to his sister, Claire. "Red licorice, stolen from my desk. I'm onto you."

Claire grinned, clearly guilty of the crime.

Then, Owen looked at Bee who grinned as cutely and as best she could. But Bee was one person he couldn't remember. "Crud," Owen said. But then, he regrouped and turned back to Dr. Grogan with a grin. "But it's only one small thing I can't remember. Otherwise, I'm fine. I remember everything."

"You're doing great," Dr. Grogan assured Owen and his parents. "And these things usually clear up in a few days or so.

You'll be fine."

Owen looked to Nick for further backup.

Nick smirked with cheeky bro-love. "You just gotta rest, my friend," Nick told Owen. "Doc Grogan knows his stuff. And where to fish. He's always got the best fishing spots."

Owen gulped, getting unexpectedly emotional all of a sudden. "I remember those spots."

Bee felt awful and poked Demi, who was right in front of her.

Demi turned to look at Bee with an annoyed "What?!" look.

Bee mouthed insistently, "Tell them!" And gestured with her chin for Demi to speak up, nudging her to reveal their truth so Owen and his family and team didn't have to suffer this fake amnesia scare.

Demi angrily mouthed back, "No!"—as if Bee were insane. "Actually...," Bee said out loud.

Everyone turned to look at Bee.

Demi jumped in, interrupting Bee and pushing her from the back of the crowd towards the front door as she feigned sincere kindness, while also using her I-know-exactly-what-I'm-talking-about leader voice, to insist to Bee, "We should give Owen some space." Then, she shot everyone an "everything's fine" super smile and forcefully escorted Bee out the front door.

Everyone who was inside watched out the front window as Demi pushed Bee down the front walk—and cheerleader Chrissie, Glenn and Drew-ster moved closer to the front window to get a better look. Clearly, there was some kind of drama happening there and they were intrigued.

"Owen needs to know he's okay," Bee whisper-yelled at Demi as they reached the street at the end of the front walkway.

Luckily, no one inside could hear a word they were saying, but everyone inside could definitely tell by the body language that something important was going down.

"You are overly emotional and overthinking this," Demi scolded with a vicious whisper-yell right back. "And I am on it, with a level head. Sticking to our plan." Demi nodded and stood up tall to show both of them that this was the reality.

"I just want to tell the truth," Bee pleaded.

"The truth is that Owen's gonna love you if I tell him the truth *later*," Demi insisted as if this were the only and smartest option. Then, she nailed it home with clenched-teeth zeal, "*Not* in front of everyone. We cannot tell him now. With everyone looking. And everything on the line. That would be more cruel than anything that has already gone down."

*Ouch.* Bee felt the sting of Demi's words and noticed everyone watching from the front window. *Crud,* she thought—

—as Chrissie, Glenn and Drew-ster waved with hopeful grins.

"Did you see how fired up they got now that Owen's awake with amnesia?!" Demi reminded Bee about Owen's crew. "We can use that! Watch," she added and turned to the window and did a big cheer, shooting her arm and fist into the air with, "Win!" Then doing a stag-leap thing with, "For Owen!"

Chrissie, Drew-ster and Glenn's arms shot up mimicking Demi with a fist pump and "Win! For Owen!" cheer that Demi and Bee couldn't hear, followed by Chrissie jumping up doing the same stag-leap thing that Demi had done.

Demi turned to nail it home for Bee again, "See?!"

Which is when Nick opened the front door. "We good out here?" he called out.

Bee deflated.

Demi jumped on the opportunity, lowering her voice again with determined insistence as she told Bee, "Nick's the one who's gonna get hurt if we don't do this right."

It was like a slap in the face to Bee.

Then, Demi called out, "Nick?!" Then, she turned away from being right in Bee's face with a smile, dousing her voice with cheer and positive, upbeat energy as if her name were Pollyanna not Machiavelli. "Can you take Bee home?" Demi asked Nick.

Bee was shocked by Demi's nerve. "What they heck?" she

snarked, not even hiding her ire.

Demi smiled at Bee as if she were an angel, "Go rest. You need it as much as Owen. Just don't let Nick find out."

Bee knew she was defeated and turned and walked off, not looking back. Then, she heard footsteps running to catch up with her.

"Hey, wait up!" Nick called out.

Bee felt anger rise up inside of her. She didn't want to deal with him and all this emotion. She didn't want him to walk her home. She hated that Demi had butted her nose in and manipulated her. She knew it wasn't Nick's fault but now she felt angry at him too for listening to Demi. And being so darn nice. And chivalrous. And making her like him so much. And she hated herself for being so cowardly.

Yeah, Bee was pissed off and steeled herself and picked up her pace.

Nevertheless, Nick caught up to Bee and walked alongside her for a while through Owen's neighborhood. The further they went, the worse Bee felt—guilt, sadness, wanting to disappear all over again, heart hurting—the whole gamut of emotions once again.

Finally, after a few blocks, Nick blurted out, "Look..."

And Bee stopped and said, "Me too," as—

—he finished his sentence, catching up to her, "Yeah, I..."

Their eyes met, then both of them quickly diverted their gazes away from each other.

"...I didn't mean that friendship thing, at all," Nick continued, finding the courage to look back at Bee but still feeling awkward, embarrassed and not knowing how to do this. "Yesterday. The thing I said. That you don't know how to be a friend. I mean, it's just the opposite. You're a good friend."

"You too," Bee admitted and looked at him now too.

"And Owen's lucky to have you," he continued with a little more courage. "And..."

Their eyes locked. Nick wanted to say something. Something more. Something about his feelings. And Bee's feelings, because he felt it for sure—that she liked him too. Or at least, he really thought so. And he wanted to say something about how awesome she was. And about how much he liked hanging with her. But he didn't. Instead, he just toyed, playfully taking the piss out of himself, "I'm just gonna have to 'man up' and find my own girl...friend. To kill the time with. Right? Since you're taking all of Owen's time." He laughed.

This was totally awkward.

Bee tried to smile. "Yeah, I guess things are gonna..."

Once again, they read each other's minds and both said, "...change," together, at exactly the same time, which felt awfully sad but they both knew it was true and nodded, which was an obvious cue to start walking in order to avoid more discomfort. So they walked in silence for another block—

—until Bee couldn't stand it anymore and told Nick that she was veering off at the next block. "I'm good. Seriously, you don't need to take me home." And then, she waved without looking at him as she turned the corner onto a street that wasn't near hers and was, in fact, going in the wrong direction.

Nick knew that. "You're gonna...it's...," he began but then turned and kept going down the street they'd been on together, feeling miserable and thinking, *Guess she's not that into me.* And teasing himself out loud with a low booming voice, "Wrong again, Wells." Then, he started air boxing while trying to convince himself, "Man up, bro. Man up," realizing he was going to have to fully show respect to himself if his life was ever going to veer in a positive direction at all after another false-girlfriend disaster. He boomed, "Truth, Wells. Truth." And it didn't help at all.

*Major bummer*, he thought again, knowing this wasn't going to be easy but that he didn't have a choice.

***

Nick was relieved when he got home and his dad showed up pretty soon afterwards and suggested they play some hoops in the driveway. "Dad and me time?" Coach Wells proposed, laughing at his corny joke. "I need a break from football."

Without having to say a word, they both agreed that the whole Owen-amnesia fiasco morning needed to be forgotten for the rest of the day.

It was a cool day, but the sun came out for them, and after warming up and several rounds of one-on-one hoops, things were heating up.

Coach Wells was getting super sweaty but was definitely in the zone. He dribbled past Nick and slam-dunked. "Yeah!" he shouted, feeling it for the first time in a long time. It was good to have his kid back. That was for sure. And it helped his game.

"Good to see you back, old man," Nick told his dad.

Coach Wells stopped to catch his breath. He wasn't in the best shape...yet. "I'm glad to be back. And glad you're back. And I'm gonna get us back in Bo's Thursday hoops game. Get you ready for the season. We're gonna have a full year." He put his hand up for a high-five.

Nick put his hand up but hesitated. "Actually, Dad, we gotta talk about that," he admitted before completing the high-five.

Coach Wells frowned, instantly worried. "Your mother wants you back," he guessed.

"No, Dad," Nick assured him. "This has nothing to do with Mom; and by the way, I pick where I live now, right? And I'm here, okay?"

Coach Wells cracked a small smile of relief. "So, it's not all about her after all," he joked.

"Not this time," Nick teased, happy that his dad could make light. Still, Nick felt the nerves jostling in his own stomach. He knew he had to speak his own truth. And that it couldn't wait any longer. And it wasn't going to be easy.

Coach Wells laughed and did a victory dribble and shot the ball. "Swish!" he cried, shooting his fist out and doing a little jig.

"This time it's about us," Nick interrupted the joy, bursting his dad's win bubble.

Coach Wells stopped and saw his son's face looking serious.

Nick hesitated, then forced himself to come clean. "Dad, I don't want to play anymore. No more football. No more kicker. No b-ball either."

"You...What? Really? I knew that," his dad croaked then had to look away, taking this in.

"Dad, I'm a mediocre kicker and you keep playing me over Vinny," Nick reminded him. "And...it's just not me. As much as I want it to be." Nick held his breath, heart pounding, hoping to God that he didn't disappoint his dad too much and make his dad's life worse.

Coach Wells looked at his son, heart hurting and filled with pride and love all at once. This was his kid and his kid...just...was everything to him. "My peewee is ready to fly, isn't he?" Coach Wells managed, doing everything to keep his tears at bay.

Nick nodded, making a "yikes" cringy funny smile.

"Darn that Uncle Al. Wins every time," Coach Wells joked while still battling tears.

Nick laughed in relief.

And Coach Wells guy-hugged his son and teared up. "You're my kinda kid and I love you." And the guy-hug turned into a bear hug, like Coach Wells just hugged Nick so hard— *squeezing, squeezing, squeezing.*

"So glad you're not gonna lose it," Nick croaked, teasing from under the squeezes.

"Me? Naw, not me," Coach Wells cried as he actually cried now.

Nick pulled back and smiled warmly at his dad who had massive amounts of tears on his face, running into his Sunday stubble. "Yeah, Dad. You've been kind of losing it lately," Nick razzed him further.

Coach Wells grinned and held Nick still by the shoulders, keeping him there to get a good look at him. "I'm proud of you, son. But you'd better play that Thursday b-ball game with us. I refuse to lose that one."

Nick laughed, "You got it," then grabbed the ball and took off dribbling, Coach Wells going after him, until Nick made the shot. Net ball. "Aaand another swish!" Nick went up for a high-five, and his dad reluctantly gave it to him.

They continued to play, Nick finally having stepped into his truth—by owning up to his truth and saying it out loud. And the burden was lifted, and he felt massive relief and joy.

# 28 DEMI GETS MACHIAVELLIAN BY THE POOL

While the Owen-assumed-amnesia situation drove Nick to own his truth and Bee to attempt to disappear into her flatfoot poetry and hip hop writing because she knew she was living a lie, Demi found herself leaning into her Machiavellian resourcefulness and clever scheming nature. She was not going to let the Lions lose or let Owen go down. She saw him as an extension of her high school and future success.

So, the next day, she set out with confidence to visit Owen so that she could nail her plan home. It was a surprisingly warm fall day again in this mountain valley town, and Owen's was one of the few houses in the Flathead Valley, like Chrissie's, that had a backyard pool, so the Fleets were taking advantage of the weather while they could.

Demi knocked at the front door several times while holding the chocolate chip cookies that she'd bought at the bakery and put in a cute tin as if she'd baked them, and she peeked in the front window—*no, Owen*. But she could see that the sliding-glass door was open. And she heard shouting and a splash. "Of course," she told herself with a smile. "The pool." This was good news. The Fleets were up and out in full-on Fleet fashion and that meant Owen was coming round.

Demi went in the side gate.

Owen was sitting up in his wheelchair with his casted right leg sticking out, supported by a wheelchair leg extender. Mrs. Fleet was feeding him a healthy green protein shake. Demi recognized the shake. It was something she used to make for Owen when they were dating briefly. *Good*, Demi thought. *They're being smart. Less inflammation.* And then, she thought that maybe she shouldn't have brought the cookies as they were definite inflammation creators.

*Whatever*, she justified in her mind, *no biggie*, and watched Claire leap off the diving board, doing a cannonball—making a giant splash and nailing Owen and Mrs. Fleet.

"Wooooooo!" Mrs. Fleet, Owen and Claire cheered in unison. Clearly, the whole family loved a thrill.

"I don't have a towel, but I did make Owen's favorite chocolate chip cookies," Demi called out as she made an entrance, walking up with the cookies and a big smile.

"Oh, sweetie, I'm so happy to see you," Mrs. Fleet gushed, the joy beaming from her smile.

"Demi Robertson," Owen stated like an announcer to drive home the point that he did not have amnesia, "5'5", 108 pounds; favorite movie: *Dirty Dancing*; TV show: *Friday Night Lights*; quarter-life goal: own and run a sports franchise, preferably football."

Demi's eyes lit up and she nodded at Owen with pride then smiled at Mrs. Fleet to nail it home, "Impressive, right?"

"That's right," Owen boasted. "No amnesia here."

"Very good, honey. And you will remember Bee," Mrs. Fleet assured her son. "No need to prove anything now. Take it easy on yourself."

Owen's confidence instantly took a dive with the mention of Bee. "What?" he grimaced.

"She's right," Demi insisted. "And I came to help. Maybe if Owen and I could talk?" she asked Mrs. Fleet with her most polite, confident smile.

"Of course, dear," Mrs. Fleet agreed. "You are always so generous. We really appreciate it. C'mon, Claire," Mrs. Fleet called out and handed Demi the back scratcher and gave her a polite hug. Then, Mrs. Fleet and Claire went inside with Demi's chocolate chip cookies.

Luckily, the pool was off on the side of the Fleets' house so Demi and Owen had some privacy. Mrs. Fleet and Claire would have to look out the side window off of the dining room to see them, which was unlikely, and as long as the window was closed, they wouldn't be able to hear anything.

So, Demi moved in. She held the back scratcher up in Owen's face. "We need to have a heart to heart."

"Why couldn't I have forgotten I was dating you?" Owen said, eyes flirting. Her assertiveness was a definite turn on.

"Because you dumped me for Jade," Demi reminded him.

"I did do that, didn't I?" Owen grinned, clearly remembering every detail.

"Stupid move, but now, I have Glenn, who's perfect for me," Demi boasted in true Lioness-pride fashion.

Owen, still grinning, appeared to be listening but was mostly taking in her perfect hair and makeup, his eyes glistening.

Which was the most annoying thing ever to Demi, and she squeezed the back scratcher handle in utter maddening frustration and shoved in down the back of his upper-body cast. And started scratching.

"Owwwww!" Owen cried in pain.

"And you've gotten insanely lucky," Demi whisper-yelled in her most intimidating voice then pulled out the scratcher.

Owen looked disappointed.

"Seriously, Owen, you may not remember Bee, but she is the best thing that ever happened to you," Demi insisted convincingly.

"You sure about that?" he flirted.

"Yes; the football gods are giving you a second chance to get your priorities straight. Namely your unbelievable talent and career," she complimented firmly.

"I love it when you get all Urban Meyer on me," Owen grinned up at Demi's scowling, serious and beautiful face.

"This is serious!" Demi shouted. "Bee Plumb not only saved you from the bees but rallied the entire Lions' football team and Reno to win the last two games!"

Owen's face brightened with recognition. "Plumb!" he cried with joy. "Her last name's Plumb! I knew that!"

"Owen! Look at me," Demi insisted, getting in his face and lowering her voice to a firm, direct, bossy coach-like whisper for effect. "You have the potential to do amazing things, like playing on my future NFL team. But that's not gonna happen if you're sneaking around distracted by a Thunderbird. So, you better raise your girlfriend bar. Before Bee leaves you."

"She's gonna leave me?" Owen was instantly worried.

"And someone else is gonna snap her up, just like that," Demi let him know.

"Like who?" Owen wondered, feeling the potential gravity of this loss.

"Anyone," Demi told him. "Everyone loves Bee, even Coach Wells."

Owen took this in.

Demi smiled subtly. Her plan was working. "So, you better think of something nice to do for Bee," she instructed. "And recommit. Even if you never remember her." Demi put the scratcher back down Owen's back again more gently this time and scratched as he considered her words. His uncharacteristic silence and absence of flirtation told her that he really was worried now about his memory and potentially losing this girlfriend Bee that everyone loved. Demi grinned, rejoicing in her perfect triumph—*total score!* And she let Owen stew in the situation, knowing that ultimately, she was going to win—the Lions would beat the Thunderbirds, go to State and be this year's State Champions. And Owen's future career would get right back on track.

And hers would *stay* on track.

Demi texted Bee as soon as she left: *Beatrix, I solved the problem. Got us back on track. Was just over at the Fleets' house. Owen now knows of your total awesomeness and is ready to keep being your boyfriend. He sees the value in it. Like we do. It is imperative that he is your boyfriend. And you have to go visit him today. He's by the pool. It's weirdly hot outside. Good weather. It's a lucky sign, I think. Go, Lions! Be cute! Not wishy-washy. You be in charge! It'll make him like you even more.*

# 29 BEE FLAILS POOLSIDE CHEZ OWEN

Bee hadn't left her room since the previous day's disaster. She was never leaving again if she could help it. Her plan was to just lie there on her bed and stare up at the ceiling forever like she was doing when she heard the ping of her phone. It was all the way over on the other side of her bed where she could better ignore it. Dread came over her. She pretended it didn't happen. Then, her phone pinged again. "Fine!" she yelled at it and grabbed it in a huff.

It was a text from Demi. She read it. Demi wanted her to go over to Owen's and take charge so that he could "keep being" her boyfriend. "Never gonna happen," Bee told her phone. "Not going over to Owen's. Not capable of being in charge." Then, she looked at Cardboard Owen and moaned, "Why did I ever have to like you? I'm never gonna exude awesomeness. I hate leading. Why is this happening? Stupid JYM!"

But Bee sat up. She knew this was her fate now and that she had caused it. She had to carry out Demi's plan—at least until she could come up with something better and have the courage to enact it, which she was lacking in that moment. So, she got up, put on her cute blue dress over jeans and headed over to the Fleets' while telling herself that maybe if she got crazy brave, she would tell Owen the truth. Or do something super-hero-esque. But Bee wasn't holding her breath at this point because she was blinded by panic, love for Nick and the fact that she was still feeling sorry for herself that Kate wasn't there for her right now when she really needed help—even though the past week had made her realize she had what it took to be Owen's fake secret girlfriend, even if just on the outside.

When she pulled up in front of Owen's house, Bee saw Claire look out the front window and yell something back inside. *Criminy*, Bee thought and got out, started up the front walk, then panicked and turned around. But before she finished two steps back towards the SFB Mobile, Mrs. Fleet opened the front door and called out, "Hi, Bee!"

Bee looked back and could tell that Mrs. Fleet was over-the-top happy to see her.

"He's round back by the pool!" Mrs. Fleet shouted and pointed to the side gate. "It's open."

"Okay," Bee said and waved awkwardly, frozen, not moving anything but her hand, unsure what to do.

"Or you can come through here!" Mrs. Fleet offered. "Through the house."

"It's okay," Bee told her. "I'll go through the side. I like the exercise." She smiled then started off, berating herself, *I like the exercise. Dumb, Bee. Super dumb.*

Mrs. Fleet cheered, "Go, Lions!"—while Claire shook her head at Bee from the front window as if confirming Bee's opinion that "I like the exercise" was the stupidest thing to say ever.

*At least we agree on something*, Bee thought about Claire and hurried through the gate and over to the other side of the house where she found Owen by the pool in his wheelchair watching Three Stooges videos on an iPad.

Bee panicked as soon as she saw Owen, *Omigosh.* Her heart started racing. She forced herself onward, lifting her head, standing taller as she approached with Owen's bag that she had gotten from Jade that first day. She tried to act as if she had all the confidence in the world—while feeling totally vulnerable inside.

"Hi!" Owen cheered when he saw Bee, his eyes flashing at this somewhat cute wonder before him. "Wow, come over here; sit down," he said warmly.

*At least it's something,* Bee thought and croaked, "I just came to bring you your bag." She held up Owen's sports bag like a dork—as if he couldn't see the bag in her hand.

Owen reimagined her outfit with his eyes. And with no subtlety at all, whispered out loud, "Pink bikini. Yes!"

Bee blushed from her toes to the ends of her hair. *If I had on a pink bikini, it'd match my face*, she joked to herself.

"I like your hair today," he complimented with that classic Owen grin that she'd longed for—

—*Since pre-K*, Bee thought, then corrected herself, *Kinder*, and said out loud, doing her best to rally and hide her utter embarrassment at being complemented so much, "Really? It's just...a lucky day...for hair." She shrugged and laughed nervously. Bee really was bad at this flirting thing.

Owen playfully squirmed to show how itchy he was. "Hey, would you mind? Back scratch?" he flirted.

"Sure," Bee replied and picked up the back scratcher on the pool patio table then awkwardly stuck it down the back of his upper-body cast. "Like this?" Bee wondered as she gently but apparently effectively scratched his back-cast itch.

Owen blissed out. "Omigosh, I think it's coming back to me now how amazing you are. And nice," he gushed, enjoying the relief for a minute then remembering how he remembered nothing about Bee, and he worried all over again. "Actually, the only thing I remember is the bees. Sort of. And that your name is Bee. Which is weirdly like some kind of kismet. And your name also maybe has an x in it. And also, there's that fort you built in eighth grade. I remember that."

"Oh, yeah, that was a cool fort!" Bee sparkled. She loved that fort too.

Owen's worry grew. Now his heart was racing. "But that's

it. That's all I remember." He looked at Bee with desperate eyes.

"Uh...," Bee panicked. "Yeah, uh...hey look, I brought your playbook. To help you remember." She gently pulled the back scratcher out of his cast and pulled the playbook, which she'd gotten back from Coach Wells, out of Owen's bag then held it out for Owen to see—with the biggest and cutest smile she could muster.

"You're just really nice, aren't you?" Owen observed and just stared at Bee, oddly feeling his heart open in a new way. He remembered what Demi had said about how everybody loved Bee and that she was great for the team and his career. And he knew that Demi had to be right about Bee because Demi was right about every single other thing. "And smart," Owen continued about Bee, stopping at the corny, hokey flowered headband she was wearing. "You're almost perfect."

"Did Demi talk to you yet?" Bee wondered, digging to find out what Owen knew and what Demi had said exactly, if she really had been there—because Bee knew that could've been a scheming-Demi lie too.

"Aren't you the one who wins the science competition every year?" Owen wondered.

"Because I'm thinking Demi hasn't been here yet," Bee continued, trying to suss out Demi's truth and ignoring Owen's question.

"Now I see why Demi said you helped them win," Owen added. "I love that."

*So, she was here,* Bee noted and grabbed her Owen collage out of his bag and jutted it up between them. "And there's this!" she exclaimed. "Maybe it'll get you to remember more about me." And she pointed to one photo from first grade that she was in too, even though it featured Owen.

"Wha..?!" Owen's eyes widened as he looked at Bee's collage of photos of him. "Wow, it's just like my screensaver! Did my mom make that?"

"No, actually, I just, uh, did," Bee stuttered.

Owen looked at Bee, genuinely moved. "Why did it take me

so long to notice you?" Owen asked, honestly flummoxed. "You're my lucky angel. Demi was right." He started tearing up.

*Omigosh*, thought Bee, this was getting stranger and more uncomfortable by the minute. She had to tell him the truth.

Which is when Owen's tears fell. "You totally saved me," he cried.

Bee hesitated, then grabbed a napkin off the table and wiped Owen's nose then hugged him, carefully, so as not to hurt him—gently, barely touching the plaster of his casted self, lightly patting it in hopes that he could tell she really cared, and wondered, *How the heck is this happening?*

And then, Bee told Owen that she had to go even though she didn't, "Sorry, yeah, I gotta go help my mom." Because she couldn't tell the truth. She was too chicken!

Owen nodded and whispered, "I'm so lucky."

And Bee grinned and bolted out the side gate. She knew she'd pulled off the ruse *again*, but this really was getting more and more awful.

For her. And everyone.

Even though Owen had just found renewed hope.

# 30 NICK AND OWEN GET SOME OZZY BRO TIME IN AND GET REAL ABOUT AMY AND BEE

Owen was in his element sitting outside by the pool the next day—another oddly warm day for fall—with his best buddy, Nick. Nick had gotten there just after noon, thanks to his dad writing him a note so he could leave school early to hang with Owen to help ease Owen's transition home. It was going great and Nick was deep into playing his third heavy metal anthem on his guitar.

Owen was rocking his head to the beat, and everything was pretty much perfect from his POV except that he felt wildly emo. This truly was not Owen-usual. He figured it was maybe the drugs getting flushed out of his system by that green juice his mom had made and that it would pass soon so things could get back to normal. He was confident in that prospect.

And when Nick finished the last wailing chords of Ozzy Osborne's "Crazy Train" and crooned, "Aye, aye, aye," for effect, Owen was totally moved. "I am honored, man," Owen croaked. "I know how much you hate that song."

"Compromise," Nick replied with a big grin and did a

performative air-high-five, lightly touching Owen's cast.

And instantly, things *were* back to normal. They laughed and sat back and chilled.

"How's the amnesia?" Nick wondered with a teasing twist. "Anything yet?"

"Nope, just the bees," Owen informed him. "As in the bees in the bush not Bee Plumb. What's her whole name again?"

"Beatrix," Nick told him.

"Ah, right, with the x! I knew that!" Owen remembered. "But you know what I decided? About her? Bee with the x? Who cares? Even if I never remember Beatrix Plumb, she's here now. And she's fairly hot right? Besides that bandana thing in her hair. And they all love her, with no drama."

"You love the drama," Nick reminded him of this obvious truth.

"And I can focus on playing," Owen continued, ignoring his buddy's observant comment about the drama. "Right?"

"Instead of focusing on Jade?" Nick chided. "I told you to focus on playing not dating. You didn't listen."

"I told you about Jade? And Bee?" Owen queried, looking at Nick for the answer and feeling a little worried again that he couldn't remember telling Nick about Jade.

Nick shook his head no. "You didn't tell me about either one."

"I'm sorry dude," Owen said—remembering that he didn't tell his best friend about dating Jade and figuring that if he hid Jade, it only made sense that he'd hide Bee. *Right?* he thought, trying to convince himself. But he wasn't sure at all. All he knew was that he didn't know. "I didn't know what I was doing," Owen continued to Nick. "Still don't, but somehow I got Bee. How'd I get so lucky?"

"I don't know, man," Nick managed. "I don't. But this one's a keeper. An original."

A light bulb went off in Owen's head. "That's it!" Owen cried. "That's what's so hot about her. Beatrix Plumb. She's an original!" Then, he commended his buddy, "You always have been the chick whisperer."

Nick laughed. The feeling of admiration for his buddy was mutual—they could razz on each other and themselves endlessly and love every minute of it. This is why Nick loved his buddy, but right now, the fact that they were so chill and accepting of each other about Bee was killing him too. He gave Owen another hand-cast high-five.

"Oh, and hey...," Owen brightened. "I'm thinkin' of giving Bee the earrings at the game. What do you think?"

It was a punch to Nick's gut. And pride. And heart. But he hid it well. "Go for it," Nick said with the most fake support and integrity he could muster. "Water under the bridge, Dude. But just so you know, you already gave them to her once."

"To Bee?...atrix?"

"Yup," Nick confirmed.

"Darn. I thought so, like she had 'em on, right? At the party. But they're in my room. Did she give 'em back?" Owen worried.

Nick's heart pounded. He so wanted tell Owen the truth—that Bee was angry and hurt by something about Owen. And had given the earrings back out of anger. And that Nick knew that *he* was a better match for Bee than Owen was. And that *he* adored Bee. Even her stupid headband that Owen thought was a bandana and found cringey. And *he* adored Bee's weird dancing. But Nick didn't go there. Instead, he put his best friend Owen and his adorable Bee first and told Owen a little white lie, "She accidentally left them behind. The earrings. You're good."

Owen saw through this fib. Nick was lying. He knew it. He knew his buddy well...when he paid attention, that is. He didn't always pay attention because he got all swept up in things. That was something he had to work on. And right now, he felt guilty about the earrings. Clearly, there must've been some drama with Bee about the earrings. This peaked his interest. But mostly, he felt guilty about his buddy's feelings around the earrings because clearly the water was not yet under the bridge. And he felt like he had to fix it right then and there. "Okay man," Owen said. "I gotta tell you this thing. About Amy."

"Dude, over it," Nick insisted. "Don't want to know."

"I dumped Amy," Owen admitted. "She didn't dump me." He grinned sheepishly.

Nick couldn't believe it. "You stole Amy from me and dumped her when you knew how much I liked her?!!!"

"She wasn't into you!" Owen defended. "I was doing you a favor. C'mon, you're my best friend; I'm sorry, bro."

This was too much right now for Nick, but he tried to hold it together. He knew Owen meant it—that he had been doing his best to help Nick. "Give her the earrings, man," Nick said and stood up. "Give 'em to Bee. She's gonna look awesome in them. She does."

"Wait...," Owen said, not sure how to fix this or deal with it. He definitely was way too emo to function.

"You're good, bro," Nick told Owen and guy-cast-hugged him without causing pain.

This helped. Owen believed Nick.

And Nick walked off.

Owen watched him go and was totally relieved. Nick clearly meant it about letting it go with Amy and Bee. And Owen had told Nick his truth about Amy finally. And now, he was off the hook and was going to try really hard to do the right thing. Always. Even though he knew that was going to be super hard for him.

But maybe this Beatrix Plumb that everyone loved could help him. Shape him up. Make him a better man.

# 31 OWEN'S GOT A THING FOR BEE AND JADE GOES THUNDERBIRD-PURPLE BALLISTIC ON BEE AND THE SFB MOBILE

Bee spotted Demi in the high school halls right after school walking to practice. Demi tried to ditch her. It was obvious.

*Why is she doing this?* Bee wondered rhetorically, because she knew exactly why Demi was doing this. She picked up her pace and caught up to Demi near the football field and jumped in front of her to block her way.

"Hey, Bee!" Demi exclaimed as if she had no clue what this was about and was super happy to see Bee and was having the best cheer day ever. Then, Demi saw the fury on Bee's normally cute and positive face. "Wow! You okay?" Demi asked as if something were terribly wrong and weird about Bee, like putting something on her that wasn't there. Like kind of gaslighting her!

"He thinks he likes me! Owen thinks he likes me!" Bee shouted in a rage. "That I'm gonna save him!"

"Shh!" Demi scolded and moved Bee around to the side of the field where they'd be out of earshot and eyesight of any Lions, especially the team and cheer squad.

Which is when, suddenly, there was a loud screech of tires, and Demi and Bee saw Jade's purple Cabrio speed by.

"Crud," moaned Demi.

"Why didn't you tell him?!" Bee continued letting Demi have it about going over to Owen's. "He needs to know the truth! You said you'd tell him!"

"I'm waiting for the perfect moment," Demi replied with the most calm and normal voice, the picture of confidence and refinement that she was—

—while Bee looked and sounded insane. "It was this morning! You needed to tell him this morning! Before school! Or yesterday! When you visited him and totally manipulated him! Brainwashed him! While he's still feeling the meds! Or whatever's in his system!"

"You didn't even mention it when I texted you," Demi tried to manipulate Bee further. "Like, that was when you should've said this. I thought you were good with what I set up. Why didn't you say anything?"

Bee fumed in disbelief that Demi was going to such lengths for this and was good at it. She couldn't think clearly or calmly or cleverly and just continued to let Demi have it. "Because you didn't give me a choice! Without hurting everyone! And you're just...mean!" Bee cried, looking more and more crazy, even though she wasn't.

"Okay, let's take a moment here," Demi said, trying a different tactic. "Because what I see is that Owen likes you. The guy you've been in love with since kindergarten."

"It's not real!" Bee shouted. "He's delusional!"

"Are you kidding me?" Demi scoffed, gaslighting fully now and succeeding wildly because she tossed in a bit of general truth about dating. She really was good at this. "That's what guys do. If they like you, they go for it. If they don't, they don't. And Owen likes you. And I'm not sacrificing him or our win or you because you can't face reality."

Bee was totally taken aback, not sure what to do or say, leaning back as if trying to get away from Demi's aggressive presence and voice.

Demi knew she had Bee in her scheming clutches in that moment and felt a surge of adrenaline at the win. Then, she deviously but sweetly whispered, "And the way he kisses...amaaaazing." Nailing it home, she thought.

Bee just stared. The nerve Demi had!

"Go get him," Demi instructed and turned and walked off to cheer practice, feeling extra Lion pride. "Yes," she cheer-whispered to herself—

—as Bee watched Demi go, feeling really, really sick knowing that the ruse would have to continue. Even though she knew Demi was completely full of it.

And winning.

This fueled fire inside, as if Bee were going to go over to Owen's and blast a hole in the plan.

But then, she thought about what Demi said about dating, about guys going for it if they like you—something about that rang true for Bee and made her feel even more disheartened. Like she couldn't stand this anymore and had to head back over to Owen's after she drove everyone home in carpool and do something out of integrity, for once. And if Owen really liked her and that was integrity, well then... *I don't know*, she cried in her head.

***

Meanwhile, Jade was feeling equally enraged and desperately frustrated by this whole scenario and her inability to love Owen, and after she'd raced past the Lions' field, seeing Bee and Demi together, she'd made up her mind that she'd had enough.

She didn't care any more about Thunderbird pride, Owen's Lion pride or anything. All that mattered was her and Owen. And being together.

So, she made a reckless choice and headed straight for Owen's house. She'd made some pre-meditated cupcakes and she was going to bring them to Owen whether anyone saw or not.

Jade sat in her car a few houses down for a bit. She knew Mrs. Fleet would go pick up Claire from school since Claire usually carpooled with Owen pre-accident and his car being in the shop, and then, she'd have at least a half an hour.

And sure enough, Mrs. Fleet came out and drove off right at the expected school-pickup time, and Jade grabbed the cupcakes and discreetly snuck across the street to Owen's house and in the side gate.

She peered in the back sliding glass door and saw that Owen's hospital bed was empty.

And then, she heard laughing. It was Owen by the pool watching shows on his iPad. She snuck up behind him and shoved the wheelchair, which had the break on, so Owen lurched forward.

"Ahhhh," he cried in pain. "What the...?"

Jade whipped around the wheelchair and straddled him.

Owen yelled in even more pain.

Jade jumped up. "Omigosh, are you okay?" she eked out with worry.

"Yes, fine," Owen croaked, clearly not. "You are dangerous. And you look amazing." He checked Jade out in her purple Thunderbird cheer outfit with orange and white trim, a giant orange T and a super cool bird on her chest. "Amazing," Owen repeated in a whisper intended for himself but that was totally audible. He had a hard time keeping his feelings in normally, and now, it was worse.

Jade smiled. She knew Owen thought she was hot. And she knew he loved her. So, she climbed back on to straddle him, more gently this time, and moved in for a kiss.

But Owen instantly squeezed his lips shut and shook his head as soon as he saw her shiny purple lip-glossed lips heading towards him. "No," he peeped out, keeping his jaws clenched and moving his lips just enough for the sound to go out through his teeth so she could hear.

Jade stopped in disbelief, looking at his stupid clenched teeth. "No?!" she berated him.

"New girlfriend," Owen smiled, as if this were the most

normal news ever.

"What?!!!" Jade raged and pushed herself off him again.

Owen cried out in pain.

"I don't believe you," Jade said, her voice pulling back, confused, hurt, her desperation showing, unintentionally abandoning her usual tough-girl exterior.

"Bee," Owen told her, trying to sound certain but not feeling it. "Her name's Bee. Or Beatrix. With the x."

"Little Neighbor With The Car?!" Jade cried in disbelief. "The groupie?!"

"She's a Lion," Owen defended unconvincingly. "She's nice."

"Since when?" Jade demanded.

"Since now," Owen told her, still unconvincing in vibe but totally leaning into Demi's persuasive story. "Look at me. I need nice. And you just want to inflict pain."

Fury shot out of Jade's eyes, and she carefully but pointedly pulled the covered tray of homemade cupcakes out of her bag. Half were blue, green and gold Lion Pride cupcakes with lion heads on them. And the other half were dark purple, orange and white Thunderbird cupcakes with orange thunderbirds with light purple wings on them. She'd alternated the cupcakes in a pattern on the tray—Lion cupcake, Thunderbird cupcake, Lion cupcake, Thunderbird cupcake—all the way across five rows to cupcake-symbolically show an underlying friendship between the two teams, a reaching across the town of sorts.

But now, things had changed. And Jade's gesture felt like dirt to her. She grabbed a Lion cupcake, bit off the frosting head of the giant cat and shoved it in Owen's face, leaving a circle of blue and green across his nose and cheeks and part of his lips. "Try that for nice," Jade seethed at Owen as the rest of the cupcake fell to the ground. Then, Jade grabbed her bag and stormed off past the sliding glass door, not caring if anyone saw her, and out the side gate.

Owen licked the frosting off his face. "Yum!" he mused, trying to get more of the blue and green frosting circle bits off his face with his tongue and hoping someone would show up soon so he could have more.

****

Luckily, it wasn't long before Owen's mom came home from picking up Claire from middle school, and she and Claire came out to the pool area to enjoy the surprisingly warm day outside with Owen.

Owen was super glad that his mom and Claire hadn't showed up while Jade was still there. Jade would've been hard to explain. His mom would've been okay with it, but Claire probably would've picked up on any lie that he told about Jade. He totally remembered Jade and that they'd been dating secretly and that Claire always gave him a hard time about Jade and would scowl whenever she came over. Claire really was a pain, but she was smart too, and most of the time, he was glad to have her in his court.

Luckily, Claire let it lie when Owen told her and their mom that the cupcakes came from a friend named Dax at a different high school in the valley, the one closer to Glacier National Park, the Snow Cats. Owen said that Dax, the Snow Cat, was razzing on the Lions and the Thunderbirds because his own school was in a league for smaller high schools, and he loved to take the piss out of Owen. The friend part was true—Dax had been Owen's friend since elementary—so that part was buyable and probably helped the fake story insinuating that Dax had made the cupcakes.

Owen's mom picked up the fallen Lion cupcake bits and fed Owen two more. Owen found them to be super dee-lish. "Thanks, Mom," Owen beamed.

Claire rolled her eyes at her spoiled, corny brother and started doing dives mixed with cannonballs into the pool. Then, she and Owen began their usual thing whereby Owen would call out a dive for Claire to do and then rate her as if he were an Olympic judge. It was a Fleet custom that they'd been doing forever. Usually, Owen did the dives too and competed against Claire with their mom, dad or both acting as the

Olympic judges. Their mom had been a competitive diver in high school in Northern California and competed in college at Stanford. Their dad grew up outside of Chicago and had played water polo in high school and at UC Berkeley. Those weren't really sports up in Northwest Montana, but hence, the pool and the super competitive family vibes.

Coming up through elementary, Owen had always beaten Claire at the backyard diving competitions, but once Claire hit fourth grade, she got good and was now leagues better than he was. Claire also was leagues better on the slopes at downhill racing. In fact, she was on the junior Olympic team, while Owen just snowboarded for fun. Football was his jam, obviously, and he was amazingly talented. But he admired Claire for her own amazing athleticism and ballsy competitive nature. He was not only Lion proud but Fleet proud as well.

So, diving rounds began when Claire and Mrs. Fleet arrived home—

—and Bee could hear the splashes and cheers when she pulled up in front of their house and then came in the side gate and approached.

Claire stood on the diving board, and Owen called out, "Double front flip!"

Claire followed his request and did a one, two, three-step jump and double flip!

*Amazing*, thought Bee. This family was crazy amazing.

"Eight!" scored Owen. "Woot, woot!"

Bee watched from the side. She felt invisible because they hadn't noticed her yet and was reminded of her entire life except for being friends with Kate, who had noticed her from the get-go. But that was then, and Bee knew she had to move forward and be bold so she managed a meek, unsuccessful, "Hi."

As Bee waited uncomfortably to be noticed, she thought about how she was there at Owen's again because she didn't have a choice thanks to Demi's annoying demands, and now, seeing Claire just made everything worse. She knew Claire was onto her. Somehow, this all made her angry again and fueled another fire of ire inside. She'd had enough of Demi's scheming and was there to tell her truth, no matter how awful it would be. Her Junior Year Manifesto was all about being seen but it was more than just getting eyes on Beatrix Plumb's outsides. It was about people seeing what was in her heart. And the person she really was.

Bee stepped forward with a loud, sing-songy, confident, "Hello!"

"You're here!" Owen exclaimed, his face brightening instantly. "Come have a cupcake. Lions and uh..." He looked at the orange Thunderbirds with light purple wings on the dark purple cupcakes, searching for something, anything to explain away the thunderbirds because he doubted that she'd buy the Snow Cat friend-razzing scenario since she was all about Lion Pride it seemed. Owen scoured his memory for a bird name. Then, he got it. "...Toots the orange robin," he chimed, truly proud that he was on his memory game. *Bye, bye amnesia*, Owen cheered to himself.

Bee's brow furrowed, and she studied the orange birds, "Looks more like a barn swallow than a robin," she observed. "With the purple wings. I mean, they're technically blue but close enough. American robin wings are brown. But I guess it could also be a red-breasted Nuthatch or spotted Towhee with the white."

"Who are you?" Owen complimented. "You know everything."

Bee blushed, "I just...remember...from that class we had? In ninth? Environmental Science? We did those presentations on local birds?"

"Oh, right, right," lied Owen, having no clue that they ever even had a class together.

"Yeah, local birds. So cute," Bee chirped then saw his look of confusion and changed gears, trying to sound as chipper as possible. "So...who made them?"

"Them?" Owen waffled.

"The cupcakes," Bee clarified.

"Uh...," Owen panicked, looking to Claire for help.

Claire was now out of the water, dripping wet with her hand on her hip, glaring at Bee. Clearly, Claire saw through Owen's lie but went with it to defend her brother from this annoying fake called Bee. "He's a Snow Cat," Claire snarked at Bee. "You wouldn't know him. Dax is his name. Stop asking so many annoying questions. Can't you see my brother's still in a cast? Two casts?" Then, she ran and did a giant cannonball off the diving board.

"Woooo!" cheered Owen as Claire flew through the air—

—and splashed down into the water, spraying both Owen and Bee.

Owen laughed.

Bee screamed.

Which pleased Claire.

Which pissed off Bee all the more and gave her another burst of anger and courage, and she decided instantly that now was the time. She turned her back to Claire so Claire couldn't hear her and said, "Owen, I have to tell you something."

"No, I have to tell you something," Owen insisted with uncharacteristic earnestness—

—just as Mrs. Fleet came out of the house and over to the pool with a tray of lemonade. "Bee!" she exclaimed, so happy to see her.

Which instantly foiled Bee's plan to reveal her truth and rescue any modicum of pride she had left.

"We've been waiting for you," Mrs. Fleet gushed as she set down the tray with lemonade in fancy glasses on the poolside patio table with a huge smile and a sigh of relief. "You have no idea," Mrs. Fleet continued, voice cracking. Then, her face started to distort, the stress of the past few days since Owen's accident and return home breaking through her tough Fleet veneer. Yes, she was starting to lose it and suddenly lunged at Bee and hugged her way too tight.

"Mom!" Owen cried out, embarrassed by his mom's display of emotion. "Give me a chance here."

"Sorry!" Mrs. Fleet apologized to Bee, pulling away from the hug but clutching Bee's shoulders as if her life depended on it. "I'm just so relieved you're here. Why don't I get the jersey?" She nodded to Owen knowingly and headed inside.

Bee watched her go. *What the heck is going on now? Jersey?!* Bee wondered and turned to Owen. "We really need to talk," she told him as leader-like as she could, channeling Demi and taking charge to the best of her ability.

"Please hold my hand...," Owen pleaded, the desperation in his eyes masked by a smile. "...first." He wiggled his fingers at the end of one of his casted arms and turned up the charm.

*Oh, gosh*, Bee thought, her plan instantly derailed again. She forced a smile and took his hand.

"I'm sorry I can't remember us," Owen told her. "But it doesn't matter. And I am so nervous right now. You do that to me. It's weird." He laughed at himself and shook his head, surprised by this revelation.

Bee turned bright red.

"But that's okay," Owen said, oblivious to her embarrassment. "Even if I never remember you. I want to get to know you. And commit to you. And I want you to be my girlfriend."

"But you're in love with Jade!" flew out of Bee's mouth, and she pulled out the Gurlple love poem Owen had written for Jade. And she put it in his hand—as it stuck out of the end of one of his angle-casted arms.

Owen gasped when he saw his handwriting on the poem, emotion suddenly overtaking him. And he began to read. "Gurlple," he said and giggled. "Gurlple, gurlple," he repeated playfully and laughed.

But Bee wasn't laughing.

"No, I mean...," Owen backpedaled, "yeah, Jade's hot. And vicious. In a hot way. But, yeah, no, not when I look at you..."

He looked up at Bee. Checked out her hair. And her weird hippy-flower headband. And then her eyes. Their eyes met. And more desperation escaped from Owen's eyes as he tried to hold onto Demi's words about how awesome Bee was and would be for him—even though he wasn't feeling it.

"But she really loves you!" Bee cried about Jade. "Your

Gurlple."

*There, that's it*, Owen thought. *Feisty. Combined with smarter than me.* And suddenly, he felt *something*. And he got it. And he knew this was real, like Demi had said. And it was good for him. And he knew that was important. "And I might love you," he blurted out.

"Omigosh, no," groaned Claire, and she did another cannonball to escape this yuckiness, splashing them both again.

Owen laughed, and Bee squeezed her fists, clenching her teeth in a tortured smile. This really wasn't working out.

And then, a beaming Mrs. Fleet rounded the corner again, coming into sight as she approached the pool with Owen's football jersey. "Got it!" she chimed. "All fresh and clean." She made a beeline for Bee, scrunching the football jersey from the bottom up to the neck and putting it right over Bee's head.

Bee looked down at the green jersey and paled.

"C'mon, arm in," Mrs. Fleet instructed as she held one jersey arm out so Bee could put her arm through.

Bee did.

"And the other," Mrs. Fleet instructed with a smile.

Bee obliged again and her shoulders slumped to match her frowny face.

"What a tool," Claire muttered under her breath about Bee and did another cannonball.

This one drenched Bee, who frowned more, and sprayed Owen and Mrs. Fleet, who laughed with glee like little kids.

Owen beamed at Bee who forced a smile and faked a chortle.

"I want you to have it, the jersey," Owen told Bee, his eyes no longer desperate. Now, he was happy, and his mojo was returning just seeing this Bee girl that everyone loved in his jersey. "...so everyone knows you're my girl."

*Omigosh*, Bee cried to herself just as her phone buzzed. It was a text from her mom in all caps, like a rude barky shout: *I NEED U TO DRIVE PAIGE 2 BALLET.* And for the first time ever, Bee couldn't have been happier about her annoying mom and sister and their constant carpool-driving demands.

Bee laughed nervously, relieved to have an out. "You know what? I have to help my mom. But I'll be back...soon," Bee told the Fleets then grinned, did a stupid wave and bolted off in the jersey, pulling her arms out as she exited the side gate and hurried round to the car.

Bee fumbled with her keys, heart racing as she unlocked the door and got in, slamming it shut—then feeling the relief of sitting there in the quiet, warm Strawberry Firecracker Bomb Mobile.

Because everything that happened—especially NOT telling her truth again—was not what she'd intended when she'd gone over to Owen's. She'd just wanted to be herself. Say her truth. And now it was worse because Owen loved her. And Demi was right.

Bee took some deep breaths and calmed down. "I'm here. In the present. In Nana's car...that's now my car on loan. Nana Jana who loves me. And it's warm. And I'm okay," she told herself.

Bee nodded for extra assurance. This positive thinking was working—

—until suddenly, coming out of nowhere, like she often did, Jade dove on the hood of the car, eyes piercing daggers at Bee, her grin menacing, a can of purple spray paint clutched in her hand. "Two seconds," Jade shouted through the windshield. "Owen'll be over you in two seconds. Why? Because he can have someone hot like me, and people date their equals. Owen is hot. I'm hot. Do the math, Math Wench."

Then, Jade jumped up on the hood of the Strawberry Firecracker Bomb Mobile and spray painted, in purple, the words "MATH WENCH" in all caps. Then, she stomped her heel twice on the hood, jumped off onto the street and ran away—

—leaving Bee in shock.

# 32 NICK STICKS BEE IN THE FRIEND ZONE

Bee's heart was heavy, but she was determined to get through this ordeal with Owen—at least until the team beat the Thunderbirds. And she was determined to get the graffiti off her Nana Jana's precious and prized SFB Mobile. Even though it was technically hers to drive, it felt like an affront to Nana Jana and Papa Robbie.

Bee looked up what to do to get spray paint off a car and started with soapy water and a sponge and nail polish remover, the non-acetone kind. That was the easiest of the recommendations she'd found. If that didn't work fully, she'd go to the auto parts store and try the thing that video on Google or TikTok, or whatever that was, recommended next—which was called "rubbing compound."

But after ten minutes, removing the spray paint was going well with the soapy water. She'd gotten off the W and e in Wench. And at least, Jade's heel stomps hadn't dented the SFB hood.

Bee was parked down the street from her house because she couldn't cope with anyone in her family seeing this ugly graffiti affront. Or Kate for that matter. Bee felt like she was failing all around. Except her song. Her song was good, and she kept singing it over and over, "Blood-pact sisters; Pride in the differences; Doin' our best to just keep it real," as she rubbed the sponge up or down to each word and beat.

Bee was also making up new lyrics for the moment: "I hate myself; and I hate me; how am I just supposed to be; Beatrix Plumb is my name; but I'm losing my truth to this fake girlfriend game."

Bee stopped to look at the hood again: N gone. "Hooray," she cheer-whispered to herself, just as she heard the wheels of a skateboard. *Uh, oh*, she thought.

And sure enough, it was Nick on his longboard with a big smile on his face. Like he truly was so happy to see the real her. "Appalachia," he called out in his amused, teasy friend voice. "Wow, look at you, all jersied up and..." He took in the purple graffiti, trying to make out the second word. "...proud to be...smart? Math...ch?"

His happy eyes met Bee's.

"Don't ask," Bee quickly told him and looked back at the hood to avoid...anything.

"How can I not ask?" Nick toyed.

Bee did a little vicious big cat "rrrraarrr."

Nick chuckled.

They look at each other again—way too attracted. Both thinking, *This stinks!*

Luckily—or maybe not so much—Nick rallied. "Yeah, so I came to bring you these," he said and pulled out a wrapped gift for Bee, like actually wrapped in red wrapping paper with white polka dots and a pink bow on top. It was the shape of a thick piece of folded paper or an envelope.

*Weird*, Bee thought as she took the gift, looking at Nick's hands up close—she liked his hands. They were strong and he moved them deftly, with expression every time. Bee felt her heart start to race in anticipation of yet another new thing.

"My dad suggested I wrap it," Nick let her know. "You know. Had to go buy some wrapping paper."

*Still weird*, Bee thought and unwrapped the gift, careful not to tear the cute paper. She was a wrapping-paper and bow re-user, and she'd definitely find something fun to do with this cute paper. Inside was a sealed, plain-white letter envelope.

Bee glanced quickly at Nick who was watching her closely with a shy, sweet look on his face.

Then, she opened the envelope and found two concert tickets of some sort inside. She pulled them out.

"Bluegrass and fiddle fest," Nick informed her before she could read what it said on the tickets.

Bee's face brightened. "Wow. That is so awesome!" She looked up.

"With Appalachian flatfooting," Nick said, voice cracking at the sight of her joy and the smile he adored and her sparkling eyes, trying to hold in his feelings for her.

Bee was completely moved. "I can't believe...I mean, I love that you know that." Her heart swelled as she looked at Nick who was still smiling bashfully at her. *And is he blushing?* Bee wondered. *He is! Is he?* She wasn't sure.

"Yeah, you and Owen'll have a blast," Nick managed.

*What?* "Me and Owen?" Bee croaked.

"Yeah," Nick said, recovering from all the emo-ness and playing it off perfectly with a teasy smile. "He'll, um...I'm sure you'll get the wheelchair in there somehow." Then, he laughed at the thought and smiled warmly. But still there was a pained heart behind that smile.

Bee was too disappointed to notice the disappointment in Nick and couldn't hide her own. "You don't want to go?" she asked.

"Nah, I'll go another time," he chimed as if unfazed, but then he saw her sadness and felt awful. "It's not totally my thing anyway," he covered. "I mean, I'd rather play than watch."

Bee wanted to disappear but covered her feelings too. "Right, right, no, of course not," she smiled.

"But hey, I talked to my dad, and he's gonna play Vinny instead of me Friday. So, after the game, I might make open mic, without guilt." Nick was so happy to tell Bee this. If anyone would understand, he knew it'd be Bee.

But Bee couldn't get past this Owen-ticket blow. Why would Nick buy tickets for her and Owen when music was their special thing? And songwriting?! And he knew Owen didn't even like bluegrass! Bee did everything in her power to muster a smile and act happy for him about the open mic. "Wow. That's so...good," she chimed.

"Thanks to you. Keepin' it real," he grinned.

Bee frowned, knowing she'd just blown her own chance of being truthful out of the water without hope of recovery.

"Okay, well," Nick finally said nervously, unsure why she was *this* disappointed. "I'll see you on the field. For one last...win for Owen!" He made a "rah" fist and started to go, thinking, *This can't be.*

"Nick!" Bee called after him.

Nick stopped.

"Since you're Owen's friend...and mine...do you think he's the right guy for me? I mean, since we're so different?" she asked.

"Uh...," Nick said and thought about it. He couldn't tell her the truth so he just reassured her. "Yeah, Owen's the best guy in the world. And you guys'll be...amazing, Dude..." Then, Nick guy-punched Bee and skated off.

And Bee watched him go, feeling instantly hopeless, as if she'd been punched in the gut. "Dude," she repeated, as if it were the worst moniker in the world.

# 33 BEE AND KATE GET SOLID AGAIN AND BEE GOES FOR IT WITH OWEN

Bee spent a couple more hours cleaning the purple MATH WENCH graffiti off the Strawberry Firecracker Bomb Mobile, getting most of it off but knowing she'd have to do another pass, maybe with that cleaner from the auto parts store. And if that didn't fully work, she'd have to bring the SFB to some kind of professional painter or body shop. There's no chance she could leave any bit of it on her nana's car. Ultimately, she knew her Nana Jana wouldn't actually be upset. Even if she pretended to be, she'd secretly love the drama and all the romantic notions behind this whole disaster, but Bee wasn't going to tell Nana Jana this melodramatic mishap tale if she could help it.

Bee parked in front of the house kitty corner and across the street from her house to avoid Diego and his curious eyes and camera—especially in case he noticed the remnants of the dreaded embarrassment on the hood and made a big deal out of it.

Kate and Torian were on the lawn as usual, and this time, Bee knew what she had to do. She had to talk to Kate in spite of Torian. Bee felt miserable about lying to Nick and hopeless about finding a solution and knew that Kate was her only way to feeling better in this moment.

She moped over from her car and said nothing when Kate chimed, "Hey, Buddy." Instead, Bee just sat down on the lawn next to Kate on her left side while Torian was on her right.

"What's up?" Kate asked.

Bee shook her head "nothing," then solemnly stared out at Diego across the street working on his Beatrix Plumb installation. She tried to hold in the tears that were rising uncontrollably. *Maybe this was a bad idea*, Bee thought to herself.

But Kate sensed something was up and made "go" eyes at Torian.

Torian hesitated.

"Go!" Kate whisper-yelled, so Torian got up and walked across the street to his old blue Subaru parked in front of the house next to the Plumbs'. He got in and turned on his music—some kind of classical symphony boomed out and ended quickly. Then, he skipped to the next song on his playlist and an opera soprano voice boomed out. They literally could hear it across the street.

"So weird," Bee muttered under her breath about Torian's choice of music.

"My weird," Kate quipped with a smile, knowing exactly what Bee meant.

"You hate classical music," Bee reminded her.

"Opera, I hate opera," Kate corrected Bee playfully.

"This is opera," Bee pointed out.

"And opera is considered classical, so you're partially right," Kate smiled. "But I do like Shostakovich and Beethoven and Schubert, somewhat, which are also classical, but that other kind."

Bee laughed, "True," and then her brow furrowed, and she dropped her head on Kate's shoulder, feeling so vulnerable and miserable.

"I miss you," Kate said.

"No, you don't," Bee razzed.

"I do," Kate defended. "I know I've been distracted. But these boyfriends, they're just like a bonus. 'Cuz you're the best friend ever."

"Stop patronizing me," Bee scoffed.

"See, and you're totally putting it out there. Like you pledged to do in your JYM. You're putting out there exactly who you are. Saying it like it is. So *you* can like *you*. And I love that about you."

Bee groaned. "I'm living a lie, and Nick's not into me."

"He said that?" Kate was truly surprised.

"Basically."

"Well, at least you're honest with me, and I'll repeat: saying it like it is," Kate stated in all earnestness. "I'm serious."

"Too bad I can't date you," Bee joked.

They both laughed.

"It's just so embarrassing," Bee said, the tough-girl shield around her heart crumbling.

"What is?" Kate pressed the issue in true Kate matter-of-factly awesome form. "That you care about stuff and try too hard? It's the best thing about you. And the right guy is gonna find you."

"Nick was the right guy," Bee groaned. "He totally gets me. He even loves poetry. He just doesn't love me."

"Another right guy," Kate told Bee as if this were the most obvious truth.

Torian waved from inside his car across the street.

Kate sternly gestured to him to "stay put," mouthing the words like a boss, then repeated them in a barely audible whisper-yell, "Stay put!"

Bee chuckled.

Torian deflated.

Kate smiled at Bee.

Bee's heart swelled.

And that's when Bee got it—that she and Kate were solid friends still: *Yes, that's it. Kate and I are solid. But it's not black and white. She loves Torian Borian, and I have to accept it. That's just who Kate is.* And Bee sat there with this truth, feeling relief come over her while they both watched Diego doing his thing and Torian singing opera in his car. And the friends were amused, just like old times. And Bee's heart opened all the way—*finally*.

Which is when Torian glanced over at Kate and Bee, for the millionth annoying time, and Bee muttered, "Okay, fine," and gestured for him to "come back over" to Kate's lawn with a giant wave and yelled, "Come. Over!"

Kate laughed. "Oh, she softens."

Bee gestured harder. "Just this once."

And Torian got Bee's gesture the second time—*thank goodness*—and walked over to them sitting on the lawn. He beamed at Kate, blinded by love for her. And then, he just stood there like an idiot and Kate shot "not now" eye daggers at him, meaning "do not sit down or attempt to show any affection towards me at this moment." So, Torian turned to look at Diego as if he weren't cheering inside about at least being near Kate again, and he shoved his hands in his pockets in an attempt to look nonchalant and heaved a sigh of relief.

Which is when Kate hugged Bee.

And Torian grinned, truly happy for his girlfriend to be connecting with her best friend.

And Bee could see that their love was real even though Torian Borian was still the most annoying person ever, because yes, he did seem to care about Kate and her feelings, and he did seem to see Kate's true self.

"And that's when I knew I had to get real about me, like *really real*, like stop-feeling-sorry-for-myself real," Bee narrated in that moment and then over and over in her head for the rest of the day and then to Cardboard Owen that night and the next morning, thinking back about her lawn moment with Kate as she stood in her room in front of the mirror in Owen's jersey and Lion cheer skirt psyching herself up. "*Real, real, real.* Which means accepting that the only guy who ever got me—Nick Wells, musician and kicker extraordinaire and all-around nice guy and hot too—isn't gonna stop me from being with Owen," Bee continued. "Not when he called me Dude or bought tickets for me and Owen to go to a bluegrass concert without him, right?" Bee looked at Cardboard Owen for an answer. He didn't give her one.

"In fact, Nick is practically throwing us together, because he isn't into me," Bee declared, narrating as she went outside and then drove over to Owen's house. She didn't know what she was going to do, but she was going anyway, even if she was going to miss first period.

It took a moment of sitting in the car outside and doing some extra psyching-up to get herself to get out and go for it, but she did, slamming the SFB Mobile car door shut with force to rouse up more of her I-can-do-this mojo and bounding across the street, head held high, and in the side gate. Her stomach lurched but she continued on, approaching Owen, who was outside by the pool again even though it was morning. And he was feeling so much better and more energized.

Owen beamed when he saw Bee in his jersey and called out with his booming voice, "Beee-a-trix with an x!"—as if he were really, really into her now.

"Like Demi said—Owen's into me," Bee told herself as she walked over with a smile plastered on her face. "And since that's what I always wanted, I have to give it a chance. I mean, what do I have to lose?"

And so, Bee gave being with Owen a chance. She marched up to him at the pool as if she were his girlfriend and it was the most normal thing ever. She scratched his back with the back scratcher, came back soon after lunch because it was early-out Wednesday and just hung out with Owen watching *The Three Stooges Show* and *South Park* on his iPad. Bee even judged a few of Claire's dives when Claire got home from early-out Wednesday too.

Bee got a little bored, especially with *The Three Stooges Show*, but overall, she felt as if this first day was going incredibly well. Wearing Owen's football jersey to school that day really was showing the world how much Owen meant to her and how much she meant to Owen. "JYM! JYM!" she cheered in her head every hour, at least, throughout the day. Sometimes Bee had to chant to herself every five minutes when her mind started to wander—to Nick, which started as soon as Bee saw him in the halls at school that day and he waved and smiled.

*Gah*, Bee cried in her head and moved on.

Then, Bee's attention went to Nick again—*but worse*—when she went to practice with Owen that early-out afternoon after watching *South Park* and judging a few of Claire's dives. Owen was feeling much better and Mrs. Fleet had hired that van to drive Owen around until he got out of the wheelchair. Once they were dropped off at school, Bee pushed Owen in his wheelchair and hung out with him and Coach Wells on the sidelines, listening closely while they talked football—which is when Bee became so hyper aware of the fact that Nick wasn't there because he'd quit football, and Cardboard Owen wasn't there either because now the real Owen was. And all Bee could think about was how the week before she and Nick and Cardboard Owen were cheering on the team together—and how good she'd felt inside.

"JYM! JYM!" Bee shouted in her head and turned her focus back to Owen and Coach Wells who were now coaching Reno, who was super eager and nervous with the real Owen there. "And Reno is like a baby giraffe," Bee joked in her head in an attempt to focus on the present and not the past with Nick. "While Owen and Coach Wells are totally in the zone."

Which is when Owen smiled at Bee like he was also totally mesmerized by her and it made her think of Nick again for no reason at all and she shouted in her head, "JYM! JYM!"—in hopes that her Nick-overwhelm would subside.

And it did, momentarily, thanks to her JYM chanting, so she invited Owen over to her house to attempt to bring him into her world. And the van driver took them from practice to Bee's, and Bee introduced Owen to Diego. And Owen and Diego stupidly hit it off. *Like crazy. I mean, how stupidly crazy is that? And annoying*, Bee thought as she watched Owen take in Diego's Beatrix Plumb lawn installation while Diego explained each part and then watched Owen tell a story too, totally animated—he really was a good storyteller. Owen even brought Bee into the conversation like the perfect boyfriend when he noticed she wasn't really paying attention. After all, Owen was an attention junkie and needed Bee to be watching his every move.

Which is when Bee's eyes wandered again and noticed *that one photo* hanging in the orbit of the sun that Nick had taken of her standing inside the house that day right before they went jumping into the freezing cold lake like idiots and had so much fun. And Bee's mind wandered—against her will—to that moment when Nick had taken the photo because Nick had made her laugh and teased her and her heart had opened and she'd laughed. And Bee remembered Nick teasing Diego too and Nick seeing the real Bee without trying and how that had made her feel so good and like herself and like the real Bee. And how she felt that way now too just thinking about it.

Which is what Bee was thinking when Owen and Diego laughed on the lawn by the installation—at who knows what— and Bee laughed too as if she knew what they were talking about. And Bee tried to forget about Nick and luckily spied Kate on her lawn, and Kate waved and did the JYM three-beat fist pump—*JYM! JYM! JYM!*—and Bee bucked it up, exhaled and kept going, throwing thoughts of Nick to the wolves. *Or maybe the Lions*, Bee thought, amusing herself and imagining the Lions taking Nick in and being nice to him, which was a good thought and allowed her to "put Nick away" in her heart, like in a friendly lions' den lockbox.

And that worked for Bee.

And blocking out thoughts of Nick continued going really well the next afternoon, the day before the big game, when Bee went with Owen in the van to visit Granny Fleet with another huckleberry pie made by Mrs. Fleet, and Granny Fleet wasn't even mean to Bee. She wasn't nice either, but Bee noticed how nice Owen and Granny Fleet were to each other—like they really loved each other's company. And Owen told tons of stories, and they ate pie and Granny Fleet looked with adoring eyes at her grandson and was happy even if there was no walking outside or uphill wheelchair racing since both Owen and Granny Fleet were in wheelchairs, and Bee couldn't possibly push them both at the same time.

And forgetting Nick continued going really well until Bee noticed the framed photo of Granny Fleet and Owen next to his suped-up blue Mustang, which reminded Bee of that day when she was there with Nick and narrowly diverted him and Granny Fleet from seeing Jade in the tree.

Bee forced herself to turn away from the photo and the memory of Nick and instead focus on listening to Granny Fleet and Owen's conversation. Granny Fleet was retelling a tale of downhill skiing in the Olympics—*maybe that's where Claire gets it from*, Bee thought—but Bee's eyes quickly wandered over to the window and her mind wandered back to the memories of Nick that day when he saved her when Granny Fleet flew out of the wheelchair and how she'd left him on the side of the road and how he'd taken her cliff jumping and how he gave her a song to write lyrics to and how Bee felt when she was with Nick and how he was so nice and hot and funny.

Which is what Bee was thinking about when she rallied and doubled down on her "JYM!" chanting and remembering that Nick had called her "Dude" and clearly wasn't into her.

Bee kept doubling down later that night when she went with Owen to the pre-game Lions vs. Thunderbirds party at cheerleader Chrissie's house. Bee also reminded herself that she really was helping the team—that being Owen's girlfriend *was* the ticket to their win and that she had been helping them all along, even when she and Nick were friends.

Bee was wearing Owen's jersey over her favorite cute yellow-on-green flowery dress that she loved because it had been a gift from her Aunt Becky the past summer when she'd visited her in Tennessee and had done a lot of flatfoot dancing. The dress felt like good luck because of that. Bee figured the good luck would carry over to help the team win the next night and help her get out of this mess without hurting anyone in the end, namely Nick—*And maybe it'll help me like Owen again*, she cried in her head as she sat with Owen, Demi and Glenn poolside at the pre-game-night BBQ.

Which is when Drew-ster and a bunch of guys from the

team picked up Reno and carried him over to the pool, which was steaming. Reno squirmed and shouted for his teammates not to dunk him. The pool had to be cold, even if the water was warmer than the air. It probably was much colder out, and in, than the day before when Claire had been diving in the Fleets' pool. *Though Claire probably would dive in if it was freezing out and the water was frozen*, Bee thought.

In spite of Reno's pleas, the team was relentless with their pre-game good-luck ritual and launched Reno into the water. And that's when Bee knew the Lions would win. They had so much spirit. And Bee being Owen's girlfriend was helping like it was supposed to, especially since Owen believed it. *How could he believe it?* she wondered and told herself to give herself more credit.

And as Reno surfaced and cried out like a cold and skinny giraffe and barreled out of the water and into the house, Owen beamed at Bee, eyes flashing. *So hot. And charming. He really is cute*, Bee thought. And she was reminded why she had always been crushing on him. And Demi hugged Bee. And then, Bee looked over at Nick chatting with some guys and felt so jealous that she couldn't be over there or flirting with him.

And Reno came outside again with cheerleader Chrissie's dad, who had given him a warm change of clothes, and everyone chanted, "Reno! Reno! Reno!"

"Yup, that's when I knew. The Lions would win, and I would break inside. And it was all Nick's fault. And my stupid romantic heart," Bee cried to herself in full force in her head to an imaginary audience. Because she had to get out of reality in that moment and that was the only way she could cope.

# 34 THE BIG LIONS VS. THUNDERBIRDS GAME

Bee's narration to herself continued Friday night at the big game. "Broken is how I felt inside as I sat on the sidelines under the Friday night lights in the stadium for the big game, and I wasn't sure how to put myself back together," Bee recounted to the imaginary audience in her head as she stood next to Owen on the field between the team and cheer squad. "I probably was looking great on the outside. At least, Owen thought so. Which was good I suppose."

"Reno! Reno! Reno!" shouted the entire crowd on the Lions' side of the bleachers.

Bee looked down past the entire team bench to the opposite end—where Nick was standing and shouting and cheering—and she wished she could be near him. A huge banner waved behind them out to the crowd: "FLEET/RENO 2 BEAT THUNDERBIRDS 4 CHAMPIONSHIP!" It was right by the scoreboard where the clock ticked towards halftime. The game was heated and tied with a score of: LIONS 7, THUNDERBIRDS 7.

"Let's do it, Reno!" Owen boomed out.

"Beat them Thunderbird pansies!" Demi cheered, beating out each syllable with her pompom and riling up the Lions.

"Pan-sies!" everyone called out in reply.

Then, play began. The ball was hiked to Reno. He moved back, looked around and made an amazing throw to Glenn, who took off, racing towards the end zone, doing everything to make it happen before he got tackled right before the buzzer sounded for halftime.

They didn't make the touchdown, but the Lions went nuts anyway. It just felt like they were sure to win.

Owen beamed at Bee, "We're on."

Bee forced a smile, "Yup," and started to push Owen in his wheelchair over the grass towards the ramp leading up onto the halftime "stage." Nick saw Bee struggling in the grass and jumped in to help. Bee's heart fluttered, and her palms started to sweat as she followed Nick pushing Owen onto the stage.

Kate and Torian, who hadn't bailed on Entertainment Club like Bee had during this whole fiasco, were doing sound and lights for the halftime show. Kate smiled and nodded at Bee, and Torian gave her a shy, awkward wave. *What a nerd*, Bee thought about Torian but also thought that at least he was trying and, *He's just who he is.*

Then, Bee's heart started pounding through her chest as they neared the center of the stage. "And I should feel better or grounded with Kate here on my side, but this time I don't. *Why? Why? Why?*" Bee cried to herself. The last time she and Kate had been manning lights at the talent show, just the thought of Kate being there had given Bee courage. Until Kate wasn't there. "But this time, she's a hundred percent here and so is her stupid boyfriend! Take in the love, Bee! Take it in!" Bee insisted to herself.

Which is when she turned away from them, and Nick did a funny little bow to Bee, gesturing for her to take her place next to Owen and his wheelchair as he stepped back and away— out of the spotlight.

Coach Wells came up on the stage and took the mic. "Welcome, Thunderbirds, Lions, to our halftime show," his voice boomed out over the field and bleachers.

Wild cheers filled the stadium.

Coach Wells gestured to Bee, who had no clue what to do, so Nick stepped up again and pushed Owen a couple feet forward on the platform stage to the mic and Coach Wells.

Coach Wells smiled and nodded "thanks" to Nick then gestured for Bee to step up next to Owen.

*Omigosh*, Bee cried to herself and shook her head *no*, preferring to stay a bit back and off to the side.

Coach Wells wasn't thrilled with Bee staying back, immediately dreading any possible issue arising from Owen drama like it always did, but he smiled out at the crowd as if all were well and began, "Before we start with our main act...Paige Plumb..." He gestured over to Paige waiting on the side of the stage.

Paige beamed and jump-clapped for herself, grinning at Bee as if Bee would be pleased for her younger sister too, rather than annoyed like she always was.

"...let's welcome back our star player and team captain, Owen Fleet!" Coach Wells finished his introduction.

Cheers and applause rang out.

Coach Wells held the mic out for Owen.

"Go Lions!" Owen boomed into the mic in response to the crowd.

The crowd echoed him, "Go! Lions!"

"It's great to be back, and there's one Lioness in particular that I'd like to give a shout out to," Owen continued and shot Bee a hot, charmed smile. "Bee Plumb!" he boomed. "C'mon over, Bee. I have something for you. For saving me. And the team."

*Oh, no*, Bee panicked. *No, no, no.*

"Yes, you," Owen insisted. "Come here."

Bee's cheeks flushed with utter embarrassment and her heart pounded louder than it ever had before. She was frozen.

"C'mon," Owen encouraged. "You're good."

So, Bee stepped forward—up to Owen's wheelchair.

Coach Wells handed Bee the mic and then a little gift box.

"What...what's this?" Bee stuttered about the box. It looked like a ring box, which was terribly worrisome.

"It's from me," Owen boasted with a gleaming smile.

Coach Wells confirmed this with a nod and a smirk. They'd been planning this whole gift surprise, and he was super happy they were pulling it off because Bee looked so surprised.

"Open it," Owen encouraged Bee, beaming as if he were about to lift off.

*Crud*, thought Bee. *Someone save me.* And she opened the little box, and there inside were the blue Italian glass earrings, the deep blue glass glistening in the spotlight.

"Blue Italian glass earrings," Coach Wells informed the crowd even though he was wondering why Owen was giving Bee the earrings that she had already been wearing that day in the hospital.

Bee paled.

Nick paled.

And Owen beamed with pride. "Go ahead, put them on," he told Bee.

Bee's head and heart spun in a million different directions. She felt like she was having an out-of-body experience, as if she were floating above herself in her fantasy mind and she could see herself standing on that makeshift stadium halftime stage below. Luckily, finally, slowly, the crazy spinning came to a halt, and from above herself in her mind, Bee could see herself, the real Beatrix Plumb, shining like a beacon. "And that's when I knew that Bee plus Owen *really* wasn't adding up to me being true to myself," Bee began to narrate to herself with truth, trying to stay focused on that stage. "Even if Nick doesn't love me, I have to love myself. And be me. Super corny, but still."

Bee came back down to earth and turned to Owen. "I can't take these earrings. I'm sorry," she told him.

The microphone picked up her voice so everyone in the stadium heard her words and her rejection of Owen's gift.

"What...?" Owen managed, totally confounded.

Gasps rang out from everyone in the Lions' bleachers—the

team, the cheer squad, literally everyone except Kate, who cheered.

"I'm not your girlfriend," Bee confessed to Owen and into the mic so everyone could hear—she had to get it out and they had to know. "And I never was. The only reason I was there that morning to stop the bees from the bush from attacking you was because I showed up at your house at 7:00 a.m. so I could give you a ride to school so you'd notice me and like me. You were running away from me outside at 7:00 a.m. in the morning because you spotted me in my car trying to cunningly trick you into being in my carpool because I thought I was in love with you."

"I remember that!" Owen called out with glee for the whole stadium to hear. "I remember trying to run away from you and hide!"

"Yup, no amnesia," Bee confirmed. "No girlfriend named Beatrix." Which is when Bee looked back and over at Nick— who was standing there in total shock.

"No amnesia!" Owen cheered. "You're amazing! Beatrix with an x!"

"So, you faked the whole thing?" Nick blurted out at Bee.

Bee ignored Nick—using every bit of strength she had to do so—and continued smiling at Owen, validating his optimism about her and his situation. "More like fake amazing," she told him.

"So, what *is* real, Bee?!" Nick demanded from behind her, not letting it lie. This was too much. Too painful. He couldn't believe this was happening.

"She is! Bee is real!" Owen yelled back at Nick, turning his head, smiling at his best friend, not at all getting anything that was going on, let alone Nick's feelings. "Bee is real! An original. You said it." Owen looked at Nick, like—*don't you get it?!*

There were gasps in the stadium. And then silence as the crowd waited to see what would happen next in the drama unfolding before them on the stage.

But there were no reactions up there at first. All that was happening was awkwardness emanating from Bee—and feelings of pride, awesomeness and joy coming from Owen's entire being.

Bee turned to see Nick's reaction. He looked so betrayed, so upset. Her heart squeezed.

And that's when Bee took charge. She couldn't let Nick sit in the not knowing. She couldn't do that to the guy she loved. Or to herself. Or to Kate cheering in the wings.

Bee stepped forward to the microphone as if she were the main halftime show entertainment about to belt out a number.

And suddenly, sparks of restless halftime energy shot through the stadium like a flash. Excitement. Like something even bigger than the drama was happening on the stage now and it was about to get better, and everyone could feel it.

Bee took a deep breath and moved the microphone forward so that she was standing right in front of Coach Wells and Owen.

Paige called out from the side of the stage with glee, "Now?! Do I go on now?!" She couldn't wait to get out there and do her performance.

"No!" Kate and Torian shot Paige down—

—just as Bee looked out over the Lion crowd and the players and cheer squad and coaches and at the Thunderbirds' side too—their crowd and team. She even looked right at the Thunderbirds' cheer squad where she knew Jade was hating on her in that moment, planning revenge because her own heart was breaking with love for Owen.

And everyone was silent, waiting for Bee to begin.

Again, things went into slow motion for Bee, but instead of being outside of herself looking down as if she were in some kind of weird, fantasy-warrior, guardian-angel-type fantasy that she was narrating, she felt heat and power and love rising up from her heart and then spreading out into her whole body as if she were a light power beacon.

Bee took another breath, told herself, *Go, now*, and started singing and flatfooting, alternating lyrics with beats of her tapping feet—

"Hello my name is Bee Plumb; Right now I feel really

dumb," she began, then flatfooted out the matching beats: tap, tap, tap, tap, tap, tap, tap, tap, tap, tap, tap, tap, tap, tap. "I always loved Owen Fleet; because I found him really neat." Tap, tap, tap, tap, tap, tap, tap, tap, tap, tap, tap, tap, tap, tap, tap. "His charm can slay any girl; and his killer arm can really hurl." Tap, tap, tap, tap, tap, tap, tap, tap, tap, tap, tap, tap, tap, tap, tap, tap. "So when you thought I was his girlfriend; I swore to be her till the end. " Tap, tap, tap, tap, tap, tap, tap, tap. "Till the championship was done and won; I tried to be his fake hun. And then I met his friend Nick Wells; who made me feel kinda swell..."

Bee faltered, feeling Nick behind her even though she couldn't see him, but then she pushed through with more flatfoot taps, then continued the lyrics, "And being real through thick and thin; was the only way I'd ever fit in. With him."

Bee stopped—then looked at Nick, who was still obviously pissed, hurt and all kinds of things.

Silence. From Nick. From Bee. From everyone.

No one knew what to do or say—

—until Owen stated the obvious, without qualm or hesitation and broke the silence, "That was...weird."

Nervous laughter rang out.

"It was amazing!" Kate cheered with her most booming voice from the side of the stage and shook the lights as if they were a blast of fireworks applause.

"And amazing!" Owen agreed.

Which gave the crowd permission to cheer.

And Bee felt a momentary surge of love and joy.

Until Nick turned and walked away.

And Bee's heart sank to the depths of epic sadness and failure.

While Owen thought it was the exact opposite, beaming up at Bee with love and awe. "You are amazing, Beatrix Plumb," he declared.

And Bee took note that Owen had never even known her actual name before, all that time growing up, since she started crushing on him in kindergarten. Which meant that the JYM was a success countering her utter love failure. And so, in keeping with her truth right then, she told him, "I can't be your girlfriend, Owen," and she put the earrings, which were still in the box that she was clutching in her hand, back in one of his hands at the end of one of his casted arms.

Owen's face dropped. "Really?" he croaked, unable to fathom this rejection, a feeling he had never felt before.

"Omigosh, she's breaking up with him!" cheerleader Chrissie cried out in disbelief and shock, as if her entire view of the world would crack if someone didn't adore Owen, especially someone in her Lion Pride universe.

Which is when the booming infuriated voice of a Thunderbird cheerleader rang out like a warrior's battle cry, "Raaaaaaaaaah.......!"—

—as suddenly Jade tore across the field and barreled onto the makeshift halftime stage, frenzied, on a mission, knocking Bee down and grabbing the box with the blue Italian glass earrings from Owen, seething, shouting, booming out proudly for all to hear, "And these are mine! Because I'm Owen's girlfriend! And we never broke up!"

"We broke up three days ago," Owen shot back at Jade with annoyance, reminding her of the incident by the pool with the cupcakes and her ire.

"You guys are ruining everything!!!" cheerleader Chrissie cried out in outrage and barreled onto the stage, spray paint can pointed out in front of her, spraying Lion gold as she ran directly at Jade, making sure to spray Jade all over as if it would take her down.

Bee, who was still on the ground from being knocked down by Jade, rolled away so as not to get sprayed.

Jade screamed and covered her eyes, trying to block herself from the blast, which was throwing her off balance.

Bee jumped up to standing.

Cheerleader Chrissie swooped in and swiped the gift box with the blue Italian glass earrings out of Jade's hand. "No one is getting these until after we win this game!" Chrissie thundered and then, with pride, confessed her truth. "It's Reno's day, and no one's taking that away from him! Because I love Reno!" Cheerleader Chrissie beamed at Reno over on the sidelines by the players' bench—his look of surprise and joy visible to her instantly because he was so tall.

Reno turned bright red.

"And no one's hurting our Owen anymore!" cheerleader Chrissie glowered at Bee then shouted into the mic. "Because we all love Owen!"

The microphone screeched.

Everyone in the stadium screamed and covered their ears.

Cheerleader Chrissie knew what to do, keeping her intensity but lowering her volume so it didn't make the microphone screech or hurt anyone's ears, repeating with passion and pride out to the stadium, forgetting about Bee, "And no one's hurting our Owen anymore! No matter who Owen loves! And Owen loves us the most! Right, Lions?"

The entire Lion crowd, players and cheerleaders went nuts.

Owen laughed, totally relieved. He winked at Jade, who grinned with love and flew off back to her cheer squad—

—as Demi ran up on the stage, seizing the moment, "Who we gonna win for?!" she called out into the mic, pumping her pompom with the answer, "O-wen!"

The Lion crowd repeated her cheer, "O-wen!"

Demi added, "Reee-no!"

"Reee-no!" the Lion side of the stadium erupted.

The Lion cheer squad ran up on the stage to join Demi, pompoms flying, waving, pumping, "Owen! Reno! Owen! Reno!"

And all the Lions joined in chanting, "Owen! Reno! Owen! Reno!"

Bee looked at the madness, confused, her thoughts paralyzed, in shock, like she'd been slammed in the face with a giant Lion roar, like from an actual lion with a giant mane standing in front of her, as if the roar were vibrating and sending out a gust of wind like a hurricane, pummeling her, blowing her hair back and making her steel herself against it so as not to get blown over or away. Bee turned like a tower of confusion and started to leave the stage—

—when suddenly she heard another bellowing voice calling out, "Beeeeeaaaaatrrriiiiix...!" This time it was Kate. Bee turned and saw Kate come barreling across the stage straight at her from where she had been manning the lights, behind the oblivious-to-her hullabaloo of cheerleaders and Owen at the front of the stage.

Kate slammed into Bee with a hug.

And Torian barreled across the stage after Kate, pumping his arms like a jock, not the classical music nerd that he was.

Kate pulled back to look at Bee, shouting at her from, like, right there—three inches from her face—with more roaring and pummeling wind, but this time it felt good to Bee because the roar was a roar of love from Kate. It felt to Bee as if she were standing on top of the highest of the Rockies or up at Logan's Pass where she and Kate always loved to hike, and she was getting an invigorating blast of fresh air. "You were amazing!" Kate shouted. "And you have to go after Nick! You stupid poet!" Kate teased.

Torian nodded in agreement.

Bee laughed but tears came too, and she shook her head "no."

"That whole poem thing that you just did with the dance was totally confusing," Kate told Bee. "No one would ever get it. Even him! Nick! Because he can't read your mind."

"...I thought he could," Bee admitted, like she really, really had thought Nick could see inside her without her saying everything out loud. "And if he didn't see me, what was it all about?" Bee wondered aloud to Kate, and tears started down her face. She just couldn't hold it all in anymore, and Kate just made the crying worse because Bee felt so safe with her, like Bee knew that Kate had her back and loved her even when she was being an idiot, ever since they moved in across the street from each other in fourth grade. And even though Bee had put up a moat and a castle wall around herself to save her heart from the disappointment about Kate loving Torian all of a sudden, right now on that stage with Kate next to her, speaking truth, loving on her, the moat and the wall vanished, like there was a friendship wizard or witch that had waved a wand in spite of Bee's moat intentions. Like the witch and wizard had Bee's best interest at heart, whoever these magical happy spell-casters were.

And Bee softened in her tears.

And Kate wrapped her arms around Bee again and just held her, like the best friend in the whole world that she was, in spite of the fact that they were standing on a stage at Lion-Thunderbird halftime and the Owen-Reno chant was booming out.

And Torian wrapped his arms around Kate as Kate embraced Bee in a funny and highly awkward group hug where Bee was at the center of their universe like a sun, and Kate and Torian were both soaking up her beautiful rays of warmth and bright love and sending them right back at her.

The hug also looked rather cinnamon-bun-esque.

And everything changed all over again.

# 35 POST-GAME RESULTS AND A FIRST AMENDMENT TO THE JYM

Bee looked gorgeous in the stand-up mirror on this fabulous day wearing a blue, green and gold "Champions 4 Reno" T-shirt and a light blue skirt, trying to keep her chin high, trying to exude her shiny new sheen of Beatrix Plumb pride and self-esteem, even though it was a quite vulnerable sheen, like she now felt like a newborn baby all over again.

"The results of the Junior Year Manifesto?" Bee narrated to herself in the mirror—because this little trick was working like magic and it was all she had to hold onto. "I'd say: successful. I put myself out there. I was an awesome girlfriend to Owen. And he noticed me. And yes, I am quite happy with myself for being true and bailing on fantasy love. And fantasy self. Finally."

Bee deflated.

"But yes, I am alone," Bee admitted to her droopy self in the mirror.

But then, she lifted her head, her shoulders, her spirit, standing up straight again. She wasn't going to let all that truth-telling and bravery on her part go to waste. Not if she could help it. "Yes, I may be alone, but the team won, against the Thunderbirds," Bee continued telling the story of the past few days, "and Kate and I are being flexible with the new boundaries of our best-friendship."

Yes, the hug on the football-game halftime stage was the start of something new and good for Bee and Kate. Shortly after the Lions vs. Thunderbirds game ended that night, Kate came over—after Torian *finally* went home for the evening—and Bee and Kate sat together on the cushion in Bee's bay window.

"Yeah, and he'll be back at like 7:00 a.m. in the morning to see you and then 7:00 a.m. on Monday for carpool," Bee teased Kate about Torian. "Like, who does that? What other obsessive romantic would be so obvious in their obsession?"

And Bee and Kate laughed together, knowing full well that Bee was talking about herself and the early morning Owen-following bee debacle.

Bee raised her hand. "Me!"

"Yeah, exactly," Kate teased back. And then Kate told Bee that she really wanted to find a way to not lose her. "I mean, I can't help it with Torian either. That I like him so much. It's just this feeling, in my heart. And he makes my stomach leap. And my heart too."

Bee nodded in understanding.

And Kate continued, "I mean, I know it's stupid. And you'll think it's stupid but it's like, it happens when he shows up in his stupid blue Subaru and I hear the car door slam from my room."

Bee nodded again, agreeing, teasing, "Yeah, that is pretty stupid."

"Shut up," Kate teased back. Now, it was getting real. "I mean, the reason he rides carpool with us in the first place is so that I can keep riding carpool with you! He knows how much I love riding carpool with you."

Kate had told her this before, but Bee hadn't believed it. But this time, in Bee's bay window after the game, Bee did, and Kate's words were like a punch of love and understanding to

Bee. She could feel how important it was to Kate to get through to Bee so that Bee would understand her feelings, and Bee teared up in the good kind of teary way. And she and Kate hugged.

"Yes, that is nice of him," Bee admitted about Torian caring about Kate's friendship with Bee. "And I'm glad he gets you. And I'm so happy to have you back," Bee gushed.

"I couldn't stand how it's been," Kate told Bee. "I need you, Bee."

And Bee admitted that she'd been way too jealous and that now she understood Kate. "Because of Nick. I just felt so happy and normal around him. Like I always do around you. And he...made me a better Bee."

Kate laughed.

"Does Torian do that too? Make you a better you?" Bee wondered.

"I don't know," Kate laughed again. "I never really thought of it like that."

And in that moment, things became even more clear to Bee because she adored her friend so much. Kate didn't even need Torian to make her be a better Kate. And Bee loved that about Kate. And she blurted out to her friend, "You make me an even better Bee," through stupid additional tears that came out of nowhere again with this profound realization. And Bee squeezed Kate so tight that Kate had to yell at her to stop.

They laughed, and Bee told Kate more about her realizations, like about her crush on Owen and how he'd always made her feel good about herself until he didn't, because maybe, she'd actually grown up a little since kindergarten, and she'd learned about real friendship by being friends with Kate. And so, when reality hit when Owen came out if his body-cast pain-med fog, it became clear to Bee that her feelings for Owen were no longer the same. They were kind of a fantasy. But her feelings for Nick were based on a real friendship like the one she had with Kate.

Then, they talked more about Bee feeling awkward when Kate made out with Torian, and Kate promised to always be aware of that fact and suggested that they have a special hand signal or wave for when she wanted to carry on with Torian alone. "And then, we can meet up later," Kate added.

"Like a 'bye 'cuz you're into face-macking with your boyfriend now but we'll see each other later and it's totally cool' hand wavy thing?" Bee mocked.

"Yeah, and then when you have a boyfriend, you can do the same," Kate defended her idea.

"I do not see myself macking in public, ever," Bee told Kate with conviction.

Kate laughed. And they both laughed together and agreed that their hand-wave-signal plan was a good start.

And it got put to use a few days later, after school, when Bee, Kate and Torian were walking out from the front of the high school to the Strawberry Firecracker Bomb Mobile to drive carpool home, and Kate and Torian suddenly stopped to make out.

Bee exhaled in extreme annoyance when she realized they weren't right behind her. And then, Kate gave Bee the little hand-wave signal while she continued to kiss Torian, right there on the grass on the side of where everyone walked from the school to the parking lot. Bee laughed because it was kind of funny and because she felt so good because she and Kate had something just for them with that special hand signal— and it was something that Torian wasn't privy to.

Bee continued to walk—self-respect intact thanks to their friend plan—towards the SFB Mobile to wait to drive carpool home whenever Kate and Torian decided they were done with their stupid make-out session.

"And there is an amendment to the Manifesto," Bee told herself in the mirror, wearing her "Champions 4 Reno!" T-shirt over her light-blue skirt, as she remembered that moment earlier that day of walking towards the SFB Mobile in the parking lot. "Don't expect to find the real deal and be happy, because real love can cause misery!"

Because in that moment, while she was waiting for Kate and Torian to finish making out, she'd spotted Nick walking away from the school too. And she noticed that their paths were about to intersect. And she veered to the left to avoid him. Like an idiot. And then, Bee saw Nick watching her walk away out of the corner of her eye. "Yes, real love can cause a lot of misery," Bee continued, remembering seeing Nick seeing her and how he looked so disappointed all over again. "Especially if it doesn't work out," Bee added.

That's what Bee was recounting to herself then and there as she looked at herself in her standup mirror trying to be optimistic. And yes, once again, Bee's hope flew out the window and she decided to take a nap. She knew she'd done her best and still it wasn't good enough. She'd done the best she could given the fact that her best friend forever had suddenly bailed on her for Torian during the talent show and she'd caused a Lion-football and Owen Fleet disaster due to her needy love for her best friend's attention and the Junior Year Manifesto, not to mention causing love distress for Jade, which she felt awful about too, even though she'd seen Jade and Owen kissing behind Owen's wheelchair van earlier that day and even though Jade had been her adversary and a massive pain in her Bee-hind. *Terrible pun*, Bee reprimanded herself for even thinking of that pun and went and flopped face first on her bed, then curled in a ball for a while, then pulled her comforter quilt from her Aunt Becky off her bed and dragged it across the room to her bay window spot and huddled up in it as if she were in a papoose and just listened to music and read until something really weird happened.

# 36 BEE'S SECOND AMENDMENT OF TRUTH ON THE OUTSIDE LEADS TO LOVE

Bee had been asleep in her bay window for some time, miserable and curled up in the blanket from Aunt Becky, trying to nurse her own broken-hearted wounds, and she only got up later that evening when Diego came by just to say, "Hola, Chica," and banged on her locked bedroom door.

Bee woke up and didn't reply to his repeated knocking and telling her that he hoped she was okay. Diego had been extra nice to Bee since her embarrassing flatfoot poet debut at the halftime show. Bee assumed Diego's hope for love with her had been reignited when the truth flew out of her mouth about Owen. But to his credit, Diego seemed to have understood that Nick was Bee's true love. Since that night, Bee realized that Diego saw her too, like Nick did. It was just that Diego's visual and intuitive clarity had previously been muddled by his stupid crush on her.

That seemed to be a theme with the events of Bee's life of late, and maybe everyone else's. Love seemed to be the elixir for many things. Like Diego had somehow become enamored with cheerleader Chrissie after her confession of love for Reno and in spite of the fact that Chrissie and Reno had been an item since that moment too. *Maybe he's just a sucker for pain and unrequited love,* Bee mused about Diego as he knocked on her door, trying to get her to come down for some "delicious pre-dinner tapas I made to soothe my beauty's soul." But then, Bee realized, *Or maybe he's just attracted to people that are really honest about themselves and their loves and awesomeness, like I was when Diego first got here. Like I was just doing my flatfooting and songwriting, which I loved, and being friends with Kate, which I also loved. He must've picked up on that truth. And then, he noticed the whole Nick thing...* It wasn't a perfect theory, Bee knew, but it was decent and probably was mostly true: expressing personal truth and love, even if it made you feel vulnerable, and just beaming it out into the world or even just in your own heart was like an attraction beacon. And Diego was passionately tuned in.

After Diego stopped trying to get Bee to come down for the pre-dinner tapas, Bee's mom sent Bee a text to ask her to drive Paige's carpool to dance class. Bee felt too down and just told her mom she couldn't. After all, Bee knew full well that her mom could do the driving and that the more she resisted all the extra carpool drives, the more her mom would push Paige to get her license as soon as she could—which was still a year and a half out. Paige was fourteen, but at fifteen and a half, she could get her driving permit and their mom could get Paige lessons and driving practice hours and then Bee would be free. Bee couldn't wait. And their Nana Jana already had in mind to give Paige her new Jag because she was now thinking about a Mini Cooper for a change. Bee assumed the Mini Cooper would never last and that Nana Jana would be onto something more sporty and speedy pretty quickly. After all, Nana Jana was pretty darn fickle.

Then, Bee's mom texted Bee to try to persuade her to at least come down for dinner.

Bee texted back: *I'll come grab something later.* Which she did when the rest of the family was done eating and her mom had brought Paige to dance class. She got some pita and hummus and Brie cheese and raspberries. Her mom complained that

Bee wasn't eating the lasagna that she'd slaved over, but Bee knew her mom was teasing, and her dad gave Bee a hug and reminded her that, "Your mom loves you and she also loves giving you a hard time because she loves you."

And Bee and her dad said in sync what her dad always told her and Paige, "People only tease those they love. If they didn't like you, they'd ignore you." Bee had gotten that lesson from her dad pretty quickly, but it was a challenge for Paige, so Paige had to constantly be reminded.

Bee hugged her dad back, kissed her mom on the cheek and told her, "Thank you," even though she hadn't eaten her mom's lasagna, and then, Bee returned to her bedroom retreat.

Bee still felt miserable, but it got better. Then, Kate texted Bee to invite her to join her and Torian on her front lawn, but Bee sent Kate the wave emoji as a joke—because she loved Kate and teased her as often as possible and vice-versa, supporting her dad's observation that people only teased people they liked. Bee also shot Kate the "I'm busy see you later" wave out the window, and Kate texted an exaggerated "ho ho ho" Santa laugh in response. Then, Bee went back to her bay window and started reading. Alone. As happy as she could possibly be in that moment.

And then, it happened. It was later. Kate and Torian had gone for ice cream, which they'd also invited Bee to, but Bee had declined. The moon was out and full. The stars glistened.

And in that moment, Bee was thinking about Nick's face when she had avoided him in front of the school earlier that day and realized that, after the first Junior Year Manifesto amendment—namely, "Don't expect to find the real deal and be happy, because real love can cause misery!"—there had to be a second amendment. "Because sometimes when you actually surrender, to whatever...like admitting it's easier to tell a million people the truth than someone you care about...," she told Cardboard Owen, who was still being a good listener. "That's when you have to own that truth and do something about it so you feel good about yourself and maintain self-respect. Like do something truthfully. Like your truth from the inside has to be seen on the outside—and you as a person have to be seen and noticed like in the original manifesto."

And so, Bee felt a rush of bravery, grabbed her flashlight from under her bed—that her dad made her keep there in case of an emergency—and took off. She ran out of the room, out of the house, drove over to Nick's house and threw a pebble at his bedroom window.

Nick appeared.

Which is when Bee turned on the flashlight and held it close to her heart, shining the light up under her chin, onto her face so Nick could see her clearly, even though she looked like a ghost, which was hilarious—Nick told her after the fact.

Nick opened the window and looked quite confused.

And Bee blurted out, awkwardly, "I didn't think you'd like me as is. Even though I was more the real me with you as Owen's fake girlfriend than the real me ever was. And I wanted to keep hanging out with you. And I got scared. And I totally have a thing for you."

Then, Bee turned off the flashlight and raced away. Like a total weirdo.

*Idiot*, Bee told herself when she got back to her room, and the moon was higher, and she cuddled up, like in a papoose, draped in her blanket from Aunt Becky, in the bay window, trying to find hope and knowing that her second manifesto amendment was still a good one. "Yes, you have to show your inside truth on the outside," she groaned.

And then, another super weird thing happened, which was weirder than the first weird thing, which is that...

A pebble hit her window.

Bee scootched over on the bay window bench cushion thingy and looked out. It was Nick, and he was smiling, and she couldn't believe it.

"And sometimes the real deal shows," Bee whispered to herself in disbelief. "The real deal that's not just you showing *your* truth." And she watched anxiously to see what would happen next, her heart racing.

Which is when Nick held up a piece of yellow cardboard

paper, from the stack of yellow cardboard papers in his hands, for Bee to see. It said: "WHAT." Then, after Nick saw Bee seeing the yellow paper, he threw it down on the ground and held up the second yellow paper. It said: "THE." Then, he threw that one down and continued holding up papers with words, one by one, and throwing them down until Bee saw the rest of the words that made up a sentence that said: "WHAT THE HECK ARE YOU DOING?"

Bee and Nick stared at each other.

It was just like in Bob Dylan's *Don't Look Back*. Bee knew that. Her dad loved that movie, even though it was super old. So did her Papa Robbie. And they loved Bob Dylan, so she'd seen the movie a few times. And Bee thought that being like Bob Dylan in his movie was a cool way for Nick to convey his super cool message. Clearly, he'd seen the movie too.

"And he might even totally get you," Bee narrated in her head, "that real deal that shows up when you're being your own real deal."

And Bee opened the window and yelled back down to Nick, "What the heck are *you* doing?"

"Lookin' for Appalachia," Nick replied quite cheekily.

"Really?" Bee managed, voice cracking, heart pounding, because this was way too good to be true.

And Nick confirmed, "Yeah."

And Bee, totally awestruck by this turn of events, thought, "And without having to have an embarrassingly painful conversation...he'll find you. The real deal. Just the way you are. Imperfections and all. And you'll just know."

Which became the third amendment to the JYM—the real deal will find you and get you if you're you.

And Bee said to Nick, "She's right here. Appalachia's right here."

Which is when they both just smiled, both knowing and not needing to say more because they totally just got each other.

***

A week later, Bee was on cloud nine still about Nick showing up at her window. It made her heart leap just thinking about it, which it had been doing ever since—leaping, that is. She also got chills whenever Nick called her and she heard his voice and thought about how everything was just flowing.

The day after the pebble-throwing incident, Nick asked Bee out for tacos after school, and she showed him her lyrics to his song, and they went to Uncle Al's and practiced the song with Nick on ukulele and Bee rapping and flatfooting the beat. Nick's Uncle Al was all about this new thing—ukelele and flatfoot hip hop—and asked Bee and Nick to perform later in the week.

"Which is today!" Bee told her fantasy audience as she put on her favorite lucky dress to go out—the green one with yellow flowers from Aunt Becky.

Bee also thought about the kiss Nick had given her after they practiced that first time at Uncle Al's, replaying in her mind how she'd driven them home in the SFB Mobile and he'd kissed her in the car. And she'd kissed him back. And it was her first kiss ever.

Bee literally had been replaying it in her mind at least every five waking minutes since then. No narration. This was just for Beatrix Plumb. For now. And she was definitely going to tell Kate.

Which is what she was thinking about right then when she saw Kate approaching outside the school. That gave her a thrill too. It was Kate on her own and she was coming with Bee on her own, carpooling home and then to Uncle Al's Bluegrass Cafe & Eatery to set up tech for that night. In spite of the fact that Kate hated poetry and therefore Bee's hip hop songs, she'd agreed to film her and Nick's set later that evening. The whole halftime football show scenario had shown Kate the impact that Bee's lyrics could have, and Bee assumed it had opened her mind a little. Bee also knew that Kate had ideas about putting Bee and Nick's music out to the world, like a manager or something. Kate was all business like that. Kind of like Demi. And Kate jumped on it in true Kate fashion.

"I'll take it," Bee remembered telling Kate as Kate got in the car.

"Okay, let's do this," Kate said.

Torian wasn't there because, as Kate had told Bee, she would focus better without him.

And suddenly, it was like old times. Kate and Bee making things happen, together as a team.

Bee started the SFB Mobile, and they headed out.

# 37 HIP HOP FLATFOOT, UKULELE AND TORIAN BELTING OUT ANGELS AT UNCLE AL'S

*So, things are actually pretty awesome now*, Bee thought—about her life as Kate's best friend, her life as Nick's girlfriend and her life as an actual hip hop flatfoot poet—as she and Nick finished their hip hop flatfoot and ukulele set at Uncle Al's Bluegrass Cafe & Eatery and she looked out at the applauding crowd and then over at Kate, who was filming the whole thing, and Torian, who was running tech without hogging Kate's attention from Bee. "Maybe when you're really in love—or even just crushing," Bee narrated to herself, "you kind of can't help just thinking about your crush all the time at first and wanting to be with that person and feeling butterflies. And maybe, it wears off a little over time and saturation. And then, you find a balance."

Nick stepped forward and took Bee's hand and lifted it so they could take a bow. There was more applause. And then, Nick smiled at her.

*He's so cool*, Bee thought and narrated, "I hope Nick and I find a balance and that the butterflies and happy thoughts last forever."

Then, Kate gave Bee a thumbs up to signal that the shoot went well and that she got what she needed to make a cool video of their live performance. Uncle Al brought them all tacos and iced tea and Bee and Nick sat with Kate and Torian on the bench under the palm tree next to the seaside mural, and Coach Wells and Uncle Al joined them.

Later, after a blues trio played a set, Uncle Al announced their weekly Friday Night Karaoke.

Torian made sure he was first on the list, got up on the stage and boasted into the mic, "This is for Kate. Kate, this is for you."

*A bit redundant,* thought Bee. *But sweet.*

Then, Torian belted out this song called "Angels" by this British singer called Robbie Williams.

"That I've never heard of," narrated Bee in her head as she watched and listened to Torian. Bee was in shock and awe. "I mean, this song is amazing. Why have I never heard it?" Bee asked Kate. Kate told Bee that Robbie Williams was a superstar in many parts of the world, except America, and especially in Europe and England. And that this song was probably his biggest hit. "I guess Torian likes Euro stuff," Bee said. "I mean, opera? And this? At least this is good."

But most amazing of all to Bee was that Torian had this incredible voice. *Like, wow, he's super good,* Bee repeated in her head and kept listening in amazement. It was as if Torian were a different person to her all of a sudden.

"Surprise, right?" Kate whispered to Bee. "It's kind of why I like him. One of the things, at least. You should hear him sing that other stuff that I hate."

"Opera?" Bee teased.

"Yeah," Kate laughed. "Hate it. But he is amaze-balls. Like, really, really good. And he's gonna be in some competitions. And wants to be a professional."

"Opera singer?" Bee couldn't hide her shock.

Kate nodded. "Classical it's called."

Bee laughed at Kate's callback to their joke from that night on the lawn, then turned back as Torian crooned. "Weird."

"I know," Kate replied.

"He's really good," Nick said to both of them.

Uncle Al agreed, and Torian got a standing taco-cafe ovation. Then, Uncle Al brought out a round of chips and guac for the house in Torian's honor.

Nick leaned over and whispered in Bee's ear, which gave her the chills, "You think they'd want to go to that bluegrass festival with us. Kate and Torian?"

"You mean with the tickets you bought for me and Owen?" Bee teased.

Nick smirked then nodded. "I'm sorry. It was bad form."

"I accept your apology," Bee grinned.

"And I am grateful that you honor me with your forgiveness, dearest Appalachia," Nick teased, adding a little bow. "As long as you agree to get up and perform in the contest at the festival. I signed you up."

"What?!" Bee exclaimed.

"Yup," Nick grinned.

"With you, I hope," Bee demanded.

"Yup," he nodded. "Our song."

Bee burst out into a smile—the kind that hurts your cheeks. "Yes," she told Nick. "Our song."

Then, Bee whispered to Kate, asking if she and Torian might want to go to the festival. Kate looked it up on her phone immediately and loved the idea. And Nick bought two more tickets right then and there, and the four of them made plans to go to the festival together.

Bee said she'd drive. And Kate said she'd film Bee and Nick doing their flatfoot-ukelele thing.

Which is when Bee looked over at her best friend Kate, feeling herself tear up with so much joy, and she hugged her tight.

And Nick lifted his iced tea, "To us."

"And by 'us,' he means all of us," Bee thought as everyone at the table—Bee and Nick, Kate and Torian, Uncle Al and Coach Wells—lifted their glasses.

"To us!" they all cheered and clinked their iced teas—

—as the DJ called up the next Karaoke singer on the list, "Coach Wells is up with the classic 'You Light Up My Life.' And on deck is Big Al with 'Margaritaville.'"

Which is when Uncle Al turned to everyone at the table and said, "And I expect you all to join me."

They all cheered. Which pleased Uncle Al immensely and spurned him on to ask, "So, what do you kids think if I start a food truck?"

They all nodded. It sounded good.

"Because I'm gonna need a partner for that too. Tacos and...boba?" He laughed. "Or just tacos. Any takers? Entrepreneurial spirits?"

Bee and Kate simultaneously shot up their hands, "Me!" Then looked at each other and laughed. And Bee thought, *Yes, we got this! Me and my best friend.*

And Uncle Al was pleased too. "Excellent!" he beamed.

And Bee knew that she and Kate had this best-friendship thing down and were ready to take on the world.

ACKNOWLEDGEMENTS

Many, many thanks to:

Kathy Nolan for winning "Best Buddies" with me in junior high...instead of either of us getting "Most Likely to Succeed" or "Most Popular" (we were such dorks!) or "Most Athletic" or any such thing. I love all our adventures, starting when we met at age nine because we moved in across the street from each other. I love our best-friendship to this day more than I can say. I love you, Buddy!

My fabulous manager Seth Nagel for being on the "Boyfriend in a Body Cast" path with me from the get-go—encouraging me to finish the screenplay version, championing it and loving it as much as I do. Next up, hopefully, we get to make that movie or TV show of this little rompy teen rom-com gem.

Illustrator and designer Carolyn Nicole for making another adorable book cover for the Teen Carpool series.

Rebecca Stout for creating flatfoot hip hop and inspiring Bee's talent. Rebecca is absolutely amazing—performing, singing and teaching flatfoot dance at festivals across the U.S. She has an instructional video called "Becky's Barnyard Buckdance," if you want to learn flatfoot, and her work is featured in the International Bluegrass Music Museum in Owensboro, Kentucky. Check her out at flatfootandfancyfree.com.

Everyone at Earnest Parc Press.

**Nicole Schubert** is an award-winning author and screenwriter with a soft spot for comedy and romance. Her debut novel, *Blues Harp Green*, delved into coming-of-age and family issues and received Independent Publisher and Readers' Favorite Award nods. Her second novel, *Saoirse Berger's Bookish Lens in La La Land*, a rom-com about a teen in a film industry family, also won a Readers' Favorite Award. Nicole began her Teen Carpool book series with Readers' Favorite five-star *Carpool to Christmas* and is excited to bring more of these YA romantic comedies to readers and listeners. Nicole occasionally dabbles in other behind-the-scenes activities, like audiobook narrating or producing *Improv Diary Show* at Santa Monica's Westside Comedy Theater. She produced a music awards TV show and European-wide photo exhibition out of Brussels and enjoyed another side of storytelling working in the editing rooms of numerous Hollywood feature films. Nicole lives with her family in Montana and Los Angeles, by way of Brussels and New Orleans, where she was born during a hurricane. Visit her at **nicoleschubertwrites.com**.